CONNIE
NOBLE

Can One Woman Change Our Destiny?

Richard Cavalieri

Published by New Generation Publishing in 2020

Copyright © Richard Cavalieri 2020

First Edition

This is a fictional novel based on fact and takes place in October/November 2018.

ISBN
Paperback 978-1-80031-772-7
Hardback 978-1-80031-771-0
Ebook 978-1-80031-770-3

www.newgeneration-publishing.com

New Generation Publishing

The Author

Richard Cavalieri has been a comedy screenwriter/director for many years, but has now decided to write about something that seriously concerns him – our future. He lives in North London, but often wishes he didn't; is a lifelong Labour supporter – but socialism's vanished, and he likes Belgian beer – but after Brexit they'll probably stop importing it.

His cup is clearly half-empty.

This is his first novel.

It could be his last.

Amen.

For my daughter and her generation's future.

Prologue

She feared death. Not pain. But being no more. No sun rises, no bird song, no trees bending in the breeze or seas breaking on the shore. Nothing. Just blankness. Forever.

She had feared death since she was seven years old, and when these thoughts occurred, she entered a dark place where the walls closed in and everything she touched felt alien.

In late middle age she feared death more than ever, but now it wasn't just her own.

She'd lived during the most privileged period of history: no world wars, education for all, the welfare state, rock and roll, youth subculture, affordable luxury goods, television, cars and flights to exotic places once beyond the reach of most people. But all this had come at a price.

She'd always been a passionate environmentalist, but contrary to popular belief this didn't mean she wore tie-dyed clothes and smelt of patchouli oil. She was a scientist with a first-class degree in physics and geography, but only succeeded in becoming a school teacher, as the competition was tough in her day – science being the sole preserve of men in glasses wearing cardigans.

She was head of the geography department, and changed some elements of the curriculum that sought to 'cover up' certain environmental truths. This directive had come from a nasty bespectacled politician she'd nicknamed 'Gollum' on account of his scheming nature.

She'd set up a petition for children to sign, but her teachers' union banned it, saying it was 'too political'. She'd written back calling them 'spineless'.

She tried again a year later, but the school headmaster said he'd have parents queuing around the block if she started telling the truth and preaching the apocalypse. She nicknamed him 'The Lie Protector'.

She got the sixth formers to join her on a climate march, but one parent complained and nearly got her fired for 'inciting subversive activism'. He worked for an investment company, and she simply called him 'a shit'.

She retired at sixty and set up her own website '11thour.com.' It posted about various issues such as rain forest destruction, warming oceans and global depletion of wildlife, though it had less than a hundred visitors.

She started an adult petition in an attempt to get the government to seriously act on the crisis. A hundred thousand signatures and they would at least have to debate it in parliament. She got a hundred and sixty-six, and this was after she'd fly posted and leafleted two thousand homes in her area. Her daughter pointed out that Al Gore's film *An Inconvenient Truth* didn't change anything either, so what was she expecting?

She felt helpless for months after. It was depressing to think so many people couldn't be bothered to even write their name to help safeguard the Earth; after all, how much effort did that require?

The signs were looking ominous – our future was a slow burning dystopian fiction, and all we could do was watch – like helpless passengers on a runaway train. What could any of us do to stop it? It was around this time she began to get the headaches.

***

Chapter 1

Connie sat in her tiny North London garden in the late October sunshine, her little oasis in an ocean of concrete and brick. The flowers had gone and only a few leaves were left on the cherry tree. Everything was now dormant, but in the summer, it was a riot of colour and a haven for wildlife. This wasn't an accident; she'd let much of the garden go wild. As she sat, she listed this year's more exotic visitors; jays, wagtails, coal, blue and long tailed tits, goldfinches, chaffinches, fieldfares, blackcaps, wrens and even goldcrests – Britain's smallest bird. In the tiny pond were three types of newt, the smooth, palmate and great crested, along with the numerous frogs. There were four species of dragonflies, twelve of butterflies, and occasionally she was visited by foxes and squirrels but alas, no hedgehogs. She used to love watching those at night as they grubbed around looking for slugs. Some things were vanishing but generally speaking England would be lucky as the climate slowly changed. However, Australia where her daughter lived wouldn't be as fortunate, and the government wasn't helping matters by re-opening oil exploration off the Great Barrier Reef. This is what you were up against every day somewhere in the world.

The sun went in and the air suddenly cooled; Connie got up and walked back into the house knowing it would no doubt be another five months before she ventured out here again. She'd miss it, almost as much as she missed her daughter.

She watched the television news; it was a double whammy. The UK government in their wisdom had simultaneously given the go-ahead to a third runway at Heathrow, and decided not to invest in a huge tidal energy project in the same day. So, it was business as usual then? This was a government whose health and safety department banned people at work from giving a colleague a paracetamol or plaster – in case they suffered an allergic reaction, and didn't allow you to stand on a chair – because you might fall two feet and break your neck. But it was fine to ignore the state of the atmosphere and slowly kill us all. Inevitably her headache started again.

She Skyped her daughter. After a few pleasantries she came bluntly to the point.

'We're all fucked aren't we, Sara?'

'I wish I could say no, but if it was up to my government then yes, now they've pulled out of the Paris agreement.'

'You'd think they'd at least care about their prime tourist asset.'

'Doesn't mean a thing Mum, the dollar rules.'

'What are we all going to do?'

'All we can, I guess.'

Connie rubbed her temple, then briefly rested her head in her hands. Sara stared at her on the screen.

'You OK?'

'Yeah, fine.' Not satisfied with the answer Sara probed further.

'Mum?'

'Oh, I've been having these headaches again, I'm sure it's nothing.'

'Maybe you should see the doctor.'

'You know about me and doctors?'

'All too well,' Sara said with a touch of irony. Whenever Connie had a complaint, she'd panic it was something serious, something terminal, and would be in a catatonic state waiting for any test results, so generally she sedated herself with a few brandies until given the 'all clear.'

'Just relax, you remember what the doctor said last time.'

'I'll most likely kill myself with stress, not cancer, yes I know.'

'A headache's a headache. I get them all the time in this heat. How he talked me into living here I've no idea.'

'How is he by the way?'

'He's fine, but a bit too much like you. The other day he tore down some posters for a BP sponsored arts event.'

'Good for him.'

'They were getting kids to paint pictures of life on the Reef. Can you believe it?'

'Yes, I'm afraid I can. It's a cockeyed world we live in.'

'Tell me about it.'

'So, how's my grandchild doing?'

'The five-month scan was fine.'

'That's good.' Her headache was getting slowly worse, so she chatted for another couple of minutes then made an excuse and finished the call.

It was the sheer helplessness she felt when talking to Sara, especially now she had a child on the way. How could she change things for them both? What as an individual could she do that she hadn't already tried? The headache got even worse. She sat in the darkened living room for a while, contemplating a visit to the surgery. She'd already taken four Nurofen and two paracetamol that day and couldn't take any more. The pain throbbed like toothache, sharp and piercing as if someone was driving a knife into her head. She flopped down onto the sofa and wanted to either scream or cry but did neither.

That night she tried to sleep but the pain wouldn't subside, she pressed her knuckles into her temples for some light relief. At midnight she took more painkillers, and prayed it would go away so she wouldn't have to call the doctors the following day.

She woke at six a.m.; the searing pain had returned. She got up and paced the living room, had a cup of tea and the pain slowly subsided. The relief was palpable and she quickly fell asleep on the sofa, however, it woke her again at nine a.m., and she took two more Nurofen. She knew she couldn't go on like this, and tried to take her mind off the pain by reading the Sunday paper; more ice melts, the first container ship to pass through the Arctic Ocean without a breaker; an area the size of the UK deforested in Indonesia to grow corn oil – essentially removing the lungs from the planet that already had a severe chest infection – and the so-called good news: an attempt to ban the production of all new petrol/diesel cars by 2040. Another twenty years of peak vehicle emissions and we hope to keep the temperature increase below 1.5 degrees Who were we kidding?

She put down the paper and her headache started again. She stared at the ceiling and watched as a spider spun a web from the lampshade to the frame of the painting above the mantelpiece, and wondered how long they would survive into the future? They could be tucked away in the corner of a room and have no idea the entire world population had vanished; they'd survive as long as there were flies, and she'd seen flies walking on lightbulbs so heat wouldn't bother them.

Her musing was halted by a knock on the door. She slowly stood up and the headache kicked in hard making her wince. A shadowy figure moved behind the frosted glass. A cheerful scruffy rotund man asked if she wanted her gutters cleaning. She slowly shook her head and gently closed the door. What a job, asking people if they wanted their gutters cleaned. This man had probably twelve years of education and ended up cleaning gutters, how sad was that? Didn't the education system manage to develop some skill he had? No doubt he was really good at something; everyone is good at something. Maybe he was? Maybe this was just a way to earn money? Maybe he was a sculptor? Maybe he was good at looking after his aquarium? Maybe he was really good at ten pin bowling? Or snooker? She analysed every thought she had, had conversations with herself. It had been like this since Jim had died seven years ago.

One night he was in laughing in the pub, the following morning gone. Just like that. An aneurism in his sleep. People said it was 'a good way to go.' Was it bollocks, it was a terrible way to go. He was fifty-eight. Even thinking about him now brought tears to her eyes. All the things they were going to do when they retired. Don't ever wait, do it now.

She hadn't slept in their bedroom for four years after that. She called it 'the before room' – before the world went to shit. Apart from the funeral she never cried in public, you weren't supposed to do that were you? Had to be strong, get through it, what crap! Why aren't we allowed to show grief? Why did we have to be so in control of our emotions? Yes, it's alright at the funeral, but that's it, you can stop grieving now, don't upset anyone longer than you need to. We are so programmed as a race to control our emotions. Why don't people cry when they see the news and shit that's happening around the world? Especially to wildlife? Why don't they cry when they see an ape clutching its young whilst its home is being bulldozed around it? Why don't they cry when they see dolphins brutally slaughtered by fishermen? Or whales killed by factory ships that claim it's for research? Or worst of all, a dead rhino on its knees with half its face hacked off, because some idiots think its horn is an aphrodisiac. The northern white rhino had now been hunted to extinction, the cruelty of man was beyond belief but few of us cry, and anger, anger is kept in check too.

Why don't we shout out when someone throws rubbish on the streets? Or are cruel to a pet? Or barges in a queue? It's because people turn a blind eye, wrap themselves in cotton wool. If they see a beggar, ninety-nine percent will ignore them and give nothing. Why? Because they've distanced themselves from reality. She couldn't help feeling constant anger toward her fellow man, anger at their indifference and lack of empathy. Closing yourself off from the world creates an indifference to nature as well, which is why its destruction is often met with nothing more than a shrug.

She thought of Jim again and smiled. He'd often say if she turned her anger into electricity, she could power a small town. But at the moment it only fuelled her headache.

*

She had few friends, just acquaintances. Most of those were teachers from school. But now she'd retired for a few years she rarely saw them. There were some couples she knew but they slowly disappeared once Jim died, it seemed they didn't like to 'hang out' with widows. But deep down she knew it was her, she was too headstrong in debate, especially when it came to politics or the environment. She could tell by the way they looked at her after a few minutes, that they were bored – the men just wanted to discuss football and cars and the women, the success of their children. Ironically, her daughter was the brightest of the lot with a doctorate in Oceanography, but she rarely mentioned it; boasting wasn't her style.

The few friends they did have were mainly Jim's from his workplace – the architect practice. He didn't have that much in common with them either, but was more adept at 'rubbing along' as he put it. She on the other hand found 'small talk' almost impossible. When at the end of her tether with conversations about hairdos or clothes she could be quite sarcastic. Even Jim blushed at some of her comments. The best example was on holiday in Greece before Sara was born.

They'd been 'cornered' by a couple from somewhere up north, who seemed to think because they were also English, they'd want to spend every evening together. Nothing could have been further from the truth, as all they talked about was their expensive possessions. They turned up at the Taverna on the third night and were about to sit down when Connie turned to the woman and said:

'Would you mind not joining us?' The woman immediately looked put out. 'Why?' she asked. 'Because my husband dared me to wank him off under the table during the desert.' The woman's face collapsed. The man was horror-struck. Both left and Jim burst out laughing. Connie smiled to herself at the memory, and also because Jim had then asked if she would, joking of course, though she would have been game.

The headache was still there. Damn it! She looked at the clock, it was alright to take two Nurofen. She made herself a tuna sandwich for lunch and within thirty minutes the headache returned. She lay on the sofa as the pain slowly subsided. She got angry again as she thought about 'Brexit'. What a bloody shambles that was, and fancy letting the nation decide on something so complex, isn't that why we have politicians? But she didn't have much faith in them either – they just towed the party line. They had no passion or real beliefs, in fact very little to endear themselves to the nation at all. They just capitalised on people's fears and prejudices and worried about their own popularity – which is why none of them would have the balls to bring in measures such as reducing driving and eating meat or taxing flying – unless of course they wanted to become obsolete.

They'd only act if they had a mandate from the people; and there was little chance of that. She couldn't see Bob from Bristol volunteering to get rid of his Range Rover, his twelve-ounce steak and holidays in Thailand. She couldn't see Bob or three quarters of the nation willing to give up anything. Then again who would of their own free will? And why should you deny someone a holiday in the sun once a year, when eighty percent of air passengers are business flyers? They needed to start having conferences and meetings on the internet, we all needed to start working more from home. Travelling to work to just sit in front of a computer terminal every day was archaic, it was a bit like driving to Grimsby to get your fish, when you could go to the local fishmongers. It was just plain stupid.

'STOP IT!' She told herself severely. You aren't helping my headache! She closed her eyes and watched the 'floaters' under her lids as they moved across her horizon one way then the other. Then Trump came to mind and it felt as if someone had hit her head with a fucking axe.

'THAT'S IT! STOP THIS INSTANT!' She closed her eyes and slowly fell asleep.

She woke around three o'clock muzzy-headed and realised that like it or not she'd have to call the doctors. She slowly got up to avoid the blood rush and went to the phone in the hallway. Even though she had a mobile she still preferred to make calls on the old black Bakelite with the dialling wheel.

The receptionist asked if it was an emergency. 'Well no, or else I'd go to casualty,' she quietly replied, not wanting to wake the now sleeping headache. In the end she had to say it was serious knowing if she didn't, she wouldn't get an appointment for at least three weeks.

'Tomorrow at nine-forty. Dr Suza?'

'Yes, fine.'

She went into the kitchen with her head tilted to one side, which worried her until she realised that was the side the headache was on, and she was trying to stop it from starting again, though why tilting her head would help she had no idea. She put on the kettle to make herbal tea and sat at the kitchen table.

Doctors, fuck the doctors, she said to herself, though this wasn't meant to be personal, just a general attitude she had toward the surgery. The tiny waiting room, the bloody stupid magazines that were ten years old and so inappropriate for ninety percent of the north London patients it was comical. *Hare and Hounds*, *Sailing Weekly*, *Devon Life* and the most ludicrous of them all *Tractor Monthly*. She could only assume these were various doctors' aspirational magazines that they'd bought in over the years. But one with a keen interest in tractors? That was odd. Then there was the unpleasant receptionist, who'd challenge everybody about their need to see a doctor at all. What bloody concern was it of hers anyway? She'd grill everyone who came into the tiny room about their complaint, which naturally would be heard by everyone waiting. But what she hated most of all was the scrolling dot matrix appointment screen, hanging on the wall over the blocked up old fireplace. Seeing her name was like a call to death, the final judgement. Even if she was only going in for a blood pressure check, she was always sure they would find something else, something terminal.

So, she was going again! Tomorrow! Fuck! She poured the tea and let it steep, and was surprised to find she didn't have a headache, hopefully she could cancel the bloody appointment in the morning. She picked up the mobile phone off the table and went onto Google. At the top of the news stories it read;

'World nowhere near on track to reach 1.5-degree warming limit.' She scrolled down to the next: 'BP receives approval to develop new oilfield in the North Sea.' She read on:

BP North Sea regional president Ariel Flores said: 'BP is modernising and transforming the way we work, with a focus on accelerating the pace of global warming.' She laughed to herself. It hadn't said that at all, rather: 'on accelerating the rate of delivery.' But it may as well have done.

Connie liked the idea of finding out where Ariel Flores lived. (What a lovely name for such an ignorant bastard.) Lock him in his sauna, and turn up the heat to one hundred and twenty-five degrees – the hottest temperature on Earth this year – and see how he likes it. Better still, just shoot him. She switched off the phone and slammed it on the table. Rage, rage, rage. STOP IT!

She thought about her daughter and wished she'd leave Australia before it was incinerated and come home. But Sara loved the country, especially Cairns where the Great Barrier Reef research centre was, and diving was her favourite activity. Sara had been in the water from six months old at the local pool and had first snorkelled unaided by the time she was four. She showed no fear even after she'd seen *Finding Nemo* and

'Bruce' the shark who scared her, although she once got a bit freaked when snorkelling with Jim and encountered the 'drop off' – where the sea bed suddenly falls away into a deep blue void.

Connie was always worried that Sara was going to get attacked and killed by a shark the length of time she spent in the water on the Reef, until she'd told her she was more likely to get hit by a drunken driver, which didn't exactly placate her fear. 'You mean Sydney is full of drunken drivers?' She sipped her tea and smiled at her own paranoia.

*

Out of curiosity she often watched climate change denial posts on YouTube – they received ten times more hits than the genuine scientific ones, even if the presenter was some red-faced American hick, or a dubious suit sitting in an office with no scientific credentials. But their success was obvious: re-assurance that everything was fine, and it was business as usual. As far as she could tell those with their heads in the sand were still winning. But she also realised when you had a medical problem you looked on the internet to re-assure yourself it wasn't serious, so it stood to reason those worried about climate change would look for evidence to de-bunk it.

A cartoon she saw perfectly summed it up. Two cinemas next door to each other, one has a tiny queue, it's showing *An Inconvenient Truth*. The other has a queue around the block, it's showing another climate change film called *A Convenient Lie*.

She settled down on the sofa to watch Netflix. *Homeland* series 8. She loved it; best TV she'd ever watched, next to *The Wire*. The kind of TV that isn't 'dumbed down' and genuinely tackles contentious issues, even if it is fictional. American dialogue was direct with a cutting edge, intelligent yet accessible.

She'd never had much time for British TV, thrillers and cop shows never matched the Americans': the plots weren't as clever and the pace too slow. And apart from great wildlife films, it was dominated by soaps, reality shows, antiques, cookery and gardening programmes – in short wallpaper. However, we were quite good at comedy, but then again so were the Americans – bastards. *Seinfeld* was genius, as was *Friends*, comedy out of nothing, both set in New York. How she'd love to go there, and maybe find Katz's Deli where they shot the great 'orgasm scene' from *When Harry Met Sally*, and visit the Washington Square Monument where Sally dropped him off. God Harry was dark, a bit like herself really. Sally called him the 'The Angel of Death' on account of his abject pessimism. Jim could have easily said the same about her. She'd never really related to Sally in the film, she was too conventional, far too 'Miss Hospital Corners' as Harry put it. And what a great a script by Nora Ephron. Connie thought how tragic it was that a talent like her should die. This suddenly triggered her own death fears, and she worried about the headache again which seemed to be returning.

She cooked tea but didn't really feel hungry. She steamed some broccoli and green beans, fried some tuna steak and boiled some rice. She sat at the table and picked at it, leaving half the tuna, most of the rice and a few beans untouched.

She stared at the painting on the wall that a friend of Jim's had done. It was from a photograph of Myrtos in Cephalonia, taken from a vantage point three hundred feet above the beach. The vivid blue sea streaked by a white milky swirl from the sediment off the limestone. That had been their best holiday, their first holiday together at the beginning of their relationship. If she concentrated hard enough on the painting, she could feel Jim by her side, his arm around her tiny waist, the warm breeze on her face and the smell of pine drifting on the air.

How wonderful to be twenty-six again, and how fucking cruel life is, and if anyone tells you it gets better with age they're lying, and the reason is simple: when you're young your dreams and ambitions are all intact, love is exciting and powerful, and sex is never better. She would sacrifice her life at this very moment to have just one day back with Jim in Greece; better still, one eternal day.

Wouldn't it be incredible if that's what death was? Eternity in the most wonderful place you'd ever been at the most wonderful time in your life? But it won't be, will it? You'll just close your eyes and never open them again forever. How could you? You're an organism, you'll simply rot down the same as a fish. All those who believe in the afterlife or reincarnation are deluding themselves, because if every living thing that had died from the year dot existed somewhere or other, surely it would be hideously over-crowded? Well that was her theory anyway.

She also doubted those who claim to have had near death experiences and seen or spoken to 'God.' And others who had an 'out-of-body' experience – floating above themselves – or those who see the white light at the end of a tunnel. Why? Because they're all clichés, the things we're familiar with that supposedly happen to people when near death, they are what we expect to see/experience. And why would it be a white light? And not blue, or green, or yellow, or pink, or orange? And why don't you float above your bed and out through the hospital ward window? And why would God look like us? And if he spoke to us how come he'd conveniently speak in our own language? She was having another one of those pointless debates with herself, which inevitably brought on the headache again.

She knew if she did believe in the afterlife, she wouldn't worry so much about death, which was of course religion's amazing marketing pitch. But try as she might she couldn't be hoodwinked with fairy tales. Death to her was final. It was a real bitch, but at least made her realise this was it, don't wait for heaven. It made her want to do the best she could while she was here, and 'doing good' had nothing to do with God – not done in hope of a reward once she'd 'passed over.'

***

Chapter 2

She sat in the surgery waiting room. Her heart was palpating and she was sure her blood pressure was approaching a world record. Ironically, the headache had now almost gone entirely, but she couldn't walk away now, could she? *Damn it, Damn it!* she thought, glancing up at the bloody dot matrix appointment screen on which her name suddenly appeared.

She sat down and Dr Suza smiled. She liked Dr Suza. She had always preferred women doctors. It had nothing to do with physical awkwardness, they were just more empathetic.

'So, how can I help you?' she said. She loved the way the doctors said that now, rather than 'So, what's wrong?' Which would have been the question twenty years ago before they were no doubt given some lessons in bedside manners.

'Let's just take your blood pressure while you're here, shall we?' Connie froze, and her heart rate quickened.

'It's going to be through the roof you know?' she said nervously.

'Just relax.' Dr Suza attached the cuff to her upper arm, and turned on the machine. The noise increased as it began to tourniquet her arm tighter and tighter. She could feel her blood pressure rising with the contraction of the bloody thing. It finally reached its limit and stopped; Dr Suza watched the monitors screen. Finally, the cuff loosened, deflating like a puffer fish, as did Connie, her blood pressure no doubt falling with it.

'A bit high. What was the reading at home?' Dr Suza knew she suffered from the 'white coat effect' and took her own readings.

'Oh, about 130 over 75,' she lied, as she often did. Even the home machine was capable of scaring her half to death, but she knew her blood pressure was moderately OK. She'd taken it a couple of months ago after a glass of wine or two when she was relaxed and it was 130 over 80. Dr Suza removed the cuff.

'OK, so what seems to be the problem?' She explained the headaches, and the doctor asked a few questions.

'Where in particular are they?'

Connie pointed to her temples. 'Here, and sometimes down toward the back of my neck.'

'Do you have any problems with your vision, or lack of balance?'

'No. But sometimes I feel a little faint on standing.'

'Do you have any vomiting or nausea at all?'

'No.'

'How about any tingling or numbness anywhere, or weakness?'

'No, I don't have any of that.'

'Does your speech seem slurred at all?'

'No.'

'How about ringing in your ears?' She thought a moment, she had been aware of a ringing in her ears for the past month or so, especially at night or when it was very quiet during the day.

'Yes, I have noticed that, sometimes.'

'OK.' Dr Suza took the torch off her desk and examined her eyes. She then asked her to follow her moving finger, left then right. Finally, she got her to touch her nose then place her finger tip on her moving one, whilst covering each eye. Dr Suza began to type something into the computer.

'I'm going to send you for a scan, we just need to take a closer look, Connie.' *She used my name, why did she use my name?* she thought, half paralysed with fear.

'You'll get a letter in a few days.' Dr Suza smiled and could read her concern. 'As I said, Connie, it's just a precaution. There's nothing to worry about at the moment.' Dr Suza smiled again and she took that as her cue to leave. She slowly rose from the chair and walked out the room. Oh my god. They're sending me for a brain scan, why would they do that if they weren't concerned? Brain scans cost a fortune; they wouldn't do that if they didn't suspect something would they? Connie walked down the corridor and her headache came back. Oh my god, oh my god, I've got a brain tumour, haven't I? Then she paused, and recalled Dr Suza's words. There's nothing to worry about at the moment she said, didn't she? And she wouldn't, couldn't say that if there was something to worry about, after all, she's a doctor. She couldn't say there's nothing to worry about at the moment if there was something to worry about, could she? It would make her look an idiot; it would make her look as if she didn't know her job. These thoughts calmed her down somewhat – until she got home.

But she said there's nothing to worry about at the moment. Which means there probably is something to worry about in a few days' time, when the results come through? Connie got scared again and against her better judgement sat down at her computer and started looking at the symptoms of a brain tumour, assuming that was what the doctor thought she may have. Blurred vision? No. Weakness? No. Slurred speech? No. Ear ringing? Yes. Imbalance? No. Headaches weren't even down as a common symptom. So there, she only had one – ear ringing – one out of five, which was pretty good wasn't it?

Then she had another thought. What if it's not a brain tumour at all she suspects? She never said that, did she? Maybe it's Alzheimer's? Or Parkinson's? Or motor neurone disease. Or something else entirely like tinnitus? Or maybe just stress? But she wouldn't send me for a brain scan if she thought it was something straightforward, would she? She checked the three serious illnesses and found she had none of the symptoms and was relieved, but there were many more possibilities, weren't there? She checked a brain aneurism, but that didn't fit either.

She remembered when she'd done health anxiety therapy, they'd said never to go onto the internet for re-assurance, because you would always find something bad, which is probably why you have health anxiety in the first place. The internet was a curse, and also full of false information.

She switched off the computer and went to make a cup of coffee, but not before she turned it back on and checked the symptoms of three more brain related illnesses; Meningitis, stroke and a rampant outsider, Lou Gehrig's disease, whoever he was, but she was all clear of those too. Then she realised all these illnesses probably didn't have any symptoms at all in their very early stages, which got her worrying again. In fact, she worried so much over the next few hours she did the only thing she knew to relax, dispel her illness fears, and become optimistic about the outcome – poured herself a brandy, or two.

*

She'd arranged a Skype call with Sara at midday, and realised her speech may well be slurred if she drank too much, so put the bottle away. She'd also decided to say nothing to her about the scan.

During the call Sara told her about the results of her recent research into the effects of plastic on the Reef. A particular bacterium seemed to be attracted to it, and this bacterium killed coral. But there was an upside. Sea grass seemed to carry an antidote, and areas where there were large amounts of it the coral was healthy.

'Some good news at last then?' acknowledged Connie. Sara agreed, and said she was amazed how nature seemed to be able to solve problems humans created, but unfortunately not often enough. She went on to tell her that Kurt had recently done an autopsy at the institute on a pelican chick, and discovered nearly a kilogram of plastic in its stomach. 'Why do they eat the stuff in the first place?' Sara said once in salt water plastic seemed to give off an odour that appealed to their appetite, though they had no idea how or why. It was depressing news, she also told her they believed nearly all ocean creatures now contained plastic, and that micro-plastic broken down in the ocean had now been absorbed by phytoplankton as well. Connie didn't need to be told what that meant.

'The organism that produces fifty percent of the world's oxygen could be fucked?' Sara slowly nodded in affirmation. 'Dear God. What are we doing?'

'It makes me scared, Mum.'

'Me too.'

'No, I mean about having a child. What the hell can we do?'

'You and Kurt are doing all you can.'

'But it's not enough, is it?'

'No, it isn't. How can it be against a juggernaut of consumerism?' They sat in silence a few moments, staring at each other on the screen.

'Oh, did you go to the doctor's?'

'Yeah, all fine. Just like you said.'

They finished the call and Connie pondered why some people labelled it 'wet' to care for the environment? Surely taking care of your back garden made absolute sense? It seemed so fundamental to her that if you take care of things, they will give you adequate returns. But now every square inch of land was up for grabs, be it for corn or palm oil, intense farming, metals, gas or mass development, the atmosphere was heating and now the ocean wasn't only warming it was choking with plastic too. Where was it all heading? It made her feel physically sick some days, she even felt ill walking down her street and seeing all the huge SUVs (Stupid Urban Vehicles) some of her neighbours owned. Didn't they know? Didn't they ever read papers that didn't lie to them? Or watch the news? Or go on the internet? Or talk to anybody who cared? These cars were obese and obscene, even the 'Mini' was now the size of a hippo. SUVs were now second to fossil fuel power generation as the world's highest emitters of CO_2.

Connie also realised that getting on her high horse was a bit hypocritical, as she was equally to blame. She didn't drive a car or fly, but she used electricity and gas and bought manufactured goods that had consumed huge amounts of power to produce and transport.

It was hard to live outside the 'grid' but at least she tried to change things. In fact, she'd marched and demonstrated since she was a student: CND, the Anti-Nazi League, People's March for Jobs, against the Falklands and Iraq wars and for the miners' strike – which on reflection was a strange thing to support, considering the impact coal has had on the environment. But it was her firm belief that if you didn't stand up and support a good cause then why should anybody else?

It wasn't self-congratulatory, or done to show others what a caring empathetic citizen she was, it was her duty, there was simply no choice; her body and soul told her to.

She often thought it was maybe genetic. Something to do with survival? But protesting was no guarantee of that, was it? She also felt if there were any justice it was her fellow protesters who should survive any impending climate Armageddon. However, she was aware the opposite would probably be true – those who didn't give a damn would be the survivors: the super-rich. They had the means to protect themselves from mass hysteria and starvation, they would survive with money they had made from destroying the planet. How ironic was that?

Later in the afternoon she found herself going through the photo albums and flicked through the Greek holiday ones. Her and Jim, slim, young, tanned and happy. On the beach, in the restaurant, on the scooters in hire boats and quite a lot of the cats, and even more of her feeding them. First those in the vicinity of the accommodation, then the ones in the square, then those on the beach and hiding in the rocks and finally those begging at the Taverna's, who often seemed the healthiest but she still couldn't help feeding them half her chicken souvlaki. Jim said it was like going on holiday with Dr Doolittle, though in her case it was Dr Dooalot. He didn't mind, but did mind having to wait an hour each night while she did the rounds with a large bag of cat biscuits.

She looked at a picture of Jim coming out of the water totally naked apart from his snorkelling gear that conveniently covered his privates. She remembered they made love a few minutes later, on the pebbles of the deserted cove. She thought about the memorable events in her life, and how strange it was they were only wonderful after they'd taken place. It was hard to appreciate things when you were 'in the moment' and if you tried, it was already gone – the moment was over. Even at a very young age she knew anything that was good would quickly pass. She knew the reason, and also why she feared death; it was watching her pet rabbit die, seeing him gasping and take his final breath as he sat on her knee as they drove to the vets. She cried for a week and started getting horrible nightmares. As an only child, Jamie was her best friend and he left her, a few months later her parents were divorced and separated. Nothing lasts, and subsequently her life was always tinged with a degree of sadness, a sense of loss. As an adult this innate sadness was fuelled by man's piecemeal destruction of the planet, along with the wildlife on it.

Yes, it was greed that depressed her now; the desire people had for possessions, the latest model of car, or TV, or mobile phone, as if these things were going to make life more enjoyable. Did they really make any difference?

If you asked people what made them happiest would they say 'When I got my new car'? Or 'When I got the iPhone 8?' Or 'When I got my sixty-inch flat screen TV'?' The answer was probably no. The more likely answer would be 'When I'm by the sea.' Or 'When I'm playing with my child'. 'When I'm dancing.' Or 'When I'm sitting in the sun.' Possessions would have nothing to do with happiness for ninety percent of people. If we could understand that without obsessive consumerism, and all the 'must-have' goods, the world could change, then we might just survive what's coming.

The big question was were more people happy pre-industrial revolution than they are now? It was impossible to answer, but she reasoned you couldn't yearn for possessions that didn't exist, and this would have been the same for not hundreds but thousands of years. But could you turn the clock back? Either way it was going to have to happen, otherwise we will be left wandering a scorched dystopian landscape like the father and son in Cormac McCarthy's *The Road*.

She paused from her rambling thoughts and looked at the picture again and remembered that Jim hadn't wanted to snorkel naked but she'd persuaded him to; she'd also persuaded him to make love to her on the beach. As much as she loved him, she wished he'd been more adventurous. She couldn't fault him in any other way. He was kind, gentle, thoughtful, generous, and a lovely husband, but lacked 'an edge', a certain spontaneity. If she was honest, Jim was never exciting to be with.

She closed the album, and suddenly had a horrible pang of guilt for thinking about him in this way. You can be really spiteful you can, she said herself.

She went to bed that night but couldn't sleep, she felt worried again about the scan, about the outcome, but even if she was fine realised how basically unhappy she was, and began to think how she could change this.

She wasn't bi-polar, she knew that. Her friend Cathy suffered from it, and when she was down, she was really down; couldn't go out for days, sometimes weeks.

No, she was just too intense about everything, too engaged with the depressing things in life, she needed to 'lighten up' for her own sake but how? Have a holiday? But she'd tried that, she'd been on her own by train to Nice for a week, and hadn't spoken to anybody. She'd wandered around the city, sat on the beach and visited Monte Carlo, but after three days felt like a ghost – invisible as she ambled around aimlessly.

Nobody wants to talk to a sixty-year-old woman on her own do they? So, after those three empty, endless days that seemed like weeks, she went home early. What else was there?

She thought of doing a class in something, a language, or creative writing, or philosophy but she'd spent enough years in a classroom. She thought about a sport, going to the gym, or playing tennis or swimming. But that didn't appeal either as she hated swimming pools, thought gyms were essentially torture chambers and although she liked tennis was rubbish at it; well, rubbish at serving. She went to the theatre a few times but found it overwritten and overlong and wanted to leave at the interval.

The cinema was fine, as long as nobody was talking or rustling sweet papers or crunching infernal popcorn, or even worse nachos (who's stupid idea was it to sell those?). But if there was something on really worth seeing, she loved going to the movies.

Other social events such as going to a pub, restaurant or even seeing a band – she loved rock music – was just embarrassing on your own, especially as an older woman. She saw it as the one major drawback of her sex, as men of any age could frequent these places without turning a hair. So, she was stuck with staying in and watching TV and getting angry with the world for a hobby, apart from the occasional drink with Cathy if she wasn't too 'out of it'.

She woke early, and, as was now habit, picked up her phone and went to Google to check the news: the usual political rants between parties and world governments, floods in India, a hurricane in the Caribbean, a train crash in China and some pointless celebrity news along with the sports results.

She checked her emails: sales junk from Amazon and Vodaphone and a report from Greenpeace about China boosting rather than reducing its coal-fired power stations. Then there were the Rainforest Rescue petitions that she always signed. They arrived about once a month.

In this batch there were appeals to save forests in Indonesia, Tanzania, Makatea Atoll, Papua New Guinea, French Guiana, Liberia, Sumatra, Temiar, the Philippines, Cameroon, Nicaragua, Brazil and Kafuga. In total 15 billion mature trees were being felled each year and wildlife was being driven out either by agriculture, mining or ironically biofuels. Forests that absorbed CO_2 were being destroyed to grow corn or sugar cane as alternatives to oil and gas, so essentially one was negating the other. It was like building a dam then putting a hole in it. At this rate all the wildlife found in rainforests around the world would only be seen in zoos or stuffed.

She signed all the petitions, and couldn't believe that man could be so hell bent on destroying something that had taken hundreds, if not thousands of years to develop and possibly never be replaced. In anger she threw the phone onto the bed wishing she'd never turned the fucking thing on in the first place. When reading the news, she was always reminded of a Pink Floyd song 'Brain Damage' on 'Dark Side of the Moon.'

"The lunatic is in the hall,

The lunatics are in my hall,

The paper holds their folded faces to the floor,

And every day the paper boy brings more."

A perfect song about politicians. She wondered why modern music didn't seem to be that political anymore, there was more than enough going in the world to protest about. Maybe there was too much? She remembered songs about money, war, greed, famine and politics by countless musicians and bands: Hendrix – 'Machine Gun'; Cream – 'Politician'; Joni Mitchell – 'Ethiopia'; Bob Dylan – 'Masters of War'; Sting – 'Driven to Tears'; Bruce Springsteen – 'Born in the USA'; The Who – 'Won't Get Fooled Again'; Stevie Wonder – 'Happy Birthday'; The Jam – 'Eton Rifles'; just to name a few. Her favourite of them all was Steppenwolf's 'Monster'– a thirty-minute epic about the arrogance and destructiveness of America, written in 1969 and more pertinent today than ever.

She decided to call Cathy, and see if she wanted to meet for a coffee. When she answered the phone her voice was slow, deliberate and sounded as if she'd just woken up even though it was eleven in the morning. It was immediately obvious she was in one of her 'down' phases. Cathy told her she'd not got out of bed for three days apart from to get snacks from the fridge. Connie offered to go over and cook her something but she declined, said she'd be OK in a few days, and the call abruptly ended

Poor Cathy, she'd suffered from bi-polar disorder most of her life. It had ruined two marriages, and she'd been on her own now for almost twenty years. When she was in one of her 'up' phases she was one of the funniest most intelligent people you could wish to meet, in fact the funniest most intelligent person Connie had ever met. They'd gone to university together and shared digs in Brighton for three years. But Cathy took drugs, too many drugs, and ended up in a clinic for a week with 'speed' psychosis. It was after she left university, she'd began to suffer extreme highs and lows, no doubt because the drugs enhanced it. Her therapist told her it was probably the disorder which made her overdo the drugs in the first place – that and a physically abusive father – the bastard.

Connie was pretty much the only friend Cathy had now, and visa-versa which was ironic considering the number of people who craved their company at university. She was dark haired and slim, whilst Cathy was blonde and voluptuous – physical opposites – yet similar in character, with razor sharp intelligence and wit. They were classic femme fatales, and subsequently had a lot of admirers. In short, university was the best fun they'd had in their lives.

Going over to Cathy's when she was in an 'up' phase was one laugh after the next, as they reminisced about their 'uni-days'. Looking at photos it seemed unfair that two such beautiful women should ever grow old.

They often decried how awful it was that when a woman lost her looks, they seemed to be ignored, whereas with bloody men it didn't seem to matter; they'd be called 'dignified' or 'distinguished' or what the fuck ever. Some even looked better as they got older – bastards. Who said there was an improving equality between the sexes? Some things would never change. Of course, some women were lucky, and by their mid-sixties didn't have a wrinkled face, ballooning arse or sagging breasts. But even those would end with their husbands drooling over a woman twenty, even thirty years their junior. Yes, meeting Cathy was great for a whinge about men, and they were lucky to have each other, especially living a few hundred metres apart. All the same they both found it strange that the older you got, the less people you saw, surely it would make more sense the other way round?

Now that Cathy would be 'off the map' for a while she tried to decide where else she could go, what else she could do. She sat on the sofa in a rare patch of sunlight that blazed through the dirt-flecked windows, and thought to herself as she had done many occasions, that they were in desperate need of a clean. But cleaning windows in sunlight only seemed to make them even dirtier, so she gave up on that idea.

She could read a book, but the last three contemporary novels she'd read weren't particularly good, and one, an autobiography, frankly annoyed her. The male protagonist was an arrogant control freak who wanted kids but his wife didn't, and when they did, complained he couldn't work and left them. So, literature was off the agenda for a while, unless Hardy, Dickens, Woolf, du Maurier or Dorothy Parker came up with a new novel. Connie loved Dorothy Parker; dark, witty, acerbic, and a great portrayer of women characters who had balls. She may have had a tragic life but at least she'd lived.

The letterbox in the hall clunked open and shut and a number of letters hit the bare stone floor with a slap. She got up off the sofa and felt the merest twinge of a headache, as if it was reminding her it hadn't gone away. She picked up the letters and sifted through them. Gas bill, three pieces of junk mail and a white envelope with 'Whittington Hospital Trust' printed on the top left-hand side. Her first thought was how it had managed to arrive so quickly, as hospital appointments usually took weeks. This worried her, had Dr Suza insisted she was seen as soon as possible while there was a still a chance of saving her?

She went into a panic and began pacing the hallway. Oh my god, oh my god, that's it, she kept saying to herself over and over again. Finally, she sat down at the kitchen table, her heart racing and slowly opened it.

Her relief was palpable when she saw it was nothing more than a routine letter offering a bowel cancer screening. She tore it up and threw it in the bin for tormenting her.

***

Chapter 3

For the next few days, she forgot about the headache and the pending appointment and kept a close eye on developments at COP24: the twenty-fourth climate change conference in Katowice, Poland. With a new UN/IPCC report outlining yet again the severe consequences of continuing use of carbon fuels, she prayed that this time real concerted action would be taken. But the US had balked at the idea of preventing its citizens from driving big cars on cheap subsidized fuel, flying till their hearts content, and eating at least two cows a week. All of which was their divine 'God-given' right as outlined in the twenty-eighth amendment. Australia had also responded with considered thought after their PM had called it all nonsense, whilst the good as elected Brazilian president said once in power, he would pretty much allow big business to do whatever they liked with the rainforests, from mass farming to mining. Then there was Saudi Arabia refusing to make any concessions whatsoever. Hadn't they earned enough money from oil as it was? She contemplated the responses with resignation. It wasn't surprising, nothing was surprising anymore. She watched the news, and the potential devastation was now outlined more clearly than ever, but she'd heard similar pronouncements for the past twenty years, and now it sounded almost meaningless – like someone drowning in a river and shouting 'help' over and over – with nobody remotely interested in saving them.

'Zero emissions must be reached as soon as possible' was now the familiar mantra, but was this remotely achievable in the next twenty, thirty or even fifty years? Especially at the increasing rate we were producing CO2? And even if we hit zero emissions tomorrow the ice caps would continue to melt, and she knew all too well the effects that would have on the planet.

But what really concerned her were the innocent people, the third world poor and indigenous tribes that had never contributed to the mess we were in. And then there was the wildlife, helpless in protecting itself from the continuous loss of its habitats.

If she was totally honest with herself, although she loved many people, she didn't care that much for the human race. They were a scourge on the planet, which would eventually consume and kill everything.

*

The appointment finally came and she took the bus to the hospital. She followed the signs to the Imaging Department and sat in the waiting area with three of four other patients. Like her, they all seemed fine. She recalled this was always the case whenever she'd been to hospital for one test or another over the years. Even on the rare occasion she'd been to A&E everyone looked relatively OK, so what was wrong with them? She could only assume those in agony or covered in blood were kept out of view, they were the emergency emergencies. One patient came out and another was called. She looked around at the walls covered in posters. She didn't read any in detail for fear of seeing something she'd rather not. She'd done this in the doctor's surgery once, it was a poster about the damage caused in drinkers who were over sixty. It listed a number of ailments and by tea time the same day she had almost all of them, so had a few glasses of wine to calm down. Reading posters was the same as going on the internet; even if you were perfectly healthy you'd find you had some illness or other.

Another patient was called and she could feel her heart beginning to pound. She knew there was nothing to fear about the procedure, but nevertheless, felt in a mild state of panic. Any exploratory medical tests made her panic.

Further down the corridor she could see a number of gurneys containing patients. One was wheeled past her, an old woman asleep with her mouth wide open and dentures removed. She looked dead. Maybe she was. It was impossible to imagine yourself in the same state one day, but you would be. Whenever she was at funerals, she could never understand why most people seemed so jubilant during the wake, then one day realised: they were glad it wasn't them. Funerals are in fact celebrations for the living. What everyone should do is stand up at some point and sing 'Staying Alive' by the Bee Gees. That would be appropriate, though somewhat disrespectful.

Her name was called, but she didn't hear it the first time, or the second, as the song had got into her head. She quickly snapped out of it on the third call.

Once in the anteroom she was told to undress and put on a gown in the cubicle. She couldn't help asking why.

'It's a brain scan, you know?'

'Yes, I know,' said the nurse. 'But we can't have any metal objects like zips or fasteners in the machine, it upsets it.' She couldn't help but imagine the machine crying as she tied the gown around her. She looked down and it didn't cover her bra and pants, and realised it was back to front. She took it off again and put it on the right way, though it still felt back to front, which in many ways it was.

She walked out the cubicle and the nurse smiled, no doubt because it wasn't her going into the machine. All hospital staff are the same. They wear that cool nonchalant expression because they're only in the hospital by default. *One day they will be here as patients*, she thought to herself. That will knock the smile off their faces. She was led into a room and told to lie down on a table.

'You don't suffer from claustrophobia, do you?' the nurse asked.

'No, lots of other phobias but not that one,' she replied. The nurse smiled.

'Any problems while you're in there just say, I can hear you and talk back through a little speaker. I could play music if you want some?'

'No, that's fine, one of my phobias is pop music.' The nurse smiled and left the room. She stared at the bright lights on the ceiling then felt the bed begin to move. Slowly it entered a tunnel, the top about six inches above her nose. After a minute or so there was a loud bang that made her jump. A voice came though the tiny speaker.

'Don't worry, that's just the machine. Are you OK?'

'Fine.'

'This will take about fifteen minutes. Let me know if you have any problems.'

'Sure.' A short while into the procedure she began to feel claustrophobic, but having said she was fine and actually cracked a joke about it, felt she was in no position to complain. She closed her eyes and had almost fallen asleep by the time the bed withdrew itself from the scanner. The nurse appeared.

'All done.' She stood up and suddenly felt light-headed and swayed slightly. The nurse quickly grabbed her arm.'

'You OK? People often feel a bit dizzy when they stand up,' said the nurse as she helped her back to the cubical.

'I'm fine now, thank you.' She pulled the curtain closed and supported herself against the wall for a few moments before she removed the gown.

As she walked out of the anteroom and into the corridor, she passed the MRI control room. The door was open and inside she could see not one, but three white-coated doctors or were they technicians? All seemed to be poring over images on a number of screens. This concerned her as she continued down the corridor, but she stopped herself. After all they could be anyone's scans, couldn't they? And even if they were hers, they were only looking. There weren't red lights flashing and alarms sounding, were they? They were just flashing and sounding in her head.

She arrived home, exhausted. All that stress, she thought, and why? She'd asked various friends in the past how they felt when going for tests, and as far as she could remember they all said something similar. It's nothing until it's something, or words to that effect, or, what was the point of worrying about something that hadn't even happened yet? But what if it was something serious? She had asked. Deal with it then, seemed to be the common response.

She couldn't believe how people could be so stoical and pragmatic about their possible demise. However, Cathy had once said to her, if you ever did get bad news, you'd probably be as cool as a cucumber. She asked why and the response was simple. You've done the worrying already. That remained to be seen.

She called her Sara that evening. The conversation revolved around the totally inept Australian prime minister, who didn't seem to give a shit about the UN report. In fact, he seemed intent on burning as much coal and oil as was humanly possible.

Sara was now one of the organisers of a huge protest they were planning in all the cities across Australia, whilst Kurt was plotting ways to kill the PM, in fact kill the entire government, saying he was going to call himself 'Bruce Fawkes'. Sara asked how the headache was, and she said it was fine, as it had been the last couple of days.

After the call she felt in high spirits; even though the current world situation was darkening, there was something joyous about people getting up and fighting back, and never giving in. She felt optimistic about the MRI results as well and settled down in the living room to watch an episode of *Homeland* – as dark as it was. She had a glass of wine or two and slept deeply for the first time in a few weeks.

*

On waking she picked up her phone and went on the Google news site. Top of the page was the headline. Climatologists are raising the alarm about a series of 'tipping points' that could have catastrophic consequences for life on Earth. She'd never seen a headline put so strongly before; scientists were now telling the world the way it really was, and not being conservative. The gloves were now off, and had to be if any progress was to be made in seriously eliminating the CO_2 in the atmosphere. Reading the article sent a shiver through her, even though it wasn't a surprise. The headline reminded her of a 1950s 'B' movie, one of those captions that spun into shot, accompanied by a crashing discord of strings. It didn't feel real anymore, none of it, it was an April fool's joke surely? Even though it was October. She read it again:

A CATASTROPHIC CONSEQUENCE FOR LIFE ON EARTH! What had we done? How had we managed to do such devastating damage to our home in a mere one hundred and fifty years? She knew why of course, but it still seemed extraordinary the atmosphere could change so quickly after eight hundred thousand years of CO_2 stability. She scrolled down to the next piece of news. Hurricane Michael, now devastating the southern US with winds up to a hundred and seventy-five mile per hour – a timely reminder for the US government to begin to act? Who was she kidding? They were set on making every last possible buck out of oil, weren't they? So was every government no doubt, but none of them had the downright ignorance and bullishness to say it, unlike the US president whose name she could hardly bear let pass her lips. She could feel the anger rising in her yet again, and got up to make breakfast before she'd lost her appetite entirely.

'FUCK THEM! FUCK THEM ALL! FUCK ALL THE DENIERS!' she said out loud as she went down the stairs. However, she'd read some good news. A group of people had taken the Dutch government to court for failing to tackle their CO_2 emissions. And they'd won. If governments could be made accountable for their miserable efforts and even fined, then there was hope, unless of course the government selected high court judges from their own ranks, which had just happened in the USA. SO, FUCK THE USA! The second biggest polluters in the world were likely to take the longest to conform to emission cuts, if at all, and what could she do? What could she do about any of it? Nothing. Nothing at all, but rant to herself.

Perhaps she could chain herself to the railings outside Buckingham Palace like Emily Pankhurst? Or better still Miss Nell, who did the same outside No 10. 'Deeds not Words', it always worked best. But she didn't really think that chaining herself to anything would accomplish much these days, unless it was Airforce One, the pile of ostentatious tin the US president flew around in. Maybe she could blow it up? But it was guarded by four giant Osprey combat helicopters and a hundred and sixty security men – she'd already checked. How could she get anywhere near that? She wasn't James Bond for god's sake. 'What a fucking world! Men with money will fuck us all!' Then she remembered a Dorothy Parker quote. 'If you want to know what God thinks of money, look at the people he gave it to.' She quietly laughed to herself.

She watched another episode of *Homeland*, then another, and another. It was addictive and also fascinating that a woman with bi-polar was the savviest in the male-dominated CIA.

She made lunch, and had a rest on the sofa. She wanted to see Cathy and tell her about the scan, but what good would that do? She was depressed enough already poor thing, telling her she might have a tumour could tip her over the edge. But she hadn't got a tumour, had she? Well, not yet anyway. Maybe she should drop round, take her a cake or something? But she'd done that once before, and Cathy never answered the door, so she'd had to eat it all herself. She decided to call her. There was no answer, so she left it at that, lay back down on the sofa and fell asleep.

She looked at the clock, it was almost four. Since she'd retired the longest hours of the day were between four and seven, why was that? Perhaps we're sick of the day by four and want the night to hurry up, and as we all know when we want time 'to get a lick on' it slows to a snail's pace. Other times of the day were fine. In the morning you were gaining consciousness and doing all the chores, then of course it was lunchtime which was usually quite early for the retired – around twelve. The early afternoon brings promise of the evening, but it's still just a mere twinkle in the day's sky. By three you're almost falling asleep, but just manage to stay awake with a stiff coffee. But then four comes. The dreaded four o'clock blues. So, to snap herself out of it she checked out the local films. *A Star is Born* was showing. The original was co-written by Dorothy Parker, which she'd never seen, but she loved the Judy Garland and Barbara Streisand ones, and it said in the reviews this one was also very good. Lady Gaga was obviously talented, pity she'd given herself such a stupid name, although it was no doubt meant to be ironic. She checked the showing times and decided to get out and shake her etch-a-sketch brain clean of depressing thoughts.

She walked out the cinema tinged with sadness, she wished he hadn't died but at least it wasn't the usual Hollywood ending. Lady Gaga was brilliant, great acting and beautiful tear-jerking songs, she never realised she was that good a singer as most of the stuff she'd heard – generally by accident – sounded like the usual run-of-the-mill over-produced pop music. She hummed the duet to herself, an Oscar-winning song without a doubt, as was Lady Gaga's performance.

She entered the hall and checked the answerphone; no messages, thank god, which meant the doctors hadn't called about the scan. They'd only call if something was wrong, so no news was definitely good news. She'd kept the old phone-line just in case some past acquaintance tried to get in touch, though she had no idea who that might be. She also knew about the damage mobile phone microwaves could cause, so used it for those calls that took forever to get through: doctors, banks, utility and insurance companies, and long calls to friends, well, Cathy.

She went into the kitchen still humming the song and put the kettle on, sat at the table and checked her phone for messages, then went on to Google. The top story caught her eye. 'Hybrid and electric car subsidies to be scrapped by UK Government.' Then she scrolled down to another that read 'UK Government to invest £4 billion into expanding oil refinery.' She felt a blind rage rise within her. BASTARDS! BASTARDS! BASTARDS! BASTARDS! THE MORONIC FUCKING BASTARDS! She texted Sara the link.

It was inconceivable that anyone with a mite of conscience could do such a thing. She knew the Tories could be a bunch of cold heartless wankers but this?

She sat down and began to think it really was the end, which she'd never really believed before, because in the back of her mind was some hope, not much, but enough to believe that in the end humanity would come to its senses. It had to didn't it?

What the hell could she do other than go on yet another march, which there was sure to be after this terrible news? She checked her phone again to re-read the stories. A new one appeared, 'Ex head of NASA says Britain is like America.' She read on; the story attacked both countries' total ignorance toward the IPCC warnings. It made her feel ashamed. What the fucking hell could she do? It was now dark outside and she went to the front door, out into the street and looked around. She had an idea; it was pathetic but she didn't care.

There was an enormous Mercedes SUV in her street that even dwarfed the stupid Range Rovers, and it was parked a hundred metres away. She approached it, lowered her hand, and with her wedding ring slowly walked around it putting a deep scratch in the paintwork with the diamond. Then walked casually back and closed the door.

She felt a lot better as childish as the act was. Fucking ostentatious piece of junk. I should have set fire to it, she mused.

She settled down to watch TV. *Newsnight* was on and they were interviewing some Republican stuffed shirt, asking him whether the US government would take any notice of the report. He said he doubted it. 'We think the damage caused to the American economy by not having a pro low-cost fuel agenda would be worse than the effects of climate change.' Who was he kidding? She immediately turned off the TV and sat motionless on the sofa. He actually said money came before the destruction of his own country! We had finally arrived at the place Karl Marx had predicted, where 'Capitalism destroys itself.' Now it was becoming clear that the only solution to the problem was revolution. But she'd done all she could hadn't she? She didn't have the energy to take to the streets anymore, that was up to the next generation wasn't it? That's what her daughter and son-in-law were now doing. If only she could do something to help them? The worrying had made her headache come back, so the cause was becoming pretty clear.

*

She had a restless night as the headache woke her up every four hours once the painkillers had worn off. She got up at 6 a.m. to make a cup of tea, and checked her phone. The news she read felt like the final nails in the coffin of reason. The US

President Donald Fucking Duck (which she now preferred to call him) had announced his reaction to the IPCC report.

What she read was nothing short of astonishing; 'All scientists have a political agenda.' By which she guessed he meant were all paid to lie by the left, so who paid them? Surely, he meant those scientists who were deniers and paid by wealthy oil companies? He also said that climate change wasn't man-made. Which was a bit like saying meat grows on trees, considering that ninety-seven percent of scientists say it is caused by us. He then added that temperatures may very well reverse on their own. So, he clearly believes that pigs can fly, and finally, it depends what it costs to fix it. Which is what the other Republican dickhead had said, in essence, 'Fuck the people, fuck the wildlife and fuck the planet.' These were clearly the words of a delusional, insane, megalomaniac. If a president can't be impeached for this they might as well put an orang-utan in the White House, at least it'd protect the rainforests.

She poured her tea and realised there were no words left to describe what was going on in the world. Catastrophe, calamity, cataclysmic cock-up all failed miserably. At this rate the world as we know it will be gone, and words with it. She went back upstairs, lay down on the bed and hoped upon hope she was wrong, but also realised it may be a good thing for the planet, as long as humans didn't recover and re-fuck-it-up.

*

It was around eleven o'clock in the morning when the hall phone rang. She was still asleep but the ringing woke her just before the answerphone cut in. She opened her eyes and heard the muffled voice but didn't recognise who it was.

As she slowly woke, she began to worry that it may have been the doctors calling, but re-assured herself they wouldn't call but send a letter if she needed any further tests or had to see a specialist about something they'd found. She drifted back to sleep for another hour, then got up and dressed.

She made herself breakfast: granary toast with marmite, fruit juice, an apple, and some de-caff coffee. She was about to check the news again when she stopped short, did she actually want to read anymore? Ever? Was there any point? Maybe she could filter out anything to do with the environment or climate change? Or even politics in general? In fact, any news whatsoever? It was all pretty dreadful. She put the phone back down and picked up her coffee and cupped it in her hands. The sun came out and shone into the kitchen warming her back, and for a brief moment she almost felt happy. Strange that something so simple could be such a mood changer.

She decided to give Cathy a visit. Her not answering the phone was in a way a call for help. She'd no doubt be in bed, surrounded by dirty plates – as she had been on many previous occasions. Initially she would tell her to leave, not wanting her friend to see the mess she was in, then slowly she would capitulate and allow her to tidy up, do some shopping and even make lunch. When Cathy was really bad, she would make her a huge vegetable stew that would last her a few days.

Cathy took drugs for her depression, but it was the malaise that really consumed her – a side effect of the Serotonin inhibitors. As with most drugs, it solved one problem yet created another. She was either awake and depressed, or half asleep and blissed out, and she preferred the latter. Of course, there were times when she was exactly in the middle, which is what most people would call 'normal'. However, that was less and less frequent these days. Her lifetime of anti-depressants was taking its toll. She took a new book to read her, the last time she was there they finished *Two on a Tower* by Hardy. That was a couple of months ago when she'd had her previous wipe out. She looked through the bookshelves and finally chose *The Years* by Virginia Woolf. It was about the way forces of society suppress the individual spirit, something they could both easily relate to.

She put on her shoes and coat and walked down the hall. The green flashing light on the answerphone caught her eye. She paused. She'd entirely forgotten about the call earlier. She hoped it wasn't the doctors, and decided she'd leave it till she got back from Cathy's, then realised it might be her leaving a message, so was forced to play it. Her finger hovered over the button a moment, then she stabbed it. There was a beep followed by;

'Hello, this is a message for Connie Noble. Could you call the surgery as soon as possible? Thank you.' She froze. Oh my god. Oh my god. Oh my god. She began to pace in the hall, toward the front door and back, toward the front door and back, toward the front door and back, six or seven times. She went into the living room. Oh my god, oh my god, oh my god. And paced the full length, back and forth, back and forth, back and forth. She sat in the armchair, and stood up again. Oh my god, oh my god, oh my god, this is it. This is really it! She was terrified, sat again, buried her face in her hands, and rocked to and fro for a few minutes. Could you call the surgery as soon as possible? Why did they say that? Why did they have to say that? Stupid bloody secretary! Now look at me! Now look what you've done to me! After a short while she realised they couldn't have really said much else. Obviously, something was serious. Or was it? Maybe it wasn't serious, but of concern to the doctor. Many people had investigations and were fine, weren't they? But she'd had investigations and they'd found something. Oh my god, oh my god. She ran for help, into the kitchen, into the cupboard, opened the bottle of brandy and poured a large measure, then a bit more. She swigged it back and felt the warmth enter her body. She poured another shot, and within ten minutes was sitting almost calmly at the table. 'It's fine, it's fine, stay calm, deep breaths, deep breaths.'

She felt her body sinking into a safe place as it had done on many occasions throughout her life when she'd had a health scare. She poured herself another drink and gradually became more optimistic. OK, so even if it is a brain tumour it might be benign. Or maybe I've got Alzheimer's or something else altogether? It could be a hundred things couldn't it? And I might live years, ten years, twenty years, who knows? Feeling in a comfort zone she went into the hall and called the doctors. It rang a good ten minutes and was finally answered by the same voice on the machine.

'Park Road Surgery, how can I help?' said the receptionist.

'I'd like to make an appointment with Dr Suza.'

'Your name?'

'Connie, Connie Noble.'

Oh yes, I left you a message earlier, didn't I? How's tomorrow morning at eight forty-five?'

'Fine, thanks.' She slowly put done the phone, the panic setting in again. Eight forty-five in the morning? That is urgent.

She sat again at the kitchen table and slowly finished off the quarter bottle of brandy. But the optimism had now gone, the effect of the alcohol neutralised by the adrenaline.

She remained sitting at the table for a further six hours and had completely forgotten about visiting Cathy's. It began to get dark outside and she got up and went to the bathroom downstairs. Returning to the kitchen she sat down again and lowered her head onto the table and fell asleep.

It was 3 a.m. when she woke stiff and cold. She went upstairs, climbed into bed fully clothed, set the alarm for 7 a.m. and instantly fell back to sleep.

*

She woke sharply at six forty-five knowing immediately something was wrong, but not what until a few seconds later when the synapses began to fire. She was too exhausted now to panic, other than issuing a flat 'Fuck.' She stared at the patterns on the curtains. They'd been put up when she and Jim moved in over twenty years ago. As a couple they had never really bothered constantly upgrading the house, never really cared much about anything material.

As she looked at them, she saw the stream, the trees and the sea beyond, even though none of these were depicted in the simple patterns, it was what she had always imagined – her way of escaping. Imaginary places were always far more interesting than real ones, as they are in dreams. She walked down the lane, past the stream, and over the hill to the sea, and stood on the cliff top staring out to the horizon. The sun slowly appeared through the material and for some reason she began to cry, but had no idea why. The alarm sounded, making her jump out of her skin. 'FUCK!' She quickly turned it off, got up and began to prepare herself for the ordeal ahead.

The name 'Connie Noble' scrolled itself in red along the dot matrix screen. 'Connie Noble. Dr Suza. Room 4.'

She walked along the brightly lit corridor and approached the door, tentatively opening it. Dr Suza's smiling face stared up at her.

'Take a seat, Connie.' Dr Suza smiled again. Connie always thought that if anyone had to give her bad news, she would want it to be her: Dr Esther Suza, warm, considerate with a wonderfully gentle Spanish accent; better than some British doctors with their slight air of arrogance. Dr Suza looked at the screen in front of her. She turned to face Connie.

'I wanted to see you before you got the appointment with the neurologist.' Dr Suza took a deep breath.

'The results have come back, Connie.' She paused. 'I'm not sure how to say this.' Dr Suza shifted her weight in the chair. 'I'm sorry, I'm sorry, you have a brain tumour, and they're pretty certain it's malignant.'

Connie froze, the moment in her life she had always been dreading had arrived. It was like walking slap bang into a black wall. Everything around her changed, and in the remaining few minutes she hardly heard anything Dr Suza said.

She eventually touched her arm, and Connie took her cue to leave saying 'Thank you,' quietly under her breath. Dr Suza watched her go almost in tears.

***

Chapter 4

The corridor she walked down had changed, the reception had changed and as she went out into the bright sunlight so had the world. The trees, the cars, the people were all muted and distanced, as if being viewed through thick plate glass. She passed smiling people, who were unintentionally mocking her predicament. The cars silently glided by with happy carefree occupants; even the trees happily swayed in the light breeze, whilst Connie felt no longer part of it, removed from the everyday. She was dying and therefore slipping into another dimension.

Arriving back at the house and turning the key in the lock she had a sudden dread of opening the door, and when she did understood why. Every picture on the wall, piece of post on the hall table, the carpet, the bannister, the hat stand, these things which she only saw an hour ago, all these so familiar things were now different. Different because the last time she saw them she was oblivious to the news, and as she looked at them, she yearned to see them again as she had then, but knew she never would. Everything she looked at reminded her of the past: the carefree, illness-free, past. Now it all reminded her of pending mortality.

She sat at the kitchen table, blank, registering and feeling nothing. It was as if she wasn't there at all. She looked down at the alien tea cup on the table out of which she'd drank only a short while ago; it now belonged to a different lifetime. The sun flooded the kitchen yet it gave out no warmth, and made all the corners in the room sharp and intense. She wanted to cry but for whom? Herself? Her daughter? Yes, her daughter. She wanted to cry as she imagined her crying at the funeral, seeing her cry made her want to cry, the same way seeing anyone cry in grief made you want to also cry.

She tried to remember what Dr Suza had told her. It was close to the brain stem, which she knew was vital in regulating the heartbeat. She did say that radio and chemotherapy might reduce it, but there was still only a very small chance that it could be operable. In other words, she was fucked.

A sudden surge of fear and helplessness engulfed her. She got up and paced the house repeating 'No' over and over to herself until there were no 'No's left. She finally sat down in the living room exhausted. She desperately wanted to drink, but realised that only made her optimistic when she was worrying about results, not when she'd got them. This time there was no escape, none at all. She'd entered a slowly darkening room, the doors had locked behind her, and she was terrified.

Sara was due to Skype her later, but she had no idea how she was going to handle the call without telling her. But she knew she couldn't. Sara had enough on her plate with the child, and the news could make her miscarry. She had to calm down, or else she would suspect something immediately.

She finally poured herself a drink, then a second, and felt surprisingly serene.

She sat at the computer in the living room and waited for the call. Bang on midday the alert light flashed and the tinny bell sounded. It was eleven at night there now as Sara always called just before she went to bed. Her image came up.

'Hi, Mum.'

'Hi, Sara.'

'Are you OK?'

'Why, don't I look it?'

'No, you look fine.'

'Well I am fine.'

'Good.' They talked for while about the US government's attitude to climate change.

'Kurt wants to nuke the fuckers, and the Oz government. Invite them all to a big party out in the desert, and boom, they vanish.'

'Sounds like a great idea.'

However, Kurt, Sara and Connie weren't naïve. They knew many countries, particularly Australia, relied heavily on the export of fossil fuels and if they were going to stop producing, they needed compensation, they needed help from other countries. Reducing atmospheric CO_2 needed to be a global effort, but it didn't solve anything to be simply in denial.

Sara told her they had planned to come back to England in the new year when the baby was a couple of months old.

'If only you could fly Mum, you could be here for the birth.'

'I can't help it if being in a toothpaste tube thirty thousand feet up scares the shit out of me, and you shouldn't be flying either, none of us should.'

'You want to see your grandchild, don't you?'

'Of course I do.'

'We know we're hypocrites, Mum. Even when we fly to the reef for research, we feel bad, but what else can we do? It takes four days to drive to Cairns. It's twelve hundred miles.'

'I know, I know. It's not easy to be morally sound in this world.' Sara stared at her mother.

'I miss you, Mum.'

'I miss you, Sara. Why the hell did you have to marry an Aussie in the first place?'

'His passion for the environment swept me off my feet, and that's your fault.' She couldn't argue with that. She finally said goodnight and felt a little better for her call. Though a few minutes after she disappeared from the screen she began to sink back into the hopeless void. Would she ever see Sara again? Or her grandchild? She would have to wait until she'd seen the specialist to find out.

She sat in the living room feeling nauseous as the anxiety had returned. She knew she must eat something, but then again, maybe starving herself to death would be quicker and less painful? She'd never thought of suicide before, but could now see why people wanted to commit euthanasia – to avoid the ticking clock and slow degeneration of the faculties.

Even though it was daytime, she pulled the living room curtains shut and sat in the dark for the rest of the afternoon. She found it comforting, rather like being in a float tank that she'd once experienced in Totnes, or Narnia as it was known because of the large number of hippies who lived there. She had nothing against hippies, but it just wasn't her thing to drop out and live in a haze of marijuana – though strangely that appealed to her now.

As the outside world receded, she realised why Cathy spent days shut away. Maybe having no stimulus re-charged the batteries? But that wasn't going to work for her as the battery was short circuiting, and her source of life was draining away. She was in two minds whether to check the stages of degeneration on Google, but realised it was a stupid idea. Someone had once said that Dr Google was a melodramatic scaremonger whose knowledge was always at least five years out of date. She heard the post box open and shut, got up feeling slightly dizzy, went into the hallway, picked up the letter and opened it. Her appointment with the specialist was in two days' time.

She barely moved from the armchair and when it was time for bed found she couldn't sleep in the main room as this was a reminder of her 'before' life. She sat on the dressing table stool and stared at the half-light coming through the curtains from the street lamp. She saw the picture, but the lane no longer led to the sea but a dark cave. She went to the spare room where she'd slept after Jim had died. She lay awake on the small single bed. She never wanted to sleep in the other room again as that was BC – before cancer – this was now AD – after diagnosis. She felt quite proud of the pun. She turned over again and again trying to get to sleep and finally crashed through sheer exhaustion.

*

When she woke the following morning, she wasn't quite as scared, although she could still feel the fear trying to kick down the wall she'd erected to keep it out. She got up, made tea, paced the house, then decided the best thing would be to try and take her mind off it.

She attempted to re-read *Rebecca* by Daphne du Maurier, but quickly put it down during the opening description of 'Manderley,' now fallen down, decrepit and derelict, and remembered the story reeked of death. It was also upsetting as she'd first read it in Greece on her first holiday with Jim – BC.

She turned on the TV and within a few moments of the crime drama a dead body lay on a mortician's slab. Even when she put on the radio it was a programme about cancer.

She was reminded of her first boyfriend, when he ditched her wherever she went songs about splitting up were playing, and it drove her crazy.

She wanted to call Cathy to see if she was alright, but wasn't sure she could hide the diagnosis from her as they shared everything. Poor Cathy. Poor Connie too, what a pair they'd make, and who would have thought it would come to this all those carefree years ago? Life is cruel, and life's a bitch, what had they both done to deserve this in their early sixties? Most women lived happily and illness free until their eighties and nineties, didn't they? But it was the luck of the draw, and she'd never won anything in her life as far as she could remember, not a premium bond, nor a lottery, or even a game of bingo or a bet on a horse. She'd couldn't even remember winning a game of Monopoly or Cluedo as a child, so surely the diagnosis wasn't exactly a surprise was it? Just bad luck. To indulge herself even further she checked on the internet for the chances of getting a brain tumour – one hundred and fifty to one. You'd never bet on a horse with those odds would you? Yet she had, and won. Fucking shit and bollocks!

She realised she was beginning to wallow in self-pity and stopped. Children in Africa and third world countries die before they can walk so shut up! She tried to be grateful for the life she'd had, tried to be positive and philosophical. But it didn't work. Fuck that! I want to live to a hundred! She was angry now. She got up, took an ornament off the mantelpiece and hurled it across the room.

'Fuck, Fuck, Fuck, Fuck.' She collapsed onto the sofa and calmed down a little. What was the point in getting angry? Somebody had to get cancer, didn't they? Why not her? On the other hand, why? There were some horrible bastards in the world who'd had long lives, look at those Nazi war criminals going to trial when they were in their nineties? What right had they got to live a full life? Even if they were wracked with guilt? Fuck them! Fuck them all!

By the early evening her system couldn't deal with the level of anxiety anymore, so endorphins had kicked in like a natural sedative. Perhaps this was the state people talked about. This was the reason some people managed to be so brave when confronting death. Some were even able to write books that tracked their demise, something she could never understand before. She lay on the sofa, the phone in the hall suddenly rang making her jump. Who the hell could that be? No doubt a cold call, it was usually around this time.

She heard the answerphone kick in, usually they'd be a continuous tone as the line went dead as they hung up, but she heard a faint voice, and quickly realised it was Cathy. Should she answer? Could she answer and not give away her state? But she may need her help? She quickly got up, went into the hall and picked up the phone.

'Cathy?'

'Hi,' came a faint voice in reply.

'How are you?'

'Not great, Connie.'

'Oh, I'm sorry.' There was a silence of at least ten seconds as Cathy didn't know what to say next. However, Connie did, but was reluctant to do so. Visiting Cathy was going to be tough, really tough, but the words seemed to come out automatically.

'Do you need me to come over?'

'Please,' came the almost desperate voice.

'Give me half an hour, Cathy.'

'Thanks.'

She put down the phone and sighed. Then realised going might be a good thing, even though Cathy may not exactly lighten her mood.

She rang the doorbell. It was quite a while before Cathy answered. She looked pale and her hair was matted and greasy. She wore a dressing gown and old trainers with flattened heels from being used as makeshift slippers. She entered the house and Cathy shuffled behind her. As she'd expected the place was a tip. Mail was scattered all over the hall floor. As they passed the lounge/bedroom she could see clothes strewn everywhere, and on the coffee-table were six mugs and two over-filled ash trays. She walked into the kitchen; piles of dirty plates, empty packets and cans. Cathy suddenly hugged her tightly.

'Thanks for coming.'

'No problem. Shall I make a cup of tea?'

'Yeah. Thanks.' Cathy sat at the table and slowly began to cry.

'I'm sorry, Connie.'

'No need to apologise to me.' Connie sat down and took Cathy's hand.

'It's OK.'

'Everything is so, so dark.'

'I know the feeling.'

They drank tea and Cathy said she couldn't live on her own any longer, couldn't cope with the cleaning and cooking on her bad days. Connie joked she hadn't noticed and the two of them suddenly fell apart laughing. Cathy then told her she was leaving the rented flat and moving into a kind of sheltered home, where they could give a hand with the chores and supervise her medication. However, it wasn't in London, but in the countryside just outside Lewes. She was sick of looking at her neighbour's brick walls for the past ten years.

'Lewes? That's near where Virginia Woolf lived, isn't it?' said Connie.

'Yes, Rodmell, but don't worry. If I kill myself, I've no intention of getting wet in the process, I'll do it in the comfort of my own fucking bed,' replied Cathy.

'Well that's a relief,' said Connie, smiling. The two women stared at each other. Connie was suspicious that something else was wrong.

'Are you OK?' Cathy looked at her and exhaled slowly.

'I've a... I've been diagnosed with the early onset of dementia.' Connie couldn't believe it.

'Oh Cathy, I'm so sorry.'

'But bollocks to it, eh?' Cathy smiled, got up and pulled a bottle of scotch out of the cupboard and poured two large shots into dirty glasses she got off the drainer.

'Well it can't fuck me up any more than I already am can it?' she said ironically.

'What, the scotch or the dementia?'

'Either.'

'I suppose not.' Connie was on the verge of telling her about the tumour, but felt it was Cathy who needed the support, to reveal her secret would almost seem like 'one-up-man-ship.' She touched her hand across the table.

'Oh Cathy, I really don't know what to say.'

'There isn't anything to say. My life's been shit for years. But I've still got you, haven't I?'

'Some consolation that must be.'

'Oh yeah sure. You've done everything for me other than wipe my arse.'

'I have to draw the line somewhere. That's one thing I never intend to do for anyone.'

'Never say never, Connie, just wait till I go really gaga.'

'You dare.'

'Oh, don't worry, it's all planned. You visit me, take me out for a stroll in the wheelchair. I crap myself, and in my far away demented gaze you will just recognise the merest hint of a perverted smile, and that my girl, will be my life's mission accomplished!'

'You scheming bastard!'

'Ah, but there's method in my madness. It's for stealing that lovely man from me at that party in Hove.'

'But you were busy throwing up outside, you didn't think he was going to want to snog you tasting of vomit, did you?'

'Men would have died to kiss me tasting of vomit, Connie.'

'I guess they would, disgusting buggers!' They drank more scotch and talked of their comedic encounters with men well into the small hours, until Connie's headache really kicked in and she had to finally leave. They stood at the door for some time hugging each other.

'You've cheered me up no end, Connie, as always.'

'You too.' Connie wondered whether she would ever see her friend again. As she walked the short distance home, she couldn't believe Cathy had a terminal condition as well, though she could live for many more years to come, but it was still ironic. Maybe she should have come clean herself? But who knows what she might have done? She'd already overdosed twice in the past year.

*

Connie woke at six a.m. the following morning with a terrible hangover. She got up, clutching her head and slowly made her way toward the bathroom. Poured a glass of water and took two painkillers. The phone downstairs rang. Who would call at this god earthly hour? The answerphone cut in and it was Cathy who began to leave a message. Worried it might be serious she went downstairs as quickly as she dared with her pounding head and picked up the phone.

'Hi Cathy?'

'Oh Connie, you're there?'

'Barely.'

'Same here, but I have to tell you something.'

'What?'

'I'm leaving this morning. They're arriving at eight, helping me pack my important stuff, then the flat's being cleared on Friday. I knew you'd want to help, which is why I didn't tell you. I didn't want to say goodbye either, as it isn't goodbye is it?'

'No, no, Cathy. It isn't.'

'I'll call you in a few days, then you can visit me, can't you?'

'Yes sure.'

'See you soon, Connie.' The phone went dead. Cathy seemed very happy, but that's how her moods sometimes went. On the other hand, it was hardly surprising as she'd finally be moving from that horrible gloomy flat after all these years. Well that was it, wasn't it? Her only friend gone. Even if it wasn't a normal friendship it was all she had, all that was left in London. Now she was totally on her own. There was one consolation however, she'd have time to come to terms with her condition before seeing Cathy again, that's assuming she lived long enough?

She went back to bed but couldn't sleep. She thought about Cathy and in some way envied her moving out of the city. She was sick of it too, but was always worried if she moved out to the country she'd be surrounded by *Daily Mail*-reading Tories. The UK was just like the USA – right wingers tended to live in the 'sticks' and the lefties in the cities. She imagined getting into all kinds of trouble surrounded by people who were fiercely patriotic and subsequently had anti-multi-cultural attitudes, not to mention being pro-Brexit and maybe climate change deniers to boot. North London had one of the strongest left-wing communities in the entire country, which is one reason she had chosen to live there after university. However, for Cathy this wouldn't be a problem, she wasn't that interested in politics. All she needed now was a comfortable home with someone to take care of her, and maybe a nice view out of the window. Connie realised in the not-too-distant future she might need that herself, and the thought petrified her.

She drifted in and out of sleep until around midday, when she got up to take more painkillers for the headache. It was hard to know whether this was the hangover, the tumour, or both. She thought about calling Cathy to see if she was OK, but she'd probably gone by now, and was travelling through open countryside, with big skies and a backdrop of the downs and the promise of the sea beyond. Connie had always wanted to live near the sea, but it had never worked out. She could now, but what was the point? She'd no doubt be dead by the time the house was sold and she'd found somewhere on the coast.

She could go and live in a hotel near the sea for a while. But how sad would that be to die alone in a hotel room. A horrible end. But why would it be less horrible than dying at home. OK, you could be surrounded by your possessions, but who cares. Surrounded by the spirit of Jim? Not really, she didn't believe in that stuff; he wasn't here anymore. No, she didn't have a reason to be at home at all. Maybe the best place for her would be in Cathy's home, with her best friend, and near the sea. But not yet, she didn't feel the time was right, after all she only had headaches, apart from that she felt fine. And she was certain there was something she could do. Something she could do before she died. Once she'd seen the specialist, maybe then she could make plans?

She lay down on the sofa, it was the time of day the low afternoon autumnal sun streamed into the lounge. She closed her eyes and imagined she was on a beach in Greece; the gentle slap of waves, smell of wild oregano, and cicadas in the trees. And for an hour she was as happy as it was possible to be, for someone who knew her end was near.

She still didn't feel hungry but tried to eat some toast. However, her throat was so dry she could hardly swallow. Was that just anxiety or her brain unable to connect to her reflexes? She wondered what the tumour looked like, a lump of red gristle or a blob of wobbly grey matter? Probably gristle, like a large walnut, a mini rogue brain crowding out the good one. But how did she get it in the first place? Did she bang her head at some point? Or was it just lying dormant till old age? One tiny cell waiting to mutate and multiply. Something must trigger it.

She lay down again and realised how crap booze could make her feel. She'd had many years of social drinking and wondered if that had caused the cancer. After all, she'd drank far more than the current accepted levels, then again who hadn't. It was one glass a night, or preferably none, even one was supposedly bad for you. If the government really wanted us to cut down drinking they should stop behaving like fucking idiots – they were enough to drive us all into the nearest bar.

As the day wore on, she became more and more fearful about her appointment. How long would she be given if it was inoperable? Would it be years? Or months? Even weeks? Or was it so far developed she could die at any moment? Like this evening?

There was a part of her that couldn't wait to discover the truth, and another that wanted to ignore it and not even bother turning up. Would that be any worse? Not knowing? Not having a proper prognosis? She could just pretend it didn't exist, couldn't she? She quite liked the way that felt.

*

It was the day of the appointment and she'd barely slept again, she got up at six a.m., and sat in the kitchen staring at the wall until it was time to leave for the hospital. She decided she had to go and face the music, if there was a slightest hope of a cure, she wouldn't receive it sitting at home in denial, would she?

She sat on the bus and overheard the conversation in front of her. Two women were talking about a close friend who had recently died…of a brain tumour. OH GREAT! What were the chances of overhearing that?

She was in two minds whether to go again, but finally decided to just get it over with.

Taking in none of the surroundings she sat in the waiting room, she blanked the man and woman who both came out the consultant's door crying. A name was called, but it didn't sound like hers.

A buzzing in her ears began, rose to a high-pitched whistle then faded, she looked up and saw a man in his late sixties wearing a suite smiling at her. She looked around, assuming he wasn't looking at her, then realised he was.

'Connie?' She nodded, 'Come in.' She got up and walked toward him, as she got nearer, she realised how small he was. 'Hello. I'm Dr Pradesh.' He beckoned her into the office, closed the door and gestured she sit down on the sofa. It was a surprise when he sat next to her. 'How are you feeling?'

'Fine.' She said, then hesitated. 'Not great.' He nodded. 'Headache, and buzzing in my ears, you know?' Dr Pradesh nodded again sympathetically. After a few other questions similar to the ones that Dr Suza had asked her he took a torch off the table in front of him and shone it into her eyes, getting her to look left then right, and put the torch down again. He got her to do the finger nose test, and finally asked if she'd stand up and walk across the room placing her toes to her heel in small fairy-like steps. She sat again next to the doctor.

'I've seen the scans. It's… it's a tough one, Connie. There are parts of the brain even a top surgeon is terrified of going anywhere near. The tumour embeds itself into the tissue and wraps itself around vital blood vessels. They're known as malignant infiltratory tumours – very tricky things. I could try radio or chemotherapy to shrink it, but I'll be honest, I would say there was little chance of that working. It's a grade four, very advanced you see.' Connie slowly nodded.

'We'd operate if we could but the tumours also too near the brain stem and cerebellum.' The doctor touched the nape of his neck. 'Right here.' Connie slowly nodded again.

'I know.'

'The treatment's up to you, Connie.'

'I'll think about it.' Connie braced herself for the question she didn't want to ask.

'So how long? How long have I got?'

'It's always hard to say. But my guess, my guess would be three to six months.' Connie lowered her head.

'I'm sorry.' Dr Pradesh put his hand on her shoulder. 'I'm so sorry.' Very gradually he removed his hand. 'I'll give you something to help the headache.' Connie raised her head and looked at him.

'What, Nurofen?'

'No, something a bit stronger than that.' Dr Pradesh got up, walked to his desk and returned with a prescription and handed it to her.

'There's also a mild sedative to calm you down if you need it.'

'No, thanks,' said Connie, 'I'll manage.' Dr Pradesh smiled.

'Make another appointment within the next few days with the receptionist and ask her for an information pack.'

'About how I'm going to bloody die?' Dr Pradesh looked forlorn.

'I'm really very sorry, Connie.' She took her cue to leave.

'Thanks. Sorry I was rude.' Dr Pradesh smiled.

'No need to apologise.'

She sat on the bus, after a lifetime of fearing death she'd now arrived at judgement day. Six months maximum, twenty-four weeks left! And who knows what she'd be like in the final months? She had the information pamphlet on her lap and as soon as she got home burned it in the fireplace. She had all the facts she needed. She had a brain tumour and was going to die; chemotherapy was a waste of time and probably make her last few months' even worse. If the specialist thought there was any hope at all he would have said so. She'd go to the next appointment out of courtesy and stock up on painkillers. In the meantime, she would try and plan her next move.

***

Chapter 5

She quickly sank back into the dark hole; she'd known things were serious but only now it really sunk in. She realised part of her had hoped it was curable, even though Dr Suza told her it probably wasn't. You needed some hope, didn't you? Because when all hope goes nothings left is there? Nothing at all.

She lay on the sofa in a foetal position, and wished she was a child again, lying in the living room with the fire burning recovering from flu, her mum bringing her hot chocolate and other treats. But there was no fire, treats, or mother to look after her. She was alone and cold and dying. She burst into tears and sobbed and sobbed like a child for a good half hour, continually wiping away the tears with her sleeve.

She was seven when she had her first panic attack thinking about death. The psychiatrist had said most people don't begin to have feelings of mortality until they're in their forties, but that wasn't going to help her was it? He said the reason she had an acute phobia was seeing her rabbit die. She could have told him that! Then he attempted to spin her lies about the after-life being a field full of white bunnies. She told him he was an idiot, and he refused to treat her anymore. Which was just as well - it was bankrupting her parents.

One day I'll be dead, gone, was her consistent mantra, but she eventually found a way of dealing with it by telling herself they'd be little to live for if all her friends were gone. And in some ways, she was right, but it still didn't mean you wanted to die, did it? Nobody wanted to die.

She remembered another psychiatrist's attempt to soothe her panics. *You know those party balloons that go up in the air when you let them go?* She'd nodded. *That's what death's like.* She'd looked at her quizzically for a while and then said *but they come down. Dad found one in the back garden and put it in the dustbin. I don't want to end up in a dustbin!* Connie couldn't help smiling to herself at the memory. The other way she'd managed to parry the fear of death was simple, it was so far away it wasn't worth worrying about. In fact, so far off into the vast universe of the future that it may never even arrive, but it had, and at an astonishing rate.

*

She slept surprisingly well that night, and didn't wake till ten a.m. The news had now sunk in so she didn't wake in a panic, though she was initially disorientated sleeping in the spare room. She got up and made tea, but still wasn't hungry. Her headache returned so she took two of the painkillers that had been prescribed and went into the living room and lay on the sofa. As she lay there, she wondered how Cathy was settling in to her new home and hoped she'd call soon, but she knew Cathy.

She began to feel scared again, she tried to resist the dark place and began humming to herself, then stopped and had a thought. Was she just going to lie on the sofa every day until the ambulance finally took her away? Maybe it was about time she accepted it? If she didn't, she would ruin what time she had left? Surely there was something she could do with these last few months? But it was hard to know what? There had to be some purpose to her life? If only she could find a way to really help stop the destructive things happening to the world. It had to be a form of rebellion. She knew that nothing peaceful was going to work, well it hadn't so far had it? So, what could she do to make everyone sit up and notice?

Re-invigorated with purpose, even optimism, she suddenly felt very hungry and went into the kitchen to make herself breakfast. She made scrambled eggs with tomatoes on toast while she checked Google News for the first time in days. It was the same shit, rising of the ultra-right in Europe, sea level rises, severe hurricane in Hawaii, Democrat supporters in the USA receiving letter bombs from far-right sympathisers. The news was either attributed to climate change or about the rise of the political movement that would ignore it. The same old helplessness set in, what could she do about any of this other than rant, march and maybe cause a bit of childish damage in the street? Nothing other than killing the man most intent on destroying the planet, Donald Fucking Duck. But it would only serve to lionise him, and no doubt increase Republican support. The headache throbbed and she felt she was slipping into the abyss again and went and lay on the living room sofa.

She desperately needed to find a way to cheer herself up; what was the point of spending your final months in a state of abject depression over things you could do nothing about? She should take a leaf out of other people's books, ignore it and carry on as if nothing was wrong, though she knew that could never happen. She was stuck with being an angst-ridden individual like it or not. Perhaps she could find a way of doing something important and cheer herself up at the same time? Surely, she deserved that? Something exhilarating and exciting she'd never done before? She knew the name for this but hated it – bucket list – it was stupid. What dickhead thought of that?

She stretched on the sofa pulled the blanket around her and began to day dream about places she'd never been, which was pretty much everywhere, as she couldn't fly. The trip to Greece had been a three-week overland drive in the early months of their relationship, then once again by train and ferry when Sara was young, but nowhere really since, other than a wedding in Ireland where it had rained all weekend, and two day trips to France, and of course the disastrous holiday on her own to Nice. What an un-adventurous life she'd had? They could have taken direct ferries to the Netherlands, Scandinavia or Spain, or driven across Europe again to Italy or Greece, but they never did. Jim didn't seem that interested in travel once he reached his thirties. His idea of a holiday was a week in a caravan at Great Yarmouth, but Connie always yearned to go further.

She pondered for a while. Where could she go? It had to be somewhere exciting she could get to without flying. Maybe she could go by ship? She loved the ocean. Where could you sail to from the UK in November? Suddenly New York came to mind, of course New York, where else? She'd always wanted to go there and remembered Cathy once saying that apart from mountains, lakes and oceans, the most breath-taking thing she'd ever seen was Manhattan at night; it had sent a shiver down her spine. They'd driven out of the underpass and up onto Brooklyn Bridge, and there it was towering above her in all its dazzling splendour. Like a city built with millions of twinkling stars. She'd described it as the eighth wonder of the world.

Thinking about it sent a shiver down Connie's spine too. And of course! She could stay at the Algonquin, the hotel where the New York literati met every lunchtime at the round table, she could stay in the same hotel as Dorothy Parker! The more she thought about it the more excited she got. She would go after the next appointment with Dr Pradesh, that's assuming you could sail there this time of year?

She picked up her phone and googled 'Cruises to New York', within seconds the Cunard website appeared.

The 'Queen Mary' sailed from Southampton on November 10th and 24th. It returned on the 18th and 2nd of December. She could go on the 10th and come back on the 2nd. That was just over a week's time, perfect, assuming it wasn't fully booked. She checked the prices, four thousand pounds, seven days cruising, two weeks in New York and back. Wonderful. But then she snapped out of her reverie. How could she? How could she go on a cruise ship knowing how much pollution they caused? She'd read they produced as much CO_2 as sixty thousand cars a day. As much soot as a million, and as much sulphur dioxide as thirteen million! But it would be the first and last cruise she would ever make, and she'd hardly been anywhere in her life, had she? And if the government brought in travel quotas, as they should, surely, she'd be owed a few air/sea miles? And the ship would still sail with or without her? But she knew that was a crap excuse, and that she'd be a terrible hypocrite if she did. She appealed to an imaginary courtroom: But I'll be dead soon, won't I? And I'll consume nothing, no electricity, no gas, nothing at all. I'll be doing my bit for the planet by dying. But the jury was still out, so she decided to hold fire on booking the trip, after all, you can't devote a large proportion of your life to protecting nature, then go and set fire to a reserve can you? Or join the 'Save the Tiger' campaign then go and shoot one? Connie was in a terrible quandary. Was she just going to die on this fucking sofa?

She got up, sat at the desk, turned on her computer, and idly browsed through photos of the Queen Mary, the grand restaurants, bars, and the opulent cabins, although she could only afford the cheapest. She looked at the Algonquin, which in many ways was just as luxurious, and day dreamed about being there. This kind of decadence wasn't something she'd normally care about, she and Jim had only stayed in a posh hotel once, and that was on their wedding night at Clivedon, and he'd thought it was a total waste of money. She had to agree that four hundred pounds for the night was a ridiculous amount, but the sunken bath, free aroma oils, robes, champagne and chocolates was pure unashamed luxury, and it was her honeymoon after all.

She looked at shots of the New York city skyline, the Chrysler, Empire State Building, Central Park and the Statue of Liberty. The more she looked the more she was determined to go. Should she ask Sara what she thought about taking a trip on a polluting ship? A thought then occurred to her, she could offset her carbon footprint. She quickly typed it into the search engine and came up with a number of sites. One of them allowed you to make a donation for reforestation in Nicaragua. She followed the steps, it worked out how much CO_2 you were producing and charged you per kg. The cost was eighty pounds for a round trip to New York, so she gave a hundred. She got her credit card and made the payment, but it still didn't feel quite right that you could pay for your guilt and pollution, it felt privileged, and of course it was. So, she sent another hundred pounds which made her feel slightly better.

Even though she'd made the donation she still deliberated about booking the cruise, was it folly? What was she doing? And where was her resolve to do something useful, something important before she died? The question kept on nagging her. She returned to the shots of New York, and scrolled through more images, Times Square, Broadway, and the Guggenheim. It occurred to her that if any country in the world needed a kick up the arse – a reminder of its lack of commitment to CO2 reduction – it was the USA, the current American government. Maybe she could demonstrate there in some way or other?

Staring at the screen began to give her a headache, so she took a painkiller and lay back on the sofa. She idly picked up her phone and skimmed through the news; only sixteen countries on track to meet Paris emissions targets. Fracking in Lancashire causes multiple earthquakes. Sixty percent of wild animals have vanished since 1970. And at the bottom an article about the 'Extinction Rebellion'. There was an inaugural gathering in Parliament Square the following day. It was a new organisation that felt it was time for direct action. No more peaceful marches, but non-violent disruption, to force the government out of their pathetic complacency. They planned to establish themselves around the world as a final attempt to stop the mounting insanity. She would go along and find out more.

*

She stepped off at Embankment tube excited about joining a group of like-minded people. She always felt a great warmth surrounding her when joining a protest of some description. It was good to be on the frontline of change, gave life a sense of purpose.

As she approached Parliament Square, she looked up at the Commons and imagined them all inside sitting by open fires playing cards and drinking tea. An exclusive club of indecisive idiots all too frightened to lay down the gauntlet of change for fear of being marginalised and kicked out of office. They should have a slogan etched over the main entrance

'Words not Deeds'. Perhaps they'd be more in touch with the real world if the building was a glass office block, and not an archaic pile of stones akin to Hogwarts. She began to see a gathering assembled in the square.

This wasn't a march but the beginning of the movement, where they would state their manifesto and demands to worldwide governments and issue a 'Rising Up' call to everyone who cares about the future. Three hundred or so people were gathered, their Rebellion flags flying in the breeze. First a shaman spoke about the dying planet, then there was a poem along similar lines and a song accompanied by the usual bongos. This was the side of environment movements that she disliked. Not because of the people concerned – they cared as much as she did – but what they represented in the eye of the press and to the man on the street; a bunch of dope smoking dropouts and street theatre performers. It couldn't be helped but they were a soft target, an easy way to discredit and ridicule the movement. The fact that ninety percent were just normal people, including teachers, doctors and lawyers was neither here nor there. However, what followed was more direct and less genteel, but some journalists would have already left with their stereotypes intact. A scientist, an MP, a church leader and a prominent journalist spoke. All decided that direct action was the only way forward.

The Labour MP – at least one politician cared about the future – said the most startling fact was that in the current budget nothing at all had been put aside for renewable energy subsidy, but thirteen billion pounds had been allocated to the fossil fuel industry. In fact, no subsidies would be handed out for clean energy at all until 2025.

She walked away from the gathering and strolled around the square. Statues of great liberators who believed and fought for their just cause; Mandela, Gandhi and Millicent Garret Fawcett – the most prominent leader of the suffragette movement. She held a banner in her hands. 'Courage Calls to Courage Everywhere' which struck Connie as the perfect slogan for an activist movement. She turned to look at the House of Commons again and wondered why there was virtually no one within those walls with a single ounce of courage. The only commitment they had was to themselves. She was aware of her headache returning and was about to leave when a show of hands agreed to block the roads. As the lights turned red at the busy intersection of the square a few protesters began to sit down, forming a human chain. Many more joined in, the few police that were present helpless. Within moments hundreds had flooded into the road to join them. The lights changed and the traffic was blocked. This was the beginning of a global revolution of civil disobedience. The poll tax riots worked, and if you could galvanise that many people over an unfair tax, then how many could you get together to protect our future? Connie watched with pride as people of all ages sat down in the road.

Glancing up again at the statue of Millicent Fawcett an idea slowly came to her, suddenly she knew what to do; it was a revelation, and if she could succeed it wouldn't fail to grab the headlines, not only in the USA, but around the world. She felt uplifted, excited, and exquisitely serene all at the same time. The idea was pure genius if she could pull it off. She watched, more people formed the roadblock, she desperately wanted to join in, but feared if she were dragged off and arrested – as some now were – it might jeopardise her entry into the USA. She sat down under the statue, looked up, and smiled at Millicent for giving her the inspiration.

*

She arrived home now totally committed to carrying out the protest – if it was remotely feasible – but still felt that travelling on a polluting cruise ship was wrong, even though she'd paid the carbon offset. Try as she might couldn't square this because she knew she'd be lying to herself.

'Bollocks!' she shouted out loud. 'Bugger and bollocks!' She switched on her phone, checked out the weight of Queen Mary 2. She'd be an extra 60 kilograms on a ship weighing 72 million. But she knew that wasn't the point, the point was she was on it, and complicit in its pollution like it or not. The question was, did the end justify the means? She'd never really know, would she? Not until the mission was accomplished, and even then? On the verge of tearing out her hair she made herself a tea and took two painkillers. She sat down and tried to think it through rationally. Millions of people were in the air or on cruise ships at this very moment, and they didn't have a hint of a conscience. She was on the front line of trying to change that, so was she allowed to partake in the same act she was protesting against? Sara did it by flying to Cairns in order to monitor the Reef's destruction, but that was being damaged further by her flying. Maybe she should put that question to her, though she already had but not pushed it. This time she would. That night she retired early and even though buzzing with excitement about her plan fell asleep almost immediately.

*

As she sat waiting for Sara to call, she wondered why Cathy hadn't contacted her yet. She said she'd phone on her arrival

76

with the new number. It didn't surprise her that she hadn't, especially if she'd sunk into one of her depressions again, but it worried her nevertheless. Why hadn't she asked for her new number when she called that morning to say she was leaving? Or at least the name of the home? But her state of mind hadn't exactly been great either had it? She just hoped she called soon that was all, poor Cathy.

Sara called on the dot of midday. Connie talked about the protest then asked the question. Sara prevaricated a while and finally said, 'I can't justify it, Mum, none of us can, but without science we wouldn't have known it was happening in the first place, would we? And a lot of research is done in remote areas where the real impact of human pollution is best measured.' Which was a fair answer, so Connie made her question more specific. 'What if a protester flew to America from the UK to make an important statement?'

'Depends on the statement and the impact of it.'

'What if that was impossible to gauge?'

'Then it's impossible to say.'

'I guess so.'

'Maybe the problem would be solved if an American made the protest.'

'I don't think you'd find an American to do it.'

'Do what, Mum?'

'Oh, nothing.' Connie realised it was a waste of time asking a hypothetical question about a hypothetical action, so quickly changed the subject.

'How's Kurt?'

'He's in Perth talking at a big Greenpeace rally.' Perth was a 4,000-mile round trip from Sydney. That was it. Her mind was made up, if Kurt can do it, so could she, as the impact of her actions could be greater than his words.

A few minutes after the call she was pacing the living room still wracked with indecision, finally she cracked and screamed at herself. FOR GOD'S SAKE CONNIE, YOU'RE DYING! AT LEAST ALLOW YOURSELF THIS ONE LUXURY BEFORE YOU PASS OVER FOR FUCK'S SAKE!

Her mind finally made up she sat down at the computer, pulled up the Cunard site, and made a note of the booking hotline. She went to the kitchen, grabbed her purse off the table, went into the hall and picked up the phone and dialled.

Her name was Samantha and she spoke in un-hurried, alluring tones, which was more akin to a psychiatrist than a travel representative.

'How can we help you today?'

'I'd like to book on the next passage from Southampton to New York.'

'That's a wonderful decision. Have you travelled with Cunard before?'

'No. No, I haven't.'

'Then you're in for a magical experience. It's on everyone's bucket list.' Connie groaned and proceeded to book the sailing on the tenth. She was asked how she wanted to return, by ship or fly. She said ship. Though she knew she may be coming back on neither. She was then asked what type of cabin she preferred. Connie went for the cheaper inside one.

'Are you sure you wouldn't prefer a balcony, Connie? Views of the sunset from your own room? Imagine sweeping back the curtains in the morning to reveal – the ocean.' What would she expect to see? The desert?

'How much extra would that be?'

'Four hundred and fifty pounds. Go on, Connie, you only live once.' She had to hand it to her, she was a salesperson with psychic powers.

'OK. What the hell.'

'That's wonderful, you won't regret it.' After the call she made a provisional booking at the Algonquin for three nights, applied for her ESTA visa from Homeland security, and hoped she hadn't been banned from the USA for her lifetime of activism. The country was currently so paranoid you never could tell. She was now so excited about the trip she'd almost forgotten about her terminal illness.

She wouldn't tell Sara until she was on the ship, that way if she had any objections, she'd be too late. Sara had a way of getting the truth out of her, and if she sensed anything was wrong, she'd fly straight back to England, and that's the last thing she wanted her to do, especially being six months pregnant. But why would Sara be suspicious? She was just going to New York for a holiday that's all, she would probably be happy for her.

She went to the local bookshop and bought a street map of Manhattan, then at home marked off places she wanted to visit, in particular Washington Square Monument, Katz's Diner, Central Park and the Loeb Boathouse where Sally met her friend Marie and talked about men. She then checked the most important place of all: where she intended to make her protest. She'd need to contact an activist group in New York to scout the feasibility of her plan. If it wasn't at all possible, she would have to think of another location in the city.

She busied herself checking out her wardrobe for dresses that still fit; not that she was one to dress up, but this was different, this was her final farewell to the world. She looked at herself in the mirror wearing a maroon velvet knee-length dress. She was still slim and shapely, but that tends to happen to 'petite' women. Her dark auburn hair only had flecks of grey and apart from smile creases around the eyes her skin was still very youthful and smooth. She had to admit for someone who was dying she looked pretty good.

Hanging out another dress and a black suit, she sorted out jewellery to match. She opened the dressing table draw to retrieve her make-up bag. On opening it she realised it hadn't been used since her 30th wedding anniversary, six months before Jim died. She still missed him terribly, she had good and bad days. Nobody tells you how to recover from grief, everyone just assumes it gets better with time. But it doesn't. It stays the same, you just find ways of not thinking about it too often. Strangely enough when he'd died it hadn't increased her own fear of death – she thought she had many years left – so much to that assumption.

She looked at the various items of make-up and swept them into the waste basket. She would go out and buy new stuff, why not? She felt buoyant, almost euphoric; in fact, she couldn't remember the last time she felt so excited.

*

She had her appointment with Dr Pradesh, he'd asked if she wanted counselling but she declined, and also said no to chemotherapy. But she did ask what to expect as the tumour progressed. He told her it was all in the brochure, and she told him she'd burnt it.

'Well, headaches, dizziness, slurring of words, memory loss, imbalance.'

'Just like a hangover then?' Dr Pradesh awkwardly smiled.

'You could say that.'

'And when I get to the end. How will I die?' Dr Pradesh was taken by surprise and stuttered a moment,

'Probably, probably loss of consciousness, caused by pressure on the brain or a haemorrhage.'

'Will it be quick?'

'Losing consciousness usually is, but you'll need to be in palliative care if you want to avoid any pain or suffering.'

'Thank you. Thanks for being honest.'

'It's the least I could do.' Dr Pradesh paused. 'You're very brave, Connie.'

'Why?'

'Some people will try anything, even if I said they only had a one percent chance of survival with chemo.'

'I'm not some people.'

'I think I've already worked that out.' Dr Pradesh smiled.

'And if you need more painkillers, you're on a repeat prescription.'

'Thanks. What if I run out abroad?'

'You going somewhere?'

'New York.'

'Then take enough with you.'

'Dear Liza. Dear Liza.'

'What?'

'Oh nothing. Just an old song about a bucket.'

'A bucket?' Dr Pradesh looked confused.

'Yes, a bucket.'

'Oh, you mean a bucket list?'

'No! I don't mean a bucket list!'

*

On waking the following day, she immediately checked the US midterm election results. The Republicans had held on to the Senate but as predicted Congress now had a Democrat majority, meaning they had more power to quash Republican policy and legislation, and above all the power to investigate the party's administration, in particular Donald Fucking Duck's tax evasion, which was a possible way to impeach the shit.

It was an increase in women voting for the Democrats that had tipped Congress, and it now had more female members than it ever had in history. Connie wondered if it was women who could sway the male-dominated world of big business to seriously begin cutting carbon emissions. One of the first countries in the world that had pledged to become carbon neutral by 2050 was New Zealand, and it had a female prime minister. Maybe women and women alone could save us all?

She switched off the phone, lay it on the bed and stared at the spare room curtains. There were no patterns in these, it had been Sara's bedroom and she had gone through an 'everything white' phase at sixteen. She missed her so much, and began to cry realising she may never see her again, or her grandchild. But in some ways, this made her feel more determined in her 'crusade'. She knew it was a tall order, but other people had made grand gestures like this before, and to great effect.

*

Two days before leaving she began to pack. Warm clothes for walking on deck and watching the sea, casual clothes for wandering around the ship during the day, and her chosen dresses for the evenings at the theatre, in the bars and ballroom. She wondered whether eight days at sea might become boring, and tried to imagine being in a hotel for that long without going out? She wondered who'd be sitting at her table for meals, as she'd read you were allocated one for the whole week. What if she didn't like them? What if she hated them? What if they were all climate change deniers and supported Donald Fucking Duck or even our own inept government? She'd have to bite her tongue, wouldn't she? But she knew that would be impossible. And would there be any other single women on the ship? Or would she be looked upon as that sad widow-spinster, all on her own. Norma no mates.

Would there be many single men? Probably a few wealthy businessmen coming back to New York the slow route, having done deals in Europe that would further pollute the world. Or widowed men from Yorkshire that would bore you to death talking about the bowling club, or where to buy the cheapest lamb chops in Wakefield. She guessed she could move tables if she wanted, or even have all her meals in the cabin? A small part of her also wondered whether there'd be anyone remotely desirable on board – perhaps a silver haired Bostonian with a degree from Harvard in politics or science, an activist like herself, a sixty-year-old George Clooney type. She found it strange fantasising about another man, it was something she'd never done for over forty years, and she had to admit it was rather exciting, but nevertheless didn't hold out any hope.

It was over two weeks since Cathy had left. She hadn't called and Connie was beginning to get worried. She wasn't reliable at the best of times, but what if the dementia had made her forget her number already? No, surely not that quickly? She was fine when they last met, and she called her the morning she left. She eventually satisfied herself that Cathy was simply 'settling in' to her new place, and that she would call once things were stable. Did Cathy have her mobile number? There'd be no point calling on the land line after tomorrow would there? Shit! Shit! Shit! Then she remembered she'd used it once, so must have it somewhere.

Cathy being Cathy never had a mobile. She didn't need one as she'd no living relations or friends apart from her. If only she could have taken Cathy with her, they could have relived old times and both gone out in a blaze of glory.

*

She woke early on the departure day and wrote the letter to Sara, telling her about the tumour, and why she was going to New York. All she could hope for was her forgiveness. She left the letter in view on the mantelpiece, and sat on the sofa briefly staring at it. She imagined Sara reading it and bursting into tears, and almost tore it up, but how else would she find out the truth? Maybe she should tell her? No, she'd already been through that a hundred times. The letter was by far the best way. The best way to say goodbye. Like Cathy she hated personal goodbyes.

She suddenly felt dizzy as if the inside of her head was moving independently to her skull. She felt briefly sick, then within few a seconds it went. It was scary and brought her condition back into sharp focus. What if this began to happen more frequently and got worse? The cruise had demanded health insurance which she'd sorted a few days ago, but hadn't told them about the tumour in case they wouldn't cover her. So, if she collapsed at sea so be it, and if she needed medical treatment in New York, who cared? They could take the fees out of her bank account, what little was in it. She just hoped she didn't deteriorate too quickly and was given time to carry out her homages and planned finale.

*

Although she still felt the darkness of death within her, it was slowly fading. Being given the prognosis allowed her commit to something she would have never remotely contemplated. Living then dying without leaving a mark had always been a fear of hers. Now she could fulfil that in a way she could have never imagined in her wildest dreams. She felt this was a privilege only allowed to the very few, and was hugely grateful.

***

Chapter 6

The countryside slid by as the train approached the South Downs. She idly glanced at the phone and was intrigued by one news item. A TV commercial about the vast areas of jungle being destroyed for corn oil, and wrecking the orang-utans' habitat had been banned on the grounds it was political. The advert had been placed by a food chain who said they wouldn't sell products containing the oil. This was honest and ethical, and no different to someone advertising that an electric car was good for the environment. So, what was the problem? A few minutes later Connie found another story that mentioned the EU was banning the import of the oil, but the UK weren't. Everything was suddenly clear; the advert undermined the government. They had censored the truth in the same way they censored the facts about climate change.

She placed the phone on the table in front of her and carried on watching the landscape out of the window. How would this look in a hundred years? Of course, she'd never know, and frankly didn't want to. Picking up the newspaper she'd bought at Waterloo station she avoided the news and looked through the supplements. Adverts and articles on exotic travel locations seem at odds with the newspaper's positive stance on climate change, but even the virtuous are culpable; everyone needs to make money. She pushed the papers aside and wondered again whether she should be making this trip at all? Even if her eventual goal was to draw attention to the crisis, wasn't she just adding to the mess? Yes, she was; she was being selfish, wasn't she? She could have made her grand gesture in London, but no, she wanted to see

New York. But she was only human, and even the most altruistic people sometimes consider their own needs first.

Having finally (almost) satisfied her doubts she continued to gaze out the window as they approached Winchester, she remembered the big demonstrations that took place nearby at Twyford Down in 1992. She'd joined the road protesters for a weekend to stop the M3 cutting through a natural beauty spot. Although they eventually failed it started other road protests throughout the county, and some say was the beginning of environmental action groups. She smiled to herself at the memory. She'd taken Sara with her and they'd camped in a nearby field. She was three years old and loved every minute of it.

The train pulled into Southampton station and she wheeled her case down the platform, through the ticket barrier and found the taxi rank. Within a few minutes she was entering the Queen Mary Terminal, and saw the huge ship rising above the surrounding buildings, its black hull and white upper decks made it regal in appearance; unlike the all-white cruise ships you often saw. But this wasn't a cruise, it was a sailing, a transatlantic crossing which felt more like an adventure than being aboard a floating holiday camp.

She tipped the cab driver and walked into the terminal, at a reception desk she was handed the letter 'J' on a card and told to enter the waiting area.

At least five hundred people sat in the huge aircraft hangar sized lounge clutching their letters. She sat next to an elderly couple, looking around she realised a large proportion were elderly. It could have been Death's waiting room; for her in some ways it was.

Within twenty minutes her letter was called and she joined the check-in queue. They took her suitcase, then a photograph, and gave her a swipe card that was used for on-board charges and a cabin key. She was in number 5111 and proceeded out of the terminal hall and up a red carpeted ramp which led into the ship on the second deck. Three uniformed crew greeted her as she entered. The red carpet continued down a wooden panelled corridor until it opened out into the Grand Lobby. She stood open-mouthed as she gazed around the huge impressive circular hall; its beige sofas, armchairs, and an elaborate flower display at the centre, with the carpet radiating outwards in red and yellow rays. Two sweeping staircases led up to the third deck where she could see a number of small upmarket shops. She looked higher still, the atrium extended another forty feet up to a stained-glass window in the roof, and to one side was a huge bronze image of the sun. She stood for a while awestruck by its sheer scale and marvelled at the quality of engineering and craftsmanship. She knew ocean liners were conceived just after the Industrial Revolution as monuments to ostentatious wealth – a display of capitalism in all its glory – but look where it'd got us? The irony wasn't lost on her. But it was still possible to marvel.

She strolled down the lush carpeted, wooden panelled 'Grand Hallway' and looked at the six by twelve-foot bronze murals of the five continents on the walls. They were all beautifully detailed and she was particularly interested in the one of the USA that depicted baseball, football, the space shuttle, the White House and images of the Wild West, all under the radiating light of Lady Liberty. The depiction of world images struck her as appropriate yet strange, the ship visited all of these places but actually belonged to none of them. It was a floating no-man's land.

Further along the corridor she noticed a sign 'The Golden Lion' and her hunch it was a pub was correct. Entering the garishly carpeted bar, with its wooden furniture and brass fittings, it felt like a London pub from the seventies. Most people were watching football on the six or so screens, which wasn't what she'd expected, but certainly gave an indication of how the clientele of these luxury ships had changed.

She was in two minds whether to have a drink, it was still only four in the afternoon and she wanted to see her cabin, but that could wait and she was on holiday after all. She sat down and ordered a glass of white wine from one of the many hovering waiters.

All were dressed in immaculate black and white outfits and seemed to be from the Far East – as far as she could tell. She gazed out of the window but there wasn't much to see except the quayside below, where various forklift trucks buzzed around with a degree of urgency as the ship was due to sail in twenty minutes. The waiter arrived with her wine and a bowl of snacks and asked for her card which he took away. He returned a short while later and placed it on the table in a leather folder. She looked at the price; seven dollars fifty, and a service charge of one-fifty, plus an optional gratuity. She wasn't expecting dollars, nor was she expecting two service charges but what the hell. She signed the receipt adding a two-dollar tip.

She sipped her wine, she was on board at last, about to cross the Atlantic. Even saying it sounded romantic. She looked out the window and briefly felt strange – as the warehouses were moving – then realised the ship was finally underway. Excited, she quickly finished her glass and left the bar. Back in the corridor she saw six lifts, and worked out from a detailed diagram next to them that her cabin was on deck five, and roughly mid-ships. She noticed a large staircase further down the corridor and decided to walk. In fact, she'd always walk as it would keep her fit, and she'd certainly need to be in approximately ten days' time.

She climbed The Grand Staircase; paintings adorned the walls, some abstract others figurative but they all seemed originals and of a high standard. She arrived on deck five slightly breathless, a sign pointed left for even cabins, right for odd. She turned right and entered the narrow corridor which vanished into infinity, like pointing a mirror at a mirror.

Within fifty yards she arrived at 5111. She took her card out of her pocket and touched it on the pad next to the handle. A green light blinked and she opened the door. There were French windows at one end with a view of the quayside slipping by. To her right was a small bathroom. In the centre of the cabin was a large queen-sized bed draped in a dark blue silk cover with matching cushions on top of the pillows. On the left near the windows was a desk and chair, opposite a small coffee table and sofa. It was all very neat, and although rather small, cosy and welcoming. She walked toward the French windows and noticed tea and coffee making items on top of a small fridge near the desk. On the coffee table was a magazine containing the day's entertainment, and a half bottle of sparkling wine in a silver ice bucket. Next to it was a card that read 'With compliments of the Captain'.

Sitting on the sofa she gazed around and felt the ship gently moving. She smiled to herself, opened the wine, and noticed another card on the table announcing her sitting time for the evening meal was eight thirty in the Britannia Restaurant. She poured herself a glass, stood up and opened the French doors and walked out onto the enclosed balcony. She looked over the rail to the water sixty feet below now being churned up by the bow thrusters as the ship began turning to face Southampton Water. She couldn't remember the last time she was so excited; all thoughts of her terminal illness had vanished as she was about to set off on the adventure of a lifetime.

She heard an announcement and went back inside the cabin to listen. It was the evacuation drill. She had to go to muster point F in five minutes with the life jacket that was in the wardrobe. She wondered if she could take her drink, but realised how ludicrous that would look. She laughed as she pictured herself staggering around the deck and falling overboard whilst trying to climb into the lifeboat. She put the glass down, found the life jacket and waited for the alarm. Of course, in a real disaster she'd be in bed asleep, or in the bar, restaurant or theatre, certainly not in the bedroom waiting with her life jacket. Evacuation drills were always pointless as far as she was concerned. If the ship was sinking people would be climbing over each other to get into the first lifeboat they could find.

The alarm sounded and she made her way with everybody else up the stairs to deck seven. When she arrived at muster point F – part of the Kings Court self-service restaurant – it was packed. She hoped to see some younger people on board as well, but apart from crew members most were in their seventies or eighties, some were in wheelchairs, others had Zimmer frames. A few were struggling to put their life jackets on, even though they had been told specifically not to. One woman had her head stuck in hers and couldn't pull it off, another had it on back to front, whilst a third was trying to step inside it. Connie wondered whether she'd made a terrible mistake; she was on a floating care home, and if there was a disaster at night, she couldn't imagine half of these people being able to get out of bed, let alone make their way to a lifeboat. However, the irony was that most of them were in better health than she was.

The drill lasted a few minutes and once everyone had their life jackets on – when they were told and the right way round – they were allowed to return to their cabins.

Her suitcase had arrived, so she unpacked, then drank the rest of the sparkling wine. Feeling pleasantly pissed she put on her coat and decided to take a walk around the promenade deck outside the muster station. She walked back up the stairs and out into the cool air. It was now dusk and they were cruising down Southampton Water, moving so smoothly and silently it felt unnatural, as if the ship were levitating. She looked toward the city as the lights slowly receded into the distance and began to walk around the deck.

A light breeze ruffled her hair which she guessed wasn't the wind but the forward movement of the ship. A few passengers strolled past her, some arm in arm, on their romantic first night at sea. This didn't concern her in the slightest, Connie had always enjoyed her own company, as restrictive as that was for a woman. At least on the ship it wouldn't be out of place to drink and dine alone.

Arriving at the bow she walked through an opening out onto the front deck. A few other passengers stood admiring the view, the Isle of Wight twinkling in the distance. She walked up to the rail. Below her was the working deck which was 'out of bounds' where winches and mooring equipment were stored. As the ship slid forward it hardly created a wave in the black water beneath it. It was impossible to imagine she was going all the way to New York at twenty-five mph. But the slow pace appealed to her, because in this instance maybe it **was** better to travel than arrive.

She continued to walk and finally arrived near the stern. The loud music took her by surprise, and below on the open-air deck disco lights flashed by a pool and Jacuzzi. She walked down the steps, to one side was a bar where a few people were drinking. She crossed the deck to the rear rail, and glanced over at the churning water below, a white ribbon trailed back toward Southampton, which was now slowly fading into the distance. She gave England a final wave goodbye and turned to face the bar. She realised the people drinking were probably the only ones on board her age or younger, and subsequently willing to brave the cold. The other 2,480 were all inside keeping warm.

She returned to her cabin, and was ravenously hungry. She couldn't possibly wait till her sitting at eight thirty, but she knew there was also one at six. Maybe she could change? Realising you had to wear a dress to eat in the Britannia Restaurant in the evening, she quickly removed her jeans and sweater and put on her blue dress. She went into the tiny bathroom and threw on some make-up, grabbed her handbag and went down the stairs to deck three.

She walked along the Grand Hallway and followed the smartly groomed diners through the upper part of the Grand Lobby, past the shops and toward the restaurant entrance and stood in the queue. Whilst waiting she casually looked down and noticed there was a stain near the hem of her dress, then saw a mark on the sleeve that looked like moths had been at it, which they no doubt had. She suddenly felt like the ugly sister at Cinderella's Ball. It'd been such a long time since she'd worn anything decent, or gone anywhere decent for that matter.

She'd been with Jim for a posh anniversary meal once, but when the bill arrived, he'd said it was a waste of money, far too much for just something to eat. They'd had a row, and never had an anniversary meal again. Dressing up and going out wasn't exactly her thing either, but once in a while it was nice to break with routine, which was something Jim never really understood.

The queue moved forward and they entered the doors of the restaurant. It was like walking into an enormous version of the Grand Lobby. She was on the upper floor and to her left and right tables swept around the atrium in a gracious curve. Behind those were two other levels separated by polished ships rails and frosted glass. The carpets were blue, the walls and Doric pillars cream, whilst the woodwork was polished mahogany. Two sweeping staircases with brass and wood rails led down to the lower deck, where many people sat at circular tables under soft lighting. In front of her from floor to ceiling was a sixty-foot-high painting of the ship having a ticker tape reception in New York harbour. She looked up to the stained-glass roof thirty feet above her from which hung art deco frosted glass circular lights. It was breath-taking, and could seat twelve hundred diners. Connie was so awestruck she didn't hear the maître d' asking for her table number. She apologised nervously, as if she shouldn't be here in the first place, and looking down again at dress realised she might be right.

'I was wondering if I could change sittings. I'm starving.' The maître d' didn't smile but officiously asked for her card. She presented it to him and he quickly took it.

'If we can fit you in, you'll get a new card tomorrow delivered to your cabin.' He was about to deal with the next people when she asked him.

'Hmm, sorry, where can I eat now?'

'Kings Court deck seven.' He said curtly, and quickly turned to the couple behind her. Connie peeled away from the queue and uttered 'Wanker' to herself. She went back up the staircase to the seventh floor and paused at the top to regain her breath.

She entered the Kings Court where she'd been earlier for the evacuation drill. She walked past many tables of elderly couples eating fastidiously. As she got near to the serving area there was an overwhelming smell of fish, or was it just a general cooking smell?

She arrived at the buffet – an array of serving counters and cooler cabinets with queues at various points. The food was laid out in sections: meats, fish, pastas dishes, rice dishes, various potatoes, vegetables, salads and sweets etc. It wasn't at all as she imagined, remembering pictures of food on cruise ships laid out in artistic colourful displays like a royal banquet. This was more akin to the self-service cafeteria in her old comprehensive school. Not that she minded. She took a plate and helped herself to some grilled swordfish, Lyonnaise potatoes and salad, then wandered back to the seating area and found a single table near the window. She glanced out and saw the odd pinpoint of light in the darkness which she assumed to be the Isle of Wight. As she was eating, she noticed most people were dressed as if they were having dinner at home, in fact some were extremely scruffy. One man shuffled by with his tray wearing urine-stained tracksuit bottoms followed by the vapour trail. It was bizarre to see such a contrast between the two restaurants. Everyone had access to the Britannia, but some preferred not to eat there at all. Clearly, they didn't like formality, and in many ways neither did Connie.

The food was fine, well adequate, and she went back to the cabin to change, but decided to take a quick look at the Champagne Bar and Chart Room on the way. The bar naturally had an 'upmarket feel' and was art deco in style like most of the ship, the walls adorned with pictures of movie stars from the forties. The Chart Room next to it was low lit and laid back with a jazz trio playing near the circular bar. A bar a single lady might sit at in an old Hollywood movie, where the handsome hero offers to buy her a drink. *Yeah, in your dreams, Connie,* she thought to herself. Against her better judgement she decided to stay and have one. What the hell, she thought, mariners should be permanently drunk. She ordered a white wine, though felt a vodka martini would have been more appropriate.

She watched the jazz band that were rather too bland to be engrossing. Looking around the large lounge with its sofas and armchairs she realised this is where the next dinner sitting had their pre-meal cocktails. Most of the men wore tuxedos, if not suits with dickie bows; the women, smart dresses or even ball gowns, their necks and wrists dripping with jewellery, their clutch bags nearby in attendance. They all possessed an air of superiority, though that may have been Connie's feeling of inferiority as she glanced down again at the small hole on her sleeve.

She wondered how many of them knew about climate change, or even cared, let alone felt guilty as she did. But there wasn't any point in having these thoughts, not in these surroundings. She must try to enjoy it best she could. She sipped her wine and saw a couple entering the lounge, they approached another couple who rose, hugged and greeted them. Clearly, they were good friends and had been on the ship before, because when the waiter approached, they all hugged him too. There was a kind of smugness to it all, an acceptance of their status. They clearly enjoyed feeling they were in 'the club.' She was being cynical again and told herself to stop it. Come on, live and let live, Connie. However, if somebody had told her that the two couples all worked hard at normal jobs and this was their annual treat, she'd be the first to say they deserved it. But somehow, she felt that wasn't the case. Her guess was both men owned companies, drove Range Rovers and exploited their work force, while the wives socialised and acted out their role as appendages. Stop it! They're all hard-working doctors, so shut up! But she couldn't help herself, and realised she judged people far too readily, but where was the fun in imagining they were all goody-two shoes? She forgave everyone for dressing like stuck up little lords and ladies, finished her drink, and took the stairs back to her cabin. On her way she mused again over the contrast between Britannia and Kings Court – upstairs and downstairs – the men in tuxedos and the one in the piss-stained tracksuit and laughed to herself. She'd put her money on piss man being the wealthiest.

She entered the cabin and on the coffee-table was a small bottle of wine, a new entertainment guide for the following day and two small chocolates – as if Santa had called while she was out. She glanced at the guide and noticed a 'Solos get together' in the Carinthia Lounge at ten thirty the following morning and decided it might be interesting, not that she was looking for a man of course. She made herself a tea, sat on the sofa and remembered she had to call Sara before the signal was out of range. It would be seven in the morning now but Connie knew she was an early riser. She turned on her phone and video called her. Sara appeared quickly on the screen.

'Hi, Mum. It's early for you to call?' Connie slowly panned around the cabin with her phone.

'Oh my god, where are you? A luxury prison?' Connie laughed.

'Funny you should say that.'

'Well?'

'The Queen Mary, on my way to New York.'

'Wow! Why?'

'Why not?'

'Well, great, great, Mum. But you know about cruise ships?'

'Yes of course. I paid my offsets, twice. And before you have a go at me, what about Kurt? He flies all over the place.'

'Fighting climate change.'

'Same here.'

'Why? What are you doing in New York?'

'You'll see.'

'Don't worry me, Mum, what exactly?'

'I can't tell you, but it's all fine, honestly.'

'If you can't tell me who can you tell?'

'Let's just say you'll be proud of me, Sara.'

'OK. But don't do anything stupid.'

'Oh, it's not stupid. In fact, it's the most sensible thing I've done in my entire life.'

'Good. So, we've decided, we're flying to England for Christmas. And we'll come over again in April after the baby is born.'

'Two trips? Now who's being irresponsible?'

'We are but to hell with it, you're my mum and I haven't seen you for three years.' She was right, if anyone needed a good excuse to fly it was for visiting family and loved ones, who could deny them that? Connie wasn't sure what to say knowing it was highly unlikely she'd be there, but could never tell her the truth.

'OK, that's great,' she said with all the enthusiasm she could muster. Sara talked about how excited she was to be home at Christmas for the first time in eight years, whilst Connie felt more and more guilty about deceiving her daughter. Maybe she shouldn't go through with her plan? Maybe it was too selfish? But would she even survive the tumour till Christmas? It was six weeks away, anything could happen? No, she'd made the decision not to die in front of her daughter and that was that. She quickly changed the subject to names they were thinking of calling the baby. Sara said if it was a boy, there was Ben or Russell after Kurt's favourite actor Russell Crowe, and if it was a girl, Connie. Slowly her eyes began to fill with tears.

'Oh don't cry, Mum.'

'I can't help it, that's so sweet of you.'

'There was no competition. Unless you consider Kurt's suggestion of Kylie a serious contender.' Connie laughed. The call finally ended after half an hour and she promised to call Sara once she was in New York and send her lots of pictures.

Connie sat on the bed and for the first time became scared about her plan, could she actually go through with it? But then realised she was equally frightened of how the tumour might finally take her. It was a fait accompli. She poured the rest of the sparkling wine and went outside onto the balcony. She could just make out a distant lighthouse and guessed it was the Needles on the south west corner of the Isle of Wight. It was strange to see everything from the ocean, it felt as if you were on the outside looking in; the land lubbers were the captives and you were free. She guessed it was this feeling that attracted many mariners over the centuries.

She lay on the bed and switched on the TV, a video about the ship played that she watched with interest. On board there was one crew member to every two passengers, and it burnt thirty thousand gallons of fuel every day, which for some reason they seemed to be proud of. The steady movement of the ship was relaxing and as she watched she slowly drifted to sleep.

When she woke the TV was still showing the ship video. She looked at her watch and it was eleven p.m.; the video must have been on a repeat cycle. She turned it off and strolled out again onto the balcony, the air was cold and the water below dark and foreboding. If you jumped overboard it would surely be impossible for them to find you, even with the searchlights shining down from the bridge, somebody would have to be watching 24/7, and even the most diligent person could miss something. She imagined jumping, hitting the dark cold water and seeing the bright lights of ship slowly vanishing into the distance until there was nothing around but darkness, pitch darkness. Part of her wanted to jump, and the thought sent a shiver through her. She'd often imagined jumping whenever she was high up, terrified an impulse in her would overcome common sense, and she'd suddenly find herself plummeting down to a certain death.

She looked out to sea and spotted another lighthouse much further away than the previous one. *That must be Portland,* she thought, *and it might be the last of England I will ever see.*

***

100

Chapter 7

She had the best night's sleep she could ever remember, and once awake couldn't work out why the bedroom was moving until a split second later. With a degree of excitement, she jumped out of bed, opened the balcony doors and stepped out. Blue swept the horizon, a vast expanse of uncluttered ocean. On its surface small waves lifted, whilst others broke, the white dot of a seabird dipped and skimmed over the gently undulating troughs. This was what she had come for, to be at sea, hundreds of miles from civilization. Everything inside the ship could vanish for all she cared, she just wanted to stare at this majestic scene for hours, not that she did as the air was damp and cold; it was only seven thirty in the morning.

She made herself a cup of tea and got back into bed and turned on her phone. She was surprised to still have a signal and checked the news. US drilling in the Arctic where the ice had melted, Brazilian prime minister thinks climate change is a Marxist hoax, expansion at another London airport and a lone woman fighting to save one of the last habitats on Earth where orang-utans, rhinos, elephants and tigers still co-existed. She knew how she felt, poor woman. It was a relief there'd be no phone signal once they were clear of Southern Ireland; she'd had it with bad news, and didn't intend to pay the ship's internet charge of fifteen pounds for thirty minutes to be more depressed than she already was. She powered the phone off, tossed it onto the sofa, and picked up the entertainment guide. There was a talk on 'Terrorism' in the afternoon, which sounded rather out of place, surely 'Surgical Supports' or 'The Songs of Max Bygraves' would have been more appropriate?

Or perhaps the talk was to help the passengers foil any attempted on-board attack? Either way, it was worth going to.

She had breakfast in the Kings Court that still strangely smelt of fish. She sat down with her cereal and juice at one of the many tables and glanced around. She could tell which passengers were English by their breakfast – fry ups – whilst the Europeans went for pastries, cooked meats and cheese, and those from the far east a bit of everything. She deduced that the really healthy eaters like herself were mainly Americans.

Through the window onto the promenade deck she saw a number of joggers, whilst the odd couple strolled by hand in hand. It was still hard to imagine all this normality going on a thousand feet above the sea bed. Looking around her most passengers seemed indifferent to the passing ocean, and may just as well be at hotel in Brighton. However, Connie couldn't take her eyes off it, and quickly finished her breakfast raring to get out on deck.

She walked to the bow of the ship and onto the foredeck. She hadn't noticed them the previous evening but bolted down were what looked like four enormous polished metal sculptures. But on closer examination a plaque explained they were in fact spare propellers, nicknamed captain's cufflinks. She walked over to the rail, the wind was quite strong and surprisingly cold when the sun disappeared behind clouds, so she decided to walk on the sheltered side of the ship. A few people lay on the sun loungers wearing overcoats, gloves and scarves. Connie stopped and scanned the cobalt blue water. Two or three very large seabirds swooped down to the surface and wheeled up again in the thermals. Skimming just over the wave tops were a number of much smaller birds with black heads and white bodies; she had no idea what either of them were and wished she'd bought a guide.

She noticed a large group of birds flying in the opposite direction to the ship, spinning, wheeling and squawking. She couldn't work out why. A moment later she caught her breath; A hundred metres out a large pod of dolphins broke the surface in unison. She felt as if she wanted to scream with joy and cry at the same time. She'd never seen dolphins before. It was a breath-taking sight as fifty or so of them surfaced and dived, surface and dived, with young ones alongside their parents. The birds were following and now it was clear why. The dolphins had got the scent and were giving chase to an unsuspecting shoal, whilst the seabirds would pick up the scraps that floated to the surface. As she watched them slowly disappear from view like a gang of frolicking partygoers, she felt sad, sad for what we may have done to the ocean and the dolphins' dwindling food supply. These beautiful creatures deserved to survive more than we did. By comparison we lacked their grace, their humility and simplicity of existence that neither harmed nor encroached on anything else. They kept the world in balance, whilst we screwed it up. She desperately wanted to see them again and wondered what life would be like permanently suspended in a deep blue void.

She'd been in a float tank once, pitch dark with just the feel of warm water on the skin; she'd felt magnificently serene and had quickly drifted to sleep. That must be what their lives felt like: heaven compared to our own.

She looked around her to see if anyone else had noticed them. A few joggers past her intent on fulfilling the morning's quota of laps, two people lay with their eyes closed on the loungers, whilst another was sitting up busy on a tablet. Through the steam of the Kings Court window she saw the diners shovelling food into their mouths with gay abandon, oblivious to the beautiful natural world outside, and wished she was a bloody dolphin.

She went back into the cabin to warm up. She cleaned her teeth, brushed her now matted hair, put on the kettle and quickly went onto the balcony to see if any other pods were passing by, but there was nothing as far as the eye could see. She felt the cool breeze coming off the Arctic icecaps some fifteen hundred miles away, and imagined narwhals, belugas and walruses, mammals seen so rarely by most of us they're almost mythical. What an amazing world we lived in, perhaps if more of us were aware of that we'd be less destructive.

After drinking her tea, she had a quick nap, then made a half-hearted attempt to look presentable and went along to the 'Solos get together'. The Carinthia Lounge was a large expanse of comfortable sofas and armchairs in blue and oatmeal. Coffee tables and lamps created small intimate areas reminiscent of a large furniture store. There was a bar at one end and views of the sea out of the windows, but again no-one seemed interested in the world outside. A large group of women sat down in one area drinking tea and eating biscuits. They were all in their seventies, some older, two men were sitting in the middle, one wearing a white tracksuit, the other a very loud Hawaiian shirt. Both were at least eighty, and grinning. She counted twenty-eight single women, no wonder. Connie immediately did a U-turn and walked out.

Climbing the staircase to deck eight she discovered the bookshop and library. She browsed in the shop. Many of the publications were about world travel or ships. One particularly caught her eye; *Titanic for Children,* with an image of it sinking in icy waters. This was a book likely to give nightmares to any child, especially one on board – not that she'd seen any.

She entered the library area with its dark polished walnut bookcases and comfortable seats overlooking the bow of the ship. A perfect place to read and dolphin watch at the same time.

Deciding to explore more she walked up to deck nine where she found the Commodore Club. It was empty, but she strolled in and was taken by the blue and cream interior, the curving polished wood bar, and the grand piano at its centre. Like the library it had windows looking down onto the bow of the ship. She liked the look of the place as it wasn't too big and felt intimate. Going up another deck she discovered it was all cabins, the expensive 'Grill Suites.'

Climbing higher still to deck eleven, she entered the Atlantic Room. It was also looking forward with panoramic views, another great place for ocean watching if it wasn't for the fact it was filled with green baize card tables and at present crammed with bridge players who all looked up in unison and gave her accusatory looks, so she quickly left.

Adjacent to the room a door led to the observation deck. Walking outside she felt the chill of Arctic air again and entered the glass-fronted viewing area. The sea was beginning to chop, with small white wisps being torn off the wave peaks by the wind. The clouds ahead in the distance were looking angry, whilst to the south the sun shone in patches onto the sea like spotlight beams.

She shivered and went back inside and up to deck twelve. Another door led to the top of the ship. She walked out and up a final flight of steps, and was as high as it was possible to go. There was a tennis court below her surrounded by high netting and a sun deck next to a café/bar but they were all closed. The large red funnel belched out fumes, and as the wind briefly changed direction it caught the back of her throat and she coughed. She walked to the stern of the ship where the kennels were situated. She'd been told on this trip they contained seven dogs and two cats migrating to America. *No doubt because they didn't agree with Brexit*, thought Connie. But when they see who is fucking president, they'll want to come back.

When she returned to her cabin the bed had been made, fresh towels were in the bathroom and more tea, milk and biscuits were on the cupboard next to the desk. There was also a card on the table that announced she was on table 27 for the six-p.m. sitting in the Britannia Restaurant. She momentarily felt dizzy and lay on the bed. *Probably the cold air or movement of the ship*, she thought to herself. A minute later she'd fallen asleep.

Waking with a muzzy head she made a cup of coffee, sat down on the sofa and picked up the book she'd brought with her entitled *Our Armageddon? The history of climate change and where it's heading*. Not exactly cheerful reading, but she needed to finally crystallise the reasons for her actions, and this was the latest book on the subject. The opening chapter entitled 'Denial' said we've known about a CO_2 build up in the atmosphere since the 1950s, and in the eighties president Ronald Reagan suppressed climate reports claiming they were 'alarmist', even when the Environmental Protection Agency said it was a matter of urgency. This sounded like a familiar comment from a certain president over thirty years later. And the attitude was the same, 'Let's wait and see'. In 1988 an extreme heatwave in the USA signalled for many that global warming had begun. In the same year the World Congress on Climate Change wanted a 30% reduction of CO_2 by the year 2000, nothing happened. We now have the highest amount of

CO2 in the atmosphere than in the past 4 million years. Connie put down the book, not sure even she even wanted to read it anymore.

She opened the balcony door and walked out. It was even cooler now and the sea state was slightly rougher. She saw no birds around either, perhaps they knew something. She guessed the ship had now passed the tip of Southern Ireland, and open sea beckoned. Two thousand miles before they'd reach Newfoundland, the route of the first European settlers over four hundred years ago. The thought of being out here in a cramped sailing ship only fifty feet long – the size of a bus – with a two-month journey through the treacherous waters ahead was too frightening to even contemplate.

She scanned the horizon but couldn't make out any surface movement from dolphins or whales as the sea was now far too choppy. She looked sixty feet down to the disturbed grey-blue water below and wondered what the depth here was. Her knowledge of geography told her they'd still be on the continental shelf, but it wouldn't be long before the sea bed dropped into the West European Basin that plunged down to 18,000 feet – over three and a half miles. Goose bumps appeared on her arms at the thought of all that blue oblivion.

Going back inside she looked at the entertainment guide again. At five it was the captain's gala in the Queens Room, a black-tie reception. Should she go? It would be fanciful and ostentatious wouldn't it? But why else was she on the Queen Mary? She knew it wasn't to wallow in luxury – but to see the ocean and get to her destination the only way possible – however, this didn't mean she couldn't indulge herself a little. She looked in the mirror: hardly any grey hair and still as slim as she was at twenty. She was lucky. Ha! She laughed to herself. She'd rather be grey and overweight and not have a tumour any day. But she did, so convinced herself to go along and try to enjoy it, without being too overtly cynical.

She'd wear her black knee-length two-piece suit that made her look demure and sophisticated, not that she ever felt it. The last time she wore it was at Jim's funeral. Poor Jim. She wondered what he'd make of this. Same as her probably, a little bit too much glitz, but he'd like the Golden Lion bar, especially on their quiz nights. He loved quizzes, no doubt because he was so bloody good at them. She hated them, as they reminded her of school – where there were too many exams and tests. She'd seen talented kids fall by the wayside because they couldn't hack the pressure. Modern education was now an obstacle course, not something to be enjoyed.

At lunch she ate in the Kings Court again. The food was fine, well, adequate, and probably gourmet for some passengers who lived at home on a diet of ready meals. She had the salmon with hollandaise sauce, potatoes and broccoli, and for a sweet had a key lime pie. None of the people sitting nearby spoke to her, she imagined some thought she was crew, being alone and comparatively young compared to themselves. She liked the idea of that, an off-duty navigating officer, or ship's doctor. She liked being an outsider, and not one of the crowd, always had. She finished off her coffee, then walked purposely out, hoping to fuel their suspicions.

The Royal Court Theatre was two decks down from her cabin, and was as lush and grand as anything in the west end. A circle, balcony, fifteen hundred red velvet seats and a large stage. A thirty-foot Cunard logo was projected onto the backcloth and under a single spotlight was a podium.

It was three quarters full for this unlikely lecture on a vacation cruise, but Cunard obviously prided themselves on having a degree of intellectualism in their entertainment. A woman in her fifties entered the stage, she was an ex-BBC journalist and proceeded to show mean-looking terrorists on the screen behind her and the acts they'd committed. This didn't just include bomb damage but dead bodies strewn around various locations.

Throughout the one-hour lecture Connie was waiting for some explanation regarding the cause – the reason a terrorist becomes a terrorist – but none came. The purpose was clearly to show the effect, the horrible things they do, which nobody could deny. But above all to get us to hate them even more.

After the talk the journalist was signing her book about terrorism outside in the lobby. Connie waited for the queue to go down and approached her.

'Good lecture,' she said in a half-hearted way.

'Thank you,' said the journalist.

'Pity it was so one-sided.'

'Sorry?'

'Well, you could have mentioned the half million innocent men, women and children killed by US and UK forces during the war in Iraq. That might have put terrorism into some kind of context.' The woman just stared at Connie for a moment, somewhat surprised by the openness of the attack.

'Yes. Maybe you're right,' she stuttered.

'I know I'm right. And I suppose you think it's right to brainwash people and give them only half of the story? It's the same with climate change, that's why we're in such a bloody mess, because most bloody newspapers and the media are biased to support the government's views. If you're a real journalist you might be brave enough to consider telling the real truth once in a while.'

Connie calmly turned and walked away leaving the woman smiling awkwardly as another eager customer thrust the book in front of her to sign. There were some good things about having a terminal tumour. You didn't have to hold back.

She found a seat in the chart room and looked out of the window as the sea grew more turbulent, rollers were now six to seven feet high and ten when they collided with the ship's own bow wave. She ordered tea and biscuits from the waiter and thought of all the lies and cover-ups people willingly made. When an American or British soldier dies it's front-page news. If ten children are killed in Iraq it's hidden deep within the paper, or not mentioned at all. Connie thought this bias and lack of value for human life was diabolical.

She'd had this argument with friends of Jim's many times, especially when certain individuals got all gung-ho about Britain going to war. She didn't support terrorists by any means, but understood their anger, and where it came from. Imagine your entire family being wiped out by an American bomb? Would you not want revenge? However, we are fed a different story by the western media; that we are good and justified in our behaviour and terrorists are evil and that BBC journalist supported the theory. Connie was giving herself a headache again, so tried to stop thinking about the stupid lecture, poured more tea and ate the biscuits and realised how lucky she was not to be born in a Middle Eastern war-torn country. It was a pity other people didn't feel the same way, but for the grace of god go they.

She finished her tea and went back to the cabin to change for the reception. Why was she so angry when confronted by people with opposing views to her own? She thought about it a while; the only answer she could come up with, even though it sounded arrogant was that she was often right, well in this instance anyway. Surely it was right to care equally about all the inhabitants of the world? However, she knew this wasn't a commonly held belief, because when people feel threatened, they will believe the lies they're fed and quickly become prejudiced, become blinded to the truth. Which in turn creates hatred, conflict and war. Connie was aware that she carried prejudices too, but it was toward those who twisted truth that wreaked damage to others.

Thinking so much stressed and exhausted her. Wouldn't it be blissful if she only worried about what to cook for tea, whether to paint the spare room, or which new handbag to buy? But maybe some of us were born to do the worrying for the rest?

She skimmed through the guide to decide what to do after the dreaded reception and meal with strangers, and noticed the film *Book Club* was on in the Illuminations cinema at eight. Four women in their sixties read *Fifty Shades of Grey* and decide to spice up their sex lives. She decided if that didn't take her mind off the troubles of the world then nothing could.

She approached the Queens Room in her slick black suit and uncomfortable heels. Couples in evening dress accompanied her along the carpeted lobby, some woman glanced at her with a degree of envy – she cut a glamorous figure when she made the effort. Walking along the plush red carpet felt like a movie awards ceremony, and best female actor is…Connie Noble for 'Saving the Planet.' She laughed to herself.

She entered the large ballroom; on the stage a full band was playing. Some couples were dancing the waltz or foxtrot or whatever it was – Connie had never formally danced in her life. She watched with amusement and was approached by a waiter carrying a tray of Champagne; she took two glasses, put one down on a nearby table and sipped the other. A couple in their seventies stood near to her, the man tall and balding, the woman small and squat. She turned and looked up at Connie to make conversation.

'Is this your first time on Mary?'

'Yes,' said Connie, thinking the familiarity was pretentious.

'This is our fifteenth isn't it, Roger?' Now she understood, it was the word frequent passengers used. The man turned.

'Yes, it is, she's wonderful, isn't she?' Connie just nodded politely and took a drink, already wishing she could vanish.

'Are you waiting for your husband?' asked the woman looking at the other glass of Champagne.

'No,' answered Connie. 'I just like Champagne.' The woman seemed briefly stumped.

'Oh. Oh. So, you're on your own then?' Connie wanted to answer truthfully but the devil got the better of her.

'Well I am now. I just threw him overboard. That's why I'm wearing black.' The woman laughed, but the man seemed un-amused and walked away, beckoning his wife to follow him. Connie smiled to herself and took another sip of Champagne.

A line of uniformed crew walked onto the dance floor and stood in front of the stage, the captain appeared and stood in front of them. He welcomed everyone and one by one introduced the senior officers who took a step forward, bowed and accepted the applause. Finally, the captain introduced the most important member of the crew, the head chef. The applause grew and Connie understood why, organising the food and cooking for almost three thousand passengers was a job of biblical proportions, and certainly harder than being the captain – anyone could steer the ship to New York using a sat nav.

She finished both glasses of Champagne and headed with the crowd to the Britannia Restaurant, and joined the queue of people waiting to be seated by the miserable maître d'. Glancing at the others in line she realised all the pomp and circumstance of dressing up and feeling important went back to the colonial days. The Victorian upper classes lording it over everyone else, and keeping the workers and servants in their place. She realised this was a way to experience the lifestyle of the old order. She also imagined a proportion of the passengers were probably Brexit 'leave' voters who somehow felt life could be like this again, once the shackles of liberal Europe could be thrown off.

She was shown to a large oval table and joined the other eight people already seated. To her left was a woman dressed in a pink silk dress, next to her the husband who wore glasses and had grey hair and a beard. To her right were another couple, who seemed similar to the ones on her left only the woman wore a bright green dress. Next to them another couple who seemed younger, the man was bald, both wore glasses and sounded American. Opposite her was an elderly man who was red faced and overweight and next to him a waif of a woman, who was probably his wife. Connie ordered with the others then sat quietly listening to the conversation. The first question to the table came from the red-faced man who asked who'd cruised on 'Mary' before. Connie sighed, while she had to admit it was a viable question, it was the 'snob' element of it that pissed her off. The couple to her left hadn't, but had been on other cruises before. 'Not the Mary then?' said the red-faced snob. The couple shook their heads in shame. The couple to her right had twice, the Americans had four times, and the waif to the man's right hadn't ever cruised before. Clearly, she was no relation at all and the red-faced man was alone. 'Your loss,' he said pointing to her and she weakly smiled. There was a silence as he was obviously waiting to be asked the same question. The American man obliged. The red-faced man took a breath. 'Twenty-four.' The table cooed. Connie didn't want to say anything, she didn't want to ruin their meals, but couldn't help herself.

'You must have a carbon footprint the size of Canada.'

'What?' said the red-faced man.

'I said with the number of trips you've done.' She thought twice before pointing the finger at him. 'Well, ships cause a lot of air pollution, that's what I'm saying.'

'Well it's better than flying.'

'It's seven times worse actually.'

'So, what are you doing on the ship if you care that much?' She couldn't help but agree, and didn't want to appear like a self-righteous prig.

'Look, I'm not criticising you, but the shipping company aren't exactly going to put the facts in their glossy brochure, are they?'

'So, what do you expect me to do? I can't walk far and I like seeing the world. So, I spend the last few years of my life in bed I suppose?' The conversation was getting awkward and Connie wished she'd never said anything in the first place.

'You could pay carbon offsets like I did,' said the waif-like woman sitting next to him.

'What?' said the red-faced man turning to her.

'It's snake oil,' interrupted the balding American. 'A con.'

'How do you know?' asked Connie.

'And how do you know it goes to the right people?'

'I don't.'

'There you go then.'

'But it's better than doing nothing.'

'Is it? Well let me tell you something. We're all screwed anyway, might as well enjoy life while we still can.'

'You mean to hell with it? Let's all burn?' said Connie, clearly annoyed.

'If it's God's will, yes,' said the American's wife.

'God's will, my arse,' said Connie under her breath. The American woman looked up as the starters arrived.

'Here's the soup.'

'And we're all in it together,' said her husband, which broke the ice and made everyone but Connie laugh. The red-faced man lifted his glass and toasted.

'To Mary.' The rest raised their glasses and joined in. Connie didn't but uttered under her breath.

'And all who go down on her.' The double entendre made her smile.

For the rest of the meal Connie spoke to the 'waif-like' woman. They talked about carbon offsets, the melting poles and Donald Fucking Duck. They were both clearly on the same page. However, during the sweet she told Connie that her son was trying to kill her for the inheritance. He'd already tried to poison her twice with drugged white wine at his house, and she was certain at this very moment he was booby trapping her house, so that when she got home it would blow up. Connie quickly finished off her sorbet and excused herself.

It was still early evening and Connie changed into casual clothes. She would see the film then have a nightcap in the Golden Lion Pub. She could now hear the sea slamming against the hull way beneath her and decided to go onto the balcony to take a look. The wind howled as she opened the door and it closed behind her with a bang.

Looking over the side she could make out white surf being tossed into the air as the cold wind blew hard from the North West, from this height it was difficult to judge the waves but she guessed they were about ten to twelve feet. She quickly went back inside before her hair became a 'rat's nest' of tangles and put on the kettle. As she sat waiting for it to boil, she momentarily thought of her imminent death, but quickly blanked it.

She approached 'Illuminations,' the art deco style cinema-planetarium. At the entrance were bronze statues of Hermes and Zeus astride two globes. Inside the 800 seats were maroon or gold, around the walls were floor to ceiling columns and art deco frosted glass lamps. At the centre the large planetarium dome was suspended high up on the roof, the viewing seats below were the maroon ones. It was the most beautiful place on the ship and reminded her of her local cinema in North London she went to as a teenager. Memories of Ki-Ora drinks, choc-ices, Jerry Lewis, Norman Wisdom, James Bond and kissing suddenly flooded her mind. The worst thing about growing up was becoming an adult. She'd love nothing more than to be in the cinema now waiting for her date and having surreptitious fun on the back row in the dark. But somehow once you're in your twenties all that's frowned upon, why? In fact, everything that's fun as a youngster is frowned upon as an adult: Getting covered in mud, climbing trees, damming streams, scrumping for plums, apples and pears, getting blind drunk on cider and having sex in somebody's shed. What happened?

There were only five other people in the cinema so she sat in the middle, halfway up from the screen. She guessed it was so empty because of the film. Most men wouldn't want their wives to see something about sixty-year-old women reading *Fifty Shades of Grey*, let alone what they might get up to after they've seen it. She guessed the two old couples present were eager to find out. The other member of the audience was a single man in his seventies. As long as he didn't come near her his life would be safe.

The film was OK. If somewhat predictable. After reading the book the 'married' woman improves the relationship with her husband, the prevaricating woman ends up with her old boyfriend, the widowed woman ends up with a new man and the avowed single woman goes on a date and has great random sex. In short, all happy Hollywood endings. At least one of them could have failed, then it would've had some bearing on reality.

She walked down the Lobby and thought about sex. Did she fancy a quick fling before the final curtain? She couldn't decide one way or the other, not that it was going to happen on this ship unless of course she'd bought some Viagra and a bed hoist with her. It was only when you thought about sex you realised how long it was since you last had it. Which probably sounded obvious. But if the opportunity isn't there you rarely dwell on it. So, she instantly forgot about it.

In the Golden Lion a quiz was starting. Connie also hated quizzes because they made you feel stupid – even if you weren't. No seats in the bar were available so she sat on the wooden window ledge and ordered a drink. Hearing some of the questions confirmed her decision not to join in. Most seemed to be about popular culture, in other words, pop music, celebrities, sport and TV, about which she knew nothing. She'd be fine on a Lawrence novel, or a physics question, but not the actress who killed her boyfriend in *Emmerdale*?

The ship lurched and she turned and peered out of the window into the darkness. She could just make out white wave tops level with her head, they were on deck two – at least thirty feet above the water – the storm was picking up. She turned back and a moment later there was a loud 'boom', she quickly turned to see they were underwater. A moment later the level fell, it was like looking into the door of a washing machine. She turned back toward the bar expecting people to be aghast, or at least surprised, but not a soul had noticed, they may just as well be sitting in their local.

Back in her cabin she noticed the following day's guide had been delivered, along with two small chocolates. She ate them both. On the front page was a reminder that clocks go back an hour at two a.m. Did that mean she would have an extra hour of life? Time-wise yes, but the body clock would still be ageing at the same rate, so no.

She wanted to go onto the balcony a final time before bed, but had to push with all her might to open the door. The wind howled in like a hurricane, or was it out? She closed the door carefully so it wouldn't wake the entire ship if it slammed. She guessed it was now easily a force 7–8, but the air had become warmer, so maybe the wind had turned away from the NW, and the storm was about to abate.

She went back inside, and for the first time since she'd been aboard felt scared, really scared of dying. Maybe she could get it over with now without the agonising wait? What if she took all the painkillers. Then drank everything in the mini-bar and faded away on the gently rocking bed.

She contemplated it for a few seconds, but what would be the point of dying without at least trying to say something? Even if it was forgotten after a few weeks? Or was she just deluding herself? Was the whole idea a load of cockeyed nonsense? Why not just stay on the ship and continue to the Caribbean like most of the passengers? Drink rum on a beach for a few weeks then drown herself in the warm waters? Why not? Who gives a fuck about climate change anyway? Very few on the ship it seemed.

She was aware of a slight headache so took a couple of painkillers. As she lay in bed she realised if she was going to see her plan through, be it crazy or not, she had to be strong and remain positive. She'd committed herself now and there was no turning back. Telling herself yet again she was doing the right thing, the noble thing (at which she smiled) the fear of dying slowly vanished and she drifted to sleep.

***

Chapter 8

She ate breakfast and took her morning stroll around the deck. She decided to do three circuits of the ship which was approximately a mile. The sea was graphite hued with a five-foot swell but no whitecaps. They were now 750 miles out into the Atlantic, and a similar distance north to Greenland and south to the Azores. The sun shone briefly and the air felt cooler than the previous day. A squadron of the small birds skimmed the wave tops whilst a group of gulls bobbed up and down on the surface like sitting ducks. It was good day for whale and dolphin watching with no deceptive surf, but she saw nothing. She wondered whether icebergs came this far south. But it was obviously the wrong time of year as the sea would be freezing in the Arctic Circle not thawing. Afterwards she quickly returned to her cabin to 'defrost'. As she arrived the door was open, and for the first time she met her steward. He was in his twenties and greeted her with a big smile after apologising for being there.

'That's fine,' said Connie. 'You're just doing your job.' He wore immaculate whites and a badge with his name 'Danillo.'

'I won't be long, madam.'

'Don't worry, Danillo. I'm Connie.'

'Pleased to meet you, Connie.'

'So, how long have you been on the ship?'

'I joined in Southampton three days ago.'

'How long will you be on it for?'

'Hmm. Nine months.'

'That long?' Danillo just smiled.

'How many cabins do you look after?'

'Fifteen.'

'Seven days a week?'

'Yes.'

'My god.'

'No, really. It's fine.' Danillo seemed to be getting slightly uncomfortable with the questioning, and quickly gathered up the dirty towels. 'Do you need anything for the mini bar?'

'Hmm, no. Thanks.' He smiled and left the cabin. It was clear that fraternising with guests was tolerated, but divulging work conditions probably wasn't. He cleaned the cabin twice a day, morning and early evening, and had to work cleverly around passengers' comings and goings. He made the bed, changed the bed linen and towels, cleaned the bathroom, the carpet, mopped the balcony floor, cleaned the French windows, restocked the tea, coffee, sugar, milk and mini bar, tidied up passengers belongings and delivered the daily programme of events and any other communications from the ship's purser, and finally, left two small chocolates on the pillow. Each time Danillo had been in, the cabin was immaculate. Connie knew most of the domestic crew on cruise ships were from the Far East and relied heavily on tips to supplement their pathetically meagre salary, reinforcing the Victorian ethos on board. Needless to say, this didn't make Connie feel particularly comfortable, but what was she going to do? Get them all out on strike?

She settled down on the newly made bed and picked up the daily entertainment guide. She noticed there was a talk on Neanderthals, our relationship, similarities and differences in the Royal Court Theatre. But that was common knowledge, wasn't it? The Neanderthals were far more intelligent than us – they existed in perfect harmony with their surroundings. Though she guessed that wouldn't be the subject of the lecture. She flicked through the pages; flower arranging, a bridge tournament, a whist drive, water colour classes, line and ballroom dancing, blackjack and bingo, none of which remotely interested her. Why did they assume all older people wanted to do these things? Or maybe she hadn't reached that age yet, when you transfer your love of just wiggling your arse for waltzes. She decided she'd take her book and go to the library, then she could read and watch the sea at the same time.

She walked past the polished wooden bookcases and found a seat directly in front of the window. Below her the prow of the ship steadily moved forward like a white tipped arrow through a grey ploughed field.

She opened the book and began to read how scientists have been ridiculed since the eighties for claiming the Earth was warming due to CO_2 emissions; some were called insane and unhinged, others physically intimidated. This reminded her of what happened to the scientist Jeffrey Wigand, when he blew the whistle on tobacco companies who claimed that smoking was safe. He was fired, ridiculed and even had death threats. This was a perfect example of the corporate bulldozer flattening all in its path. Oil and cigarettes have a lot in common: manmade, huge profits and bad for our health. As she read, she began to feel nauseous, not about corporations, but from the gentle movement of the ship which was magnified here at the prow. It was the first time on board she'd felt sea sick; she quickly got up, walked out the library, and along the endless corridor on deck seven until she reached mid-ships, where the movement was less magnified. Desperately trying not to vomit she went down the staircase to deck five and into her cabin, took two motion sickness tablets, lay on the bed and fell asleep.

She woke two hours later and was initially groggy, but soon her head cleared and she felt overwhelmingly hungry. She decided rather than eat again in the Kings Court she'd try the Britannia Restaurant once more. At lunch you didn't have to dress up and could sit at any table you liked, so she could avoid sitting with the people from the previous night.

When she arrived only the lower level of the restaurant was open, so she walked down the sweeping staircase and eyed up possible places to sit. Two or three occupants at a table could be awkward as they might be related, and to sit down with them would feel like gate crashing, so she looked for a large table with at least six guests.

She spotted one that had three couples and a single man who sat in the middle with empty seats either side of him, she took a deep breath and sat down, and as she did, he looked up.

'That'll be ten pounds please.' The man grinned to himself smugly. Connie wasn't sure what to stay, but within moments he turned his attention back to the group with whom he was obviously holding court.

'When she died, it was, it was heart breaking. I was by her bedside for three days without sleep, and the moment, the moment I dropped off, she was gone, dead. I never even had a chance to say goodbye.' The man took a handkerchief from his top blazer pocket and dabbed his eyes. The rest of the table looked awkward. Connie was on the verge of getting up when the man turned to her, his mood completely changed.

'What's your name then? And what do you do?' Connie was taken aback by his sudden forwardness.

'I'm… I'm Connie. And what I do is my own business.'

'Please yourself.' And the man turned back and studied his menu. Connie felt guilty, but at the same time annoyed, there was something about him, his manner and air of superiority. He could be in his eighties, but it was hard to tell. He was balding, tanned, but had very smooth, wrinkle-free skin. He wore a navy blazer, white shirt, striped tie and white slacks, like the commodore of a sailing club, but his strong northern accent somehow betrayed that. It was difficult to pinpoint what he did, but Connie's best guess was he'd been a salesman or even the owner of a small company. She turned and said hello to the couple next to her and was soon chatting with them until the man interrupted.

'What are you talking about?'

'Brexit,' said the husband

'Oh, we should get out as soon as we can,' he said, almost shouting.

'I don't agree,' said the husband.

'Then you're talking poppycock,' said the man shouting again. The husband ignored him and the man turned away to order his food from the waiter. Half way through the main course the man suddenly blurted out to nobody in particular, 'Did anyone go to that Neanderthal lecture?' Before anyone had the chance to answer he continued. 'What a load of crap that was.' Nobody really wanted to argue but Connie couldn't help asking him.

'Why was it crap?'

'Why? We aren't related to the Neanderthals.'

'We are in a way, they're just a different species.'

'We're related to ancient man.'

'A Neanderthal is ancient man.'

'That's rubbish.'

'Two percent of our DNA is Neanderthal. It's science.'

'What, like climate change? That's all rubbish too, a Chinese conspiracy.'

'And why would the world's largest burner of fossil fuels blow their own whistle?'

'How would I know? I'm just saying it's all poppycock.'

'You know all about science then?' said Connie, her blood beginning to boil.

'And you do I suppose? What would a woman know about science?' Connie was speechless, as was the rest of the table. She'd experienced too many times like these throughout her career and had to remain silent, so, on this occasion she didn't. Connie looked the man in the eye, and held it a while to make him sweat. Then with very measured words she quietly began;

'You fucking arrogant piece of shit, you big mouthed empty-headed moron. How dare you denigrate women with a comment like that? Not capable of understanding science? Marie Curie discovered radiography and won two Noble Prizes, her daughter Irene got a Nobel Prize for Chemistry, Dorothy Hodgkin got a Nobel Prize for Molecular science and Barbara McClintock one for Medicine.'

'Never heard of them apart from Marie Curie. My wife was in one of her care homes.'

'Was she?' Well I'll tell you something, I pity her. I'd cut off my arms and legs rather than be married to you.' Connie got up, threw her napkin on the table and walked away. One woman at the table lightly applauded and the rest tried not to smile.

Later in her cabin Connie was still trying to calm down. A part of her felt guilty, even though she meant what she said and he thoroughly deserved it. She still shouldn't have mentioned his wife though; after all, he may have been a kind, loving husband, even though he was clearly a sexist pig. It was a generational thing after all; men worked, women looked after the kids and home. It was only during the war when women did men's jobs there was an acknowledgement of equality, and even then, it took another thirty years before they were on any kind of parity, and some might argue they still aren't. Connie knew that sticking up for your sex wasn't that different to campaigning for the environment; you got ridiculed and marginalised, and were never going to make many friends when pushing the limits of convention. But someone had to do it.

She picked up her book and read about the continued unwillingness of various US administrations to act seriously on CO2 emissions. Reagan, George Bush Senior, Junior and Clinton. Even Barack Obama seemed to side-line the issue, preferring to push health reform as his major legacy, and as for Donald Fucking Duck. She put down the book, got up and went outside onto the balcony. The air was cold and she wrapped her arms around herself as she stared at the water. The ship *was* beginning to feel more like a prison, and she was missing the sight of green grass, the sound of birdsong, and the normality of home life. But above all, it was the self-indulgence that felt wrong, even though she enjoyed the comfort the ship offered, it was partying while Rome burnt. She was reminded of the film *WALL-E*, and the spaceship full of overfed, overweight humans waiting for the planet to become habitable again. She'd taken her daughter to see it when she was fourteen. On the way out she'd asked whether humans would ever destroy the planet like they had in the film. Connie had replied, 'Of course not, even the stupidest people aren't that stupid.' How wrong she had been.

The wind swept a gust of fumes down from the funnel high above her, she coughed and quickly went back inside the cabin. She'd read the amount of fuel the generators and engines used per Atlantic crossing was equivalent to every passenger on board driving twenty-four cars non-stop. It was a sobering thought, and made her wonder, not for the first time, whether the entire escapade was a sham? Regardless of what she intended to do in New York, was she really doing more harm than good?

She wandered around the ship, and noticed people were always eating in the Kings Court. It was now afternoon tea of cakes and sandwiches. Didn't they ever stop? For want of something better to do she joined them, took a piece of fruit and poured herself a tea. This is where she would eat most of her meals from now on. Even if it wasn't glamorous, it was better than sitting at a table with strangers and having to put up with listening to idiots. She sat down near the window and looked outside as the light was fading from the grey sky. Suddenly she felt dizzy, only for a matter of seconds, but as always it was a sharp reminder of things to come; loss of memory, slurring of speech, imbalance and black outs, and felt lucky that so far she'd had none of these, and prayed she wouldn't for the next five or six days at least. Being on the ship in an alien environment had helped her not to dwell on the tumour too much, as if it were a manifestation of terra firma, and not the ocean. Sipping her tea, she wondered how Cathy was, and hoped she could speak to her before, well, she did what she was going to do. With only four days left before they arrived in New York, she was now beginning to worry if she was remotely capable of the act – did she actually have the courage?

She put on her coat and went for a walk around the deck before the light finally faded. In the far distance she spotted a large container ship; these behemoths carried up to 16,000 containers filled with everything from car parts to coconuts.

She'd read that due to world trading agreements one ship could carry TVs from China to Europe and TVs made in the EU back to China, or cheese from Europe to Canada and Canadian cheese back to Europe. An utter nonsensical action, especially considering the Maersk fleet of sixteen container ships produces more sulphur than all the world's cars put together. However, gliding slowly on the horizon it looked no more offensive than a desert island.

She looked below at the churning water, the ship was now passing over the Mid-Atlantic Ridge – a range of subterranean mountains – their peaks three thousand feet below, and when crossed, would return to over ten thousand. Depths like these meant nothing to most people, but she'd appreciated the extraordinary beauty of it once when snorkelling in Greece. Gliding effortlessly above the terrain below – valleys, cliffs, vast forests of Neptune grass and fish going about their daily business – she came to the point where the gentle landscape gave way to deep blue depths at the edge of the subterranean world. She lay still for a while, staring down; it was like floating in the atmosphere, not the ocean at all. However, imagining being in this water made Connie shiver with cold, so she stepped back into the ship through the nearest door, and found herself in the Carinthia Lounge. On the small stage a man was playing a guitar – a Beatles song in flamenco style.

She removed her coat and sat down on one of the comfortable sofas to watch. As he played the man smiled, something she'd never really seen before as most musicians tend to be stern-faced as they concentrate, and this piece certainly required some concentration. 'Here Comes the Sun' segued into 'Eleanor Rigby', followed by 'Yesterday'. She heard an elderly woman near her complain to her husband that it sounded nothing like the original.

'It's a rendition, you idiot,' she thought, then immediately chastised herself. *Oh, stop being a snob, Connie.* But she couldn't help it.

The man stopped playing and received mild applause from the twenty or so elderly couples present. Connie clapped considerably louder; he was good, very good. The man nodded politely and took a sip of water. 'Any requests?' He asked. A voice shouted, 'An Abba song.' Connie rolled her eyes. The man happily strummed an intro and broke into 'Waterloo' followed by 'Take a Chance on Me' and finally 'Dancing Queen', which had a few old ladies singing along, though with some difficulty given the fast tempo. He took another sip of water as the applause died away and asked for any other requests. Connie was unsure but then raised her hand. He looked toward her and smiled. She felt slightly embarrassed and returned the smile. 'Anything by Paco Pena?' The man nodded his appreciation. 'Good choice, some real flamenco then,' he said in an American accent and began to play 'Salobre' which showed his true talent.

Connie watched him perform the sombre yet virtuoso piece. It was so beautiful the odd tear fell down her cheek. At the end she applauded almost too loudly, whilst the rest of the gathering were mild in their appreciation. The man said thank you, and packed his guitar away. She'd obviously come to the performance late and cursed herself for not checking the programme. As he left the stage and passed her, he smiled. Connie blushed.

Lying on her bed she looked through the entertainment guide. Three till four p.m. Carinthia Lounge. Russell Ellis–Flamenco Guitarist. Russell Ellis? He didn't sound that American.

She drifted to sleep, and woke two hours later still feeling unrested. She sat up. Her head began to buzz, accompanied by a high-pitched ringing in her ears. It faded after a few moments but was still disconcerting.

She shook off her worry and poured herself a gin and tonic from the mini bar, knowing full well it would cost at least ten pounds – but who cared? She sat on the sofa and found herself thinking about Russell. Where did he sleep? How long was he aboard? What did he do on his days off? Did he get days off? She checked herself, why on earth did she even care? She'd be off the ship and gone in a few days, he was probably on board for months like Danillo.

Day dreaming about Russell segued into Jim, it was still incomprehensible he wasn't around anymore. She couldn't help imagining what he looked like in the coffin, dried skin on bone and empty eye sockets.

STOP IT! STOP IT! She blanked the images with another gin and tonic.

She ate in the Kings Court, which seemed to smell more pungently of fish every time she visited. Or was that her sense of smell giving up on her? She imagined all kinds of things could go wrong once the brain began to shut down. She sat in an alcove near the window so she wouldn't have to talk to anyone, though that was unlikely in here as most people kept themselves to themselves and were at single tables. Eating here was a business not a social event, which suited her fine. She'd always liked buffets; choose exactly what you want without the wait. She guessed this had a lot to do with her life with Jim. They rarely ate out, but even when they did, he'd complain about the time it took to get served. This would stress her out and generally ruin the meal. So, in the end it was her choice as well as his to eat in. She wondered whether it was this subconscious stress that had caused her to have arguments in the Britannia Restaurant, but then smiled to herself, knowing full well that was a pathetic excuse. She'd argue with anyone anywhere if she disagreed with their politics.

She finished off her sweet and strolled down to the Chart Room. Jazz was playing again and she sat at the bar as before and had a gin and tonic whilst looking at the other guests on the sofas.

Many sat in groups of four, mostly two couples who'd no doubt teamed up on board so the men could talk sport or money, and the women their families. She knew it was a huge generalisation, but would put her money on the fact nobody was discussing climate change or the multifarious fuck ups of Donald Fucking Duck. But they were on board to enjoy themselves, not slash their wrists.

She sipped her drink and watched the band, the drummer smiled at her briefly between songs. God, was she becoming a groupie! She quickly finished her drink and left.

Back in the cabin she was beginning to get the classic 'fever'. If you were in a group or a couple you could hang around the ship without any problem, but sitting on your own for an hour or two in the bar, or one of the lounges made it look as if you were 'on the make' especially as a woman. It wasn't that she cared about this too much, it was being looked upon as 'the lonely spinster' she didn't like. She could try to find a single female companion, but she'd probably seen most of them at the 'Solos' meeting and they were old enough to be her mother. There was the 'waif-like' woman – whose name was Joan – that she'd spoken to at dinner, and they did have a fair bit in common, but she seemed slightly unhinged and the last thing she wanted was somebody tailing her around the ship. And now they were almost halfway across the Atlantic, and nearing their destination, she would need time for mental preparation – whatever that meant.

She picked up the guide. Seven p.m. 'Singers in Concert' in the Royal Court Theatre with Queen Mary's musicians. Would Russell be one of them?

She took her seat and sank into the plush red velvet. It was still impossible to believe this vast theatre was levitating two miles above solid ground. She noticed some of the audience were dressed up, having just come out of the Britannia Restaurant's first sitting, whilst others were wearing clothes you would walk the dog in. She found this contrast amusing, and also levelling. The band appeared on stage: a brass section, drummer, bass and electric guitar, all behind their Cunard motif music stands. Connie saw Russell sit down on a chair behind his and lay out his music.

Four singers, two men and two women, entered into the spotlights and bowed to applause. Each gave their name, then three of them sat down on high stools.

The band struck up and the lone singer began to croon some old song that Connie didn't recognise. Each singer then took it in turn to take centre stage. The singing wasn't great, neither were the songs. Neil Sedaka, Andy Williams and Petula Clark weren't exactly her thing, and they were performed in a rather cheesy fashion with exaggerated grins and twirls that didn't impress Connie at all. However, Russell did, as he sat casually playing with that huge grin on his face. Maybe he was grinning and bearing it? Perhaps he was on drugs? But surely that wouldn't be allowed on board? Either way, watching him was far more interesting than the singers. At the end of the show he disappeared backstage, where Connie imagined they put him back in his box until morning.

**

Chapter 9

The following day the air on deck was chillier than ever as Connie did her usual three circuits, but more briskly on the starboard side due to the prevailing north westerly wind. She went back inside her face numb from the cold, something she'd not experienced in London for twenty, even thirty years. If anyone needed proof the Earth was warming, surely that was it. She could remember a winter when she and Jim rented their first flat, and the pipes in the bathroom froze solid for three months. The standing joke being they had kept the milk in the fridge to prevent it freezing solid in the kitchen, and they both slept in thermals. Only once in the previous ten years had it snowed in London and stayed more than a day. 2018 was the warmest Arctic winter on record and this warm air pushed cooler air south creating the stupidly titled 'Beast from the East'. Young people in London today didn't know what cold was.

She warmed up in the cabin and dutifully checked her guide. RADA were presenting *Much Ado About Nothing* in the afternoon. She wasn't a huge fan of Shakespeare, but it would kill the time, probably four hours knowing Shakespeare's love of hearing his own words. She noticed Russell was playing again at six. Seeing his name made her heart quicken, how long was it since she felt like that? There was a chemistry teacher at school when she was in her forties, she was happily married to Jim with a four-year-old daughter, but he entranced her. It was just as well he was gay, or else she may have done something foolish. Was this foolish? To feel like this for a man on a ship? A clichéd shipboard romance? Not that anything was going to happen of course, and did she need the complication of a relationship considering her condition and objective once in New York? She sat down and sighed. No, it wasn't a good idea at all, and he'd only smiled at her for god's sake! Was she that stupid? If she went to see him in the afternoon, what then? Was she going to sit and watch him like a lovesick schoolkid with a dumb grin on her face and hope he might stop and say hello as he leaves the stage? Of course not. And he smiled because that's his job, he's an on-board entertainer, what was she thinking? He no doubt smiles at everyone, has to, it's in his contract to be cheerful, you idiot Connie. He was smiling all the way through the concert, so were the singers, and the drummer in the jazz band. You can't have an entertainer on a ship looking as if he's about to commit suicide, can you? Connie convinced herself to stop being foolish, and not to watch Russell in the afternoon. She noticed there was something on in the planetarium at eleven; she'd never been to one and now was a good time. She could cast the thoughts of him into oblivion and down a black hole.

She sat in the cinema's central seats as the giant dome lowered itself above her head, until all she could see was the white screen surrounding her. It reminded her of being in the MRI machine, only a giant one. The lights lowered and three separate projectors came to life, all pointing upwards. A title appeared. *Asteroid-Mission Extreme*. She was floating in space, suddenly a large rock hurtled toward her making her shrink in the seat. It was an asteroid, and climbing up a ladder attached to its side was the tiny figure of a man in a spacesuit.

The idea was that if another asteroid was on collision course for the Earth, like the one that wiped out the dinosaurs 250 million years ago, we could land on it, attach a bomb and blow it up, hence avoiding a possible extinction – it didn't take into account we'd probably do that ourselves, but it was interesting to watch nevertheless. However, for at least three quarters of the audience floating around in space was sleep-inducing, as Connie noticed when suddenly snoring became part of the soundtrack.

She came out of the cinema and walked along the corridor on deck three – forty feet above the water. Through the large portholes the big waves silently glided past. That was one of intriguing things about the ship, there was no sound of the engines whatsoever. She sat down at the small green baize games tables that ran the entire length of the passageway. Looking out through the glass she saw the squadron of small black-headed birds again, but they quickly disappeared over the wave crests to god knows where. She guessed at some point they must touch land to breed, but until then it was life on the wing, and no doubt a prayer when the weather became ferocious. If only she knew what they were called?

A large wave suddenly crashed against the window, and for a brief moment she was underwater – as it had been in the bar, but that was at night. As the next wave collided, she could make out some organic debris, and a school of tiny fish. She decided this was the best place to be on the ship, and sat transfixed for over an hour, during which time she didn't see another soul.

She walked back along the Grand Lobby, the busy main thoroughfare and realised how easy it had been to find a quiet place to sit, even with a total of four thousand people on board.

Not wanting to eat lunch again in the Kings Court she found a table on her own in the Britannia Restaurant. The service was good, as was the salmon wellington and baked pears in cognac, though a little rich for lunch. Connie drank coffee and looked around her, she didn't see any of the diners she'd sat with recently. In fact, she'd not seen anyone on the ship more than once, even though she had a good memory for faces.

She went up to the library too see if she could find a book on sea birds, which you would expect in a library on the ocean, but there were none, which didn't surprise her at all. The ship was beginning to pitch and roll again and she felt mildly nauseous so returned to her cabin.

She lay on the bed and idly picked up the book. One passage particularly intrigued her:

The Head of the World Bank Nicholas Stern said in 2006 'We need to act now to avoid huge costs in the future due to global damage caused by climate change. Whatever we spend now to prevent it, will be increased ten-fold if we ignore it.'

USA, Saudi Arabia, Russia, Kuwait, Australia and other oil and coal producing nations have ignored it. Maybe climate change denial is associated with the fear of death – the death of the dollar – which is ironic considering it will eventually guarantee it.

Connie didn't want to think about death either so put the book down and closed her eyes.

She woke just in time to rush to the Royal Court and take her seat for the play. The RADA players were ex-students of the famous London drama school and performed it well. It was a typical Shakespeare comedy about love, loss, broken promises, double-crossing and mistaken identity that all ends well with the two couples marrying each other, and as far as Connie was concerned all the better for being just over an hour long without losing the plot.

She walked out the theatre and saw Russell walking toward her. She wasn't quite sure what to do, whether he'd seen her amongst the crowd, or even recognised her. When he was a few feet away, she smiled, and to her surprise he stopped and spoke.

'Hi. Enjoy the play?' Connie wasn't sure what to say.

'Hm. Yes. It was OK. But I'm not mad about Shakespeare really. Though if you're educated, you're supposed to be aren't you? Or pretend you are.' Russell laughed.

'I guess so.' After a few moment's awkwardness Connie spoke.

'Did you see it?'

'Not allowed.'

'Really?'

'We aren't supposed to fraternise with passengers either.'

'You're kidding?'

'I wish.'

'You're in trouble already then?'

'Yup. The cat of nine tails for me at six bells.' Connie laughed.

'I'm playing again, in the Carinthia Lounge.'

'I know.' Connie felt awkward. 'Well, I guessed you were, I mean.'

'See you later maybe?'

'Maybe,' replied Connie. Russell walked away into the theatre leaving her wondering what had happened to her resolve, but she couldn't just ignore him could she? But was there any point if he couldn't fraternise? Or maybe he could? Connie decided to treat herself to a drink in the champagne bar and mull it over.

She sat nursing her glass, and gazed around. It was art deco in style like most of the ship. On the walls were black and white paintings of movie stars: Bogart, Bacall, Monroe, Sinatra and Cary Grant, whose face reminded her of Russell's, kind, open, and with a big smile. Of course, he was much older than the Grant in the picture; she guessed Russell was late-fifties. He was tallish, maybe five eleven, had thick grey hair, but his skin was young and un-creased. In another life she may have fallen for him, but now? If an affair was even possible how could she get involved when she was going to die sooner rather than later? But on the other hand, didn't she deserve some comfort, maybe even passion, a final fling? No, maybe not if it caused him pain and she didn't want to hurt him, didn't want to turn that smiling face into a morose one.

She had another glass of champagne, and began to feel warm and fuzzy, began to feel great, she had a third, fuck it, why not? She deserved it. She had a fourth, and giving Russell a wide berth had now vanished. She would go and see him play, but leave it a little late to try and gauge how happy he was when he finally saw her. She looked at her watch, fuck! It was already six thirty! He'd been on half an hour already.

She quickly walked down the Lobby and took the lift to deck seven. She could hear him playing as she opened the Carinthia lounge doors. She steadied and giggled to herself realising she was slightly pissed, and tried her best to walk in a straight line which was quite difficult as the ship was now pitching considerably more, being nearer the bow.

She laughed as one moment she was tiptoeing like a ballet dancer as the floor dropped beneath her, and the next walking like Grouch Marx as it came up to meet her. She paused a moment to regain herself before the stage came into view. She'd hardly make a good entrance staggering in like an alcoholic. She took a few careful steps and sat down in an armchair on the perimeter. As she did Russell turned and smiled briefly, even though he was in the middle of a tricky piece by Rodriguez. Yes, he had been waiting for her.

Connie lay back into the deep armchair and closed her eyes as she listened to the soothing music, and very quickly fell asleep.

She woke an hour later to an almost empty lounge with no music playing. 'Oh shit!' she said under her breath and quickly sat up. Oh shit! Shit! Shit! What had she done? Insulted the man in the worst possible manner, fallen asleep during his music, Shit! Shit! Shit! Well that was it, wasn't it? She didn't have to agonise over the pros and cons of having a fling with him any longer, did she? Idiot! Bloody stupid idiot! When she'd finally calmed down, she began to see the amusing side, and realised that Dorothy Parker would have been proud of her being a fellow inebriate. 'I'm not a writer with a drinking problem, I'm a drinker with a writing problem.'

Dorothy drank – like a fish, and scorned men for their weaknesses, but was happy when their weaknesses led them to her door. She was a true maverick, and in many ways, Connie wished her life had been more like hers, less routine, less dull, and less formal. But she could live her last days a little more like hers, couldn't she? There was nothing to lose was there? Go out with a bang? Why not? She still felt guilty about Russell though, and hoped she'd have a chance to at least apologise to him before they docked at New York. However, for now she needed to eat, so slowly got up and made her way to the Kings Court just along the corridor.

Grabbing a plate, she piled it high with a stir fry, and dumped some prawn crackers next to it on the tray. A few people in the queue cast sideways glances, on account of her extreme rigour and purpose. Sensing this she slowed down and tried to show a little more decorum as she dumped some Tempura prawns on the plate to accompany the stir-fried vegetables.

She walked away with her tray and sat down at the nearest seat she could find to devour the food, not caring if anyone was watching or not. After she'd cleaned the plate she got up and helped herself to another portion of prawns, after which she ate two bowls of lychees and a banana.

She'd hadn't eaten so much in years, nor drank that much champagne. She went back to the cabin sat on the sofa, put her feet up and stared at the ceiling.

The cabin was moving considerably and the walls creaked and the sea growled as the wind howled outside. The whole ship was listing to port as the wind rammed into the starboard side. It was exciting, and after listening to the 'boom' of big breakers striking the side of the ship, she got up and tried to open the patio door to take a look outside. It was dark and the windows were misted up with spray; she pushed the door with all her might but it wouldn't open.

Putting on her coat, scarf and gloves, she climbed the stairs to the promenade deck, but the exit doors were cordoned off with a sign reading 'Danger High Winds'. She quickly looked around her, ducked under the cordon and tried the door but it was locked. She went back to the cabin, determined to open the door. What harm could it do? She wasn't going to be swept overboard sixty-feet up was she? She prepared herself, planted her feet firmly on the carpet and gave an almighty push. The door moved fractionally. She tried again this time using every bit of strength she could muster. The door moved slightly, then suddenly it opened with relative ease accompanied by a gargantuan whoosh of wind.

She stepped outside and the door slammed shut with an almighty bang making her jump.

White water flared up in the ship's 'man overboard' searchlight. As she moved toward the rail the wind hit her, tearing at her face and hair. It was a maelstrom out there, some of the waves colliding with the ship nearly came up to eye level. As they did the wind tore off the crests and sent the spray directly into face, at first it was a shock as the freezing salty water hit her, a few seconds later another hit, she started to laugh, and waited for the next one. Within a few minutes she was soaked and exhilarated.

She didn't want to move, it was one of those moments when you feel vividly alive, stingingly alive. She didn't want it to end, but after a while she began to feel her face and hands go numb and knew it was time to go inside. Maybe they'd be another day like this?

She knew they were approaching the Flemish Cap from the daily magazine. An area of the ocean where the depth suddenly goes from ten thousand, to three hundred feet. The area was notorious for storms, because huge seas piled up as the depth dramatically diminished. Famous for tuna and swordfish, the Portuguese were willing to sail over two thousand miles to fish the area three hundred years ago.

More recently the sword boat 'Andrea Gale' went down with all crew in waves over a hundred feet high. Surely nobody could survive in seas like that, and how small birds did was beyond belief. She imagined their boat now somewhere below her with the dead bodies trapped inside their watery tomb. It sent a shiver through her, not long she'd be joining them in their oblivion and quickly abandoned the thought.

She climbed into the warm bed as the cabin swayed and jolted around her. However, she found the ship's movement soothing, and even when she closed her eyes, didn't feel remotely sick. She'd found her sea legs at last.

*

She was awake at seven am, and by the lack of movement in the cabin could tell the sea state had calmed. She got up, dressed and went for a walk on deck. The ocean had now flattened into a dull grey slab – extraordinary how wind could demolish it so effectively. She walked toward the bow; only three or four other people had ventured out on the bitter cold day. Ahead of her stood a man at the rail wearing a heavy coat and Klondike-style fur hat with the flaps pulled down firmly over his ears. He was looking out to sea with a pair of binoculars. Connie followed his line of sight and saw the small squadron of black-headed birds again flitting over the surface. She was desperate to know what they were called so walked up to the rail and stood alongside him. So as not make him jump out of skin she waited until he lowered the glasses.

'Excuse me, but what are those small birds with the black heads called?' The man turned. It was Russell.

'Oh. It's you?' said Connie, biting her tongue.

'Well if it isn't sleeping beauty.'

'Oh my god. Look, I'm, I'm really sorry.'

'It's fine.'

'No, no it's not. I, I sat down, closed my eyes and your music was so relaxing I just fell asleep.'

'Don't worry about it.'

'But it's disrespectful.'

'Well, it did hurt… a bit.'

'See, I'm a horrible person.'

'Look, if you were tired you had to sleep. You think I'm not used to people falling asleep on this ship?' Connie decided to come clean.

'OK. I wasn't tired. I was drunk. I'd had four glasses of champagne.'

'Lucky old you. I wish I could have one.'

'You mean you can't drink on board?' Russell shook his head.

'God, it's worse than a slave ship.'

'But it saves me money. I don't drink much anyway these days.' Russell raised his binoculars and looked out to sea. Connie wasn't sure whether to move on or not, then looked out and saw the squadron of small birds again.

'What are those called? The ones with the small black heads?'

'Those are… sorry what's your name?' Russell lowered his binoculars and turned to her.

'Connie.'

'I'm Russell.'

'I know. It's in the programme.'

'So it is. Right Connie, they're petrels. Wilson's petrels to be exact.'

'How the hell do they survive in a storm like the one last night?'

'By a miracle of evolution, I think. I guess they hunker down on the surface and ride the waves. If one breaks on them and they go under, it's no problem because they're divers and flyers.'

'Wow, and we can't do either.'

'That's because we haven't had to evolve that much physically.'

'Just mentally, and now look what we're doing to the world. Clever, aren't we?' Russell put his binoculars back to his eyes.

'Did you know we're only ninety miles from where the Titanic sank?' He pointed. 'Somewhere over there I think.'

'Not much chance of that happening again once all the ice has melted,' said Connie.

Russell didn't comment, lowered his binoculars and began to walk. 'I do three circuits, three times a day,' he said as Connie began to follow.

'Is it alright if I join you, or would you rather be alone?'

'No join me please.' They walked in silence for a while until Connie not being able to help herself took up her earlier point.

'Funny isn't it? The phrase "tipping point" of a ship is now used as a term to explain the planet's own point of no return. Melting ice, no sun reflection, bare tundra releasing CO_2 and methane, sending temperatures spiralling out of control. And it could all happen a few years from now.'

'Maybe, maybe not,' said Russell almost casually. Connie wasn't sure how to take this, either he was a climate denier or an optimist so she decided to remain schtum on the subject for the time being. Why did she have to bring up climate change all the bloody time anyway? Of course, she knew the answer to that, because it was the singular most threatening thing man has had to deal with since the last ice age. And she was now at the point of no return herself, and her worry for the future was so all-encompassing she could talk about little else. But she knew if she wanted to have a companion for these final few days, she should consider avoiding the subject, unless of course he brought it up first. Russell paused at the rail again and lifted his binoculars.

'Two skuas out there.' Connie could see them in the distance, circling above something or other. 'It could be a whale they're following, hard to tell.'

'Wow! A whale? Do you see many out here?'

'Hundreds, especially in spring when they migrate.'

'Do you think we'll see one today?'

'It's possible if the sea doesn't rough up too much.'

'Tell me, won't you?'

'Yeah, sure.'

They walked their third circuit, not saying very much apart from telling each other about their immediate family and where they were from. Russell came from Houston, was divorced and had two grown up children. They finally lent against the rail as Connie noticed something on the horizon. Russell gave her the binoculars.

'That's the Hibernian oil well.'

'Well. Let's hope it sinks,' said Connie. Russell didn't respond and checked his watch.

'I've got to go to rehearsal. Do you want to meet later?' Connie wasn't sure it was a good idea; they didn't exactly hit it off during their walk.

'Are you sure you want to?'

'Why wouldn't I?'

'Well, you seem, I don't know.'

'Uninterested?'

'Yeah, kind of. And I thought you said you weren't allowed to fraternise with passengers?'

'Screw that, if anyone sees me, I'll say you're my sister.'

'Alright then.'

'Shall I meet you at five in the Chart Room?'

'OK.' Russell weakly smiled and disappeared back into the ship, leaving her somewhat confused – he smiled like a

Cheshire cat when on stage, but hardly smiled once in the last half hour.

Feeling cold, she entered the Kings Court, removed her coat, gloves and scarf, went to the buffet and served herself a hearty vegetarian breakfast of fried eggs, beans, mushrooms, tomatoes, hash browns and toast. Sometimes a British fry up was the best meal on earth.

Danillo was in her cabin when she returned. 'Caught you,' she said as a joke. Danillo smiled. Connie sat on the sofa as he finished off replenishing the tea and coffee sachets.

'What will you do when your nine months is up?'

'Go back to my wife in the Philippines.'

'You're married? Doesn't she miss you?'

'Yes. But one day we will have enough money to buy a shop.'

'Must be very hard being away from home all that time?' Danillo nodded and handed her two small chocolates.

'Do you want your tablets?' Connie nodded and smiled.

'Thanks, Danillo.' He quickly left. There was something about the crew, they must have strict rules of engagement which was maybe why Russell behaved strangely earlier on. However, she imagined Danillo and the domestic crew were on a very tight rein compared to him.

She read the daily programme. That BBC journalist was speaking again so she'd give her a miss. Four different singers were giving renditions of 'Songs from Stage and Screen' no doubt something from *The King and I*. Thigh slapping songs from *Annie Get your Gun* and no doubt opening with 'There's No Business Like Show Business.' No thanks. The only thing to see was the RADA group reciting love poems in the evening. Why on earth that interested her she hadn't a clue.

147

Maybe she needed reminding what passion was after years without any, even if it was only in verse.

She decided to have a lazy day, not that the others had been particularly active. She'd stroll aimlessly around the ship, read a bit, have a rest and think about Russell and her one-hour date – as she assumed he'd be in the band again for the show at seven. She made herself a coffee and read her depressing book. It seemed that to have a remote chance of stopping the world's temperature from rising above two degrees, each westerner would have to keep their CO_2 emissions down to 2.7 tons per annum.

Currently the average western home emits that in four weeks, the USA being the worst offender having the highest per capita emissions in the world – hence their intransigence in reducing it. However, the USA claimed that China is the worst emitter. It was ironically called 'passing the buck.' It was true, China was planning to build three hundred new coal fired power stations, however, that was simply to keep up with the world's demand for their products. It was kind of "quid pro quo."

Connie decided that was enough bad news for the day and wished she'd brought a Dorothy Parker book with her. There was of course the ship's library, but it hardly seemed worth taking a book out now with only two more days left at sea. Two more days, then New York, then? Well it was up to her wasn't it?

She found herself thinking about having sex with Russell. But that was highly unlikely with his schedule and the ship's draconian rule book. She hadn't even considered when his stint aboard might come to an end, maybe it was on their arrival in New York? Or months away? She wondered if he did the same gruelling stretch like Danillo, but doubted it. No,

Russell wouldn't be on board nine months, he'd go mad. She was beginning to go a bit stir crazy after five days. Maybe they could sneak away and have clandestine sex in the freezing Jacuzzi outside, or up on the top deck next to the funnel, or even in the cinema after it was closed at night? Oh, stop being stupid, Connie! There was of course her cabin? But he'd be far more likely to get caught there. There must be security cameras along the corridor outside? She finally stopped day dreaming, although it was fun while it lasted, and had passed the time.

She decided to eat alone in the Britannia restaurant again and took her seat at a single table. Next thing she knew Joan was sitting opposite her.

'I've been looking for you everywhere,' she said earnestly. Connie smiled. They ate lunch together and talked about the environment and what was to become of it. She said they'd found a dead whale in Indonesia, and in its stomach were twenty-five plastic bags and one hundred and fifteen cups. Connie said nothing surprised her anymore, and plastic was maybe the least of our problems. If the ocean got much warmer there'd be no whales left to eat it.

During the sweet Joan turned the conversation to her son's continued attempts to kill her. She was sure he was going to blow her house up when she got back, but Connie pointed out that if he wanted to kill her for the inheritance, he'd be foolish to blow up one of her major assets. She saw the logic and said in that case he'd probably try to blow up the cab on her return home. As on the previous occasion Connie quickly finished her meal, made her excuses and left.

It was extraordinary how she could be so coherent one moment, and completely irrational the next. Maybe she had the onset of dementia? Or her son was trying to kill her?

Connie lay on the bed; the slight headache she'd had after lunch was now getting worse. She decided to take a prescription headache pill, and within half an hour she felt fine, but somewhat drowsy and drifted to sleep.

When she woke, she lay on the bed and thought about Jim. Was it a good marriage? It seemed so for the first five years, until Sara was born, then what happened? Same as any marriage she guessed? It became a dull routine, and when sex was off the agenda – a hearth without a fire. It wasn't her, but Jim. She was still game but he wasn't. But women don't divorce the father of their child because of sex, do they? It just isn't done. Nor can a woman drop into a local grooming parlour for light relief, god forbid! She'd just have to be her own pleasurer, forever. Because she was going to have to remain married to Jim for the rest of her life, wasn't she? Unless of course he ran off with someone else, but that was unlikely. He wouldn't have the time or inclination; it would be too much trouble for him.

The big problem was apart from a low libido, which he had admitted to, Jim was a lovely man, and everybody would have hated her if she divorced him. Especially her mother who doted on him like a son, which, of course, he loved.

She always cooked his favourite food when they visited, laughed at all his jokes, told him how he reminded her of Ronald Coleman, a famous actor from the forties, and even talked football with him about which she knew nothing. He should have moved in with her. There is nothing worse than seeing your mother flirt with your husband, and having him reciprocate. The only relief was they'd never have sex together as he wasn't capable. Or was he? Maybe he just never fancied you Connie? She suddenly shook herself free of the thought. My god don't go there! But she continued to chew over the past.

If she could have her life again who would she have chosen for a partner? Cathy probably, with a man on the side for sex. She couldn't imagine herself and Cathy having sex together. They'd both be in fits of hysterics or throw up, or no doubt both. How was Cathy? She hoped she'd not lost her number, or even her mind?

Connie glanced at her watch; it was nearly four thirty! She jumped up, pulled off her jeans, slipped into a skirt and clean blouse, quickly brushed her hair, daubed on some lipstick and was ready.

She sat out of view from the jazz quartet as she didn't want Russell's fellow musicians to see her with him, but wouldn't imagine they'd grass him up if they did. He turned up bang on five, sat down on the opposite sofa and asked if she wanted a drink. The waiter quickly approached. Connie had a gin and tonic and Russell ordered himself a coffee. They smiled at each other.

'So?' said Russell leaning forward. 'How long are you on the ship for?'

'Two more days.'

'Getting off in New York?' Connie nodded.

'And how long are you staying?'

'A few days.'

'And then flying back to the UK?' Connie nodded again; she didn't want to complicate matters.

'Staying anywhere nice?'

'The Algonquin?'

'Oh yeah that's cool. The famous literati hang out. Well it was.'

'I know, that's why I'm staying there.'

'You're a Dorothy Parker fan then?'

'You bet. "If love is blind why is lingerie so popular?"' Russell laughed.

'My favourite's "A hangover is the wrath of grapes"' Connie smiled.

'It's unusual for a man to know about Mrs Parker.'

'I'm an unusual man.'

'Oh really?'

'No, just a run-of-the-mill guy.'

'Pity.' They both smiled then chatted about the *New Yorker* magazine until the waiter arrived with the drinks. Russell seemed different this time, more relaxed and Connie was warming to him.

'So, how long are you on board?' she asked.

'Three months, I've got one left. Down to the Caribbean back to New York, Southampton, New York. Then three months off.'

'How long have you been doing that?'

'Five years.'

'Doesn't it get boring?'

'How? I'm playing music every night, composing in my cabin, hanging out with other musicians, and it's cheaper than living back home in Houston.'

'I guess. But it must get claustrophobic, surely?'

'No more than being stuck at home on my own in the apartment.' Russell sipped his coffee.

'You don't have someone back home then?' Russell shook his head.

'Not unless you count the mice.' Connie smiled.

He was sad in some ways, she felt he'd had a hard time with the divorce maybe? It seemed all he lived for was his music, so she decided to talk about that for a while.

It turned out they both loved the same stuff from the seventies; Led Zeppelin, Canned Heat, Cream, Free, Yes, Crosby Stills and Nash, The Who etc. Connie asked him who his favourite guitarist was.

'Hendrix, without a doubt. He showed the world how to play an electric guitar. Hendrix and his guitar were joined at the hip.'

'A friend of mine slept with him,' said Connie.

'My god, who is she? We must meet. Maybe if we slept together his genius would rub off on me? Oh sorry, that was rather crude, wasn't it?' Connie laughed.

'Disgusting.'

'I sincerely apologise. And we have to thank you Brits for adopting him.'

'You're welcome,' said Connie as he checked his watch. 'Time to go already?'

'Yeah. You could come along?'

'Songs of stage and screen? No thanks. Now if you were playing stuff from Electric Ladyland?'

'I wish. I wouldn't be on this ship if I could.' There was a brief pause where they both looked at each other with a kind of mutual attraction. Russell reluctantly broke the spell.

'I better go. Sorry it's only been an hour.' Connie glanced at her watch.

'Forty-five minutes actually. Can I ask you a question?' He nodded and took his last sip of coffee.

'What's it like having a dumb, lying, racist, misogynistic cunt for a president?' Russell nearly spat out his drink, he put down the cup and began to laugh.

'You should be a CNN reporter!' his laughter continued and when it finally abated, he asked Connie if she would like to meet on deck at muster point F the following morning. She agreed and he quickly left. She had to ask him about Donald Fucking Duck, it was important to know where he stood politically.

There was nothing to do next but eat, again. Sitting in the Kings Court she was beginning to feel bloated, lethargic and fed up with food. She was sure if they all ate half as much on board, the majority of passengers would still disembark at the end of their voyage overweight. It was eating for the sake of it, over indulgent and rather obscene. If everyone stayed on board for a few months many of them wouldn't fit through their cabin doors. Yes *Wall-E* was very prophetic about the future, the passengers on the spaceship grew so fat they needed to be transported around on electric armchairs.

She finished the small amount of salmon she'd served herself and decided three circuits around the deck was what she needed. Grabbing her coat from the cabin she sprinted back up the stairs to deck seven and walked outside.

It was getting dark and cold, very cold, but the fresh air immediately woke her up. She briskly walked toward the bow, around the front through the glass protected walkway, and down the port side. There was one single person ahead of her, leaning on the rail watching the water glide by below. As she neared him, she realised it was the patronising man she'd sat next to at lunch; there was no mistaking that bald suntanned big fucking head of his. She wondered how hard it would be to rush him, lift up his legs, and hurl him overboard. A lot harder than she thought probably. It would have to be a quick clean movement executed with precision. She'd grab him, be unable to lift him, then he'd grab her, arrest her, and she'd go to prison for attempted murder as there were numerous safety cameras around the deck. When she was almost level with him, he turned.

'Good evening, madam,' he said in a courteous voice. Connie ignored him and kept walking. *The two–faced bastard,* she thought to herself, and purposely aborted the second circuit just in case he was still there.

Later in the Carinthia Lounge the RADA group did a nice job of selecting and reading a number of love poems from Shakespeare, Elliot, Auden, McGough and Thomas amongst others. But somehow it was Roger McGough that captured the simple beauty of love in a poem called 'Summer with Monica.' One of her favourites:

'For I locked the door and threw away the key, and I spent summer with Monica, and she spent summer with me.'

It was about a young couple so in love that the rest of the world outside didn't exist, and how they turned their small room into an adventure. 'Making sandcastles on the blankets, paddling in the pillows, swimming in the sink and playing with shoals of dishes.' It perfectly described the excitement of those love sick early days, which most of us have experienced, but unfortunately not for long. It was both beautiful and bitter sweet.

By the end of the poem Connie had tears in her eyes thinking about Jim. It was his favourite poem too, and she now realised she missed him enormously, regardless of the sex.

She drifted to sleep that night listening to the low 'boom' of waves hitting the ship, but she could also hear cicadas, smell pine and oregano, and was lying next to Jim in the small bedroom in Assos, Cephalonia, when like Roger McGough's poem, they were young and madly in love.

***

Chapter 10

They stood on the deck; it was bitter cold, barely above freezing. Russell had his binoculars and was scanning the horizon, whilst Connie had her arms wrapped around herself for warmth.

'Bloody hell. This weather could freeze the nuts off a polar bear,' she said through gritted teeth. Russell just chuckled to himself. The sea was rolling with a twenty-foot swell and bad weather was on the way. Only the odd jogging couple were brave enough to be outside.

'Not too cold then?' quipped Russell.

'No, I was an Inuit in my former life.'

Russell let out a short laugh again at her comment. He lowered the binoculars pulled the strap over his head and handed them to Connie.

'Here. Straight ahead, three hundred metres out.' Connie lifted the binoculars to her eyes. She looked a few moments.

'What? I can't see anything.'

'Just wait.' Connie continued to look.

'Where?'

'Wait,' said Russell again. Something burst the surface, a spume of water shot into the air followed by a huge rolling mass of grey tipped by a small fin. Within seconds a huge tail appeared as it dived and was gone.

'Oh my God!' exclaimed Connie. 'Oh my fucking God!' Russell smiled as she looked up at him.

'Keep looking, it's surfacing to breath every thirty seconds. I counted.' Connie put the binoculars back to her eyes and waited with anticipation. Russell guided her to look further to her right. 'Remember, we're going twenty-five knots in the opposite direction, and the whale is doing about twelve.'

Moments later it surfaced again, the spume, the great roll of its back, and finally the tail as it disappeared again. Connie was speechless. It was simply the most magical, extraordinary thing she'd seen in her entire life. She'd seen a whale, she'd seen a whale, and couldn't stop repeating it to herself. She continued to look but it was now too far away to see. She passed the binoculars back to Russell and spontaneously hugged him around the waist.

'I've seen a whale, I've seen a whale, thank you, thank you, thank you.' Russell smiled at her childlike excitement as she clung on to him. Realising her behaviour may not be quite appropriate she released him.

'Sorry!'

'That's OK. It's nice to give someone that much pleasure.' Connie smiled awkwardly.

'What was it?'

'A Sei whale, about forty foot long. It's a bit north for November.'

'Wow.' I've seen a Sei.'

'You certainly have.'

'I just hope it's not full of plastic.'

'Probably not, it's the Pacific and Indian Oceans that have the worst pollution. Largely caused by South East Asia.'

'The western world just specialises in CO2,' replied Connie spontaneously, even though she promised herself she'd avoid the subject. Russell looked slightly perturbed and shrugged.

'What about China?'

'Well I just read they produce thirty percent of the world's goods, and are responsible for their emissions, take that away and the USA are by far the world's biggest CO2 polluters per capita.'

'Really? I'm not sure about that. 'Connie nodded in the affirmative. Russell began to walk.

'Can we go inside? I can't feel my feet,' said Connie. Russell turned.

'Yeah. Sure thing. Sorry.'

They both sat quietly drinking coffee in the Carinthia Lounge. Connie felt she'd hit a nerve again. Whenever she brought the subject up, he seemed defensive. Where did he stand? Why was he awkward with it? He'd laughed when she'd abused Trump but that didn't mean he wasn't a climate change denier did it? Either way she decided she wasn't going to ask now and questioned him about his day.

'Well I'm rehearsing till six, then I have the evening off. I was going to ask if you wanted to have a meal with me.'

'You were?'

'Well I am.'

'Then I'll be the cheapest date you ever had,' she said tongue in cheek.

'What do you mean?' he said slightly confused.

'A meal on a ship with free food?'

'No, no, you have to pay in the Veranda Restaurant,' he said earnestly.

'Oh, I didn't realise. I accept then, as long as we split the bill, sorry check,' he smiled.

'Agreed.' They arranged to meet in the Chart Room at six. She still wasn't sure where this was going, there was definitely something amiss. He was defensive, or perhaps just nervous? She guessed if having a relationship with a passenger on board was banned, it would certainly put you on edge, especially if you could lose your job. She still knew little about him, which wasn't a surprise considering they'd only spent a couple of hours together. This evening there would be longer, and she would have a chance to get to know him better, not that it made a great deal of difference with the time they had left. Nevertheless, now there was a vague possibility of something happening she'd go along with it, as she quite fancied the idea of sex once more before she died.

She walked the short distance to the Kings Court – she'd be glad to see the back of the place. However, she enjoyed her hearty breakfast, all fried again, and why not? Who cared anymore? She could eat anything she wanted and it wouldn't hasten her demise one jot. After she'd had the vegetarian fry-up she decided to have some ice cream – god knows what that was doing on the breakfast buffet – but she had it anyway. Then she realised Americans have sweet maple syrup with pancakes and bacon for breakfast so she guessed anything goes.

She went out onto her balcony, as it was sheltered from the cutting raw wind on the promenade deck. She desperately wanted to see another whale, but with an increasingly rough sea and without binoculars it wasn't going to happen. But what a sight it was, one thing everyone should see before they die, the behemoth of the ocean, maybe the only thing on earth that's truly god like, and other worldly, and who knows how intelligent they are? Far brighter than Donald Fucking Duck probably.

Lying on the bed she read about the solutions to climate change by SRM (Solar Radiation Management): sulphur or small mirrors in the upper atmosphere to deflect the suns heat. Problem was this could create another catastrophe – no sunlight on Earth for months – and wasn't messing with nature just as bad as producing CO_2 in the first place, only in reverse? Then there was CDR (Carbon Dioxide Removal): using carbon sinks such as forests, marshes, estuaries, or by scattering volcanic dust on fields. But the forests were being cut down, the marshes too few or being reclaimed and the estuaries were disappearing under rising sea levels. As for scattering basalt dust on fields? Well, the claim is that 2 billion tons of CO_2 could be captured each year, but we produce 32 billion tons, and then there's the 375 billion excess tons that already exist in the atmosphere.

Finally, there was CCUS (Carbon Capture Utilisation and Sequestration) And DAC (Direct Air Capture). Both remove carbon from the air with machines and bury it in the ground. CCUS would have extraction units at factories and power stations, but couldn't remove what already exists. Whereas DAC could, but would need 30 million container-sized units to absorb it, and a quarter of the world's electricity to run them. However, even if these solutions worked, they created a moral hazard, because if we did solve the problem, we'd no doubt continue to burn carbon fuel.

It was even doubtful that clean energy was making that much difference to CO_2 emissions, considering there are seven million more vehicles every year in the US, and six hundred thousand in the UK, the majority of them still petrol or diesel powered. Also, one single airport (Heathrow) wants to increase its capacity by 25,000 flights a year, which would then produce as much CO_2 annually as Portugal.

Connie already knew most of the facts, but it was still being ignored by the majority of the world's governments. They seemed to be relying on a wing and a prayer that scientists would solve the problem for them. If they didn't, they would have to bring in extreme measures and she could never see that happening – until of course it was far too late.

After reading she felt the sharp headache returning and took another painkiller and slept for two hours. When she awoke the pain was still there, so she took a single tablet as a stop gap to the next dose in another couple of hours. Might she die in her sleep? It was a thought she hadn't had until now. Maybe it would be a blessing?

She closed her eyes and slept again till lunchtime.

'God, it was lunch again!' She now realised that meals aboard the ship weren't for sustenance but simply to pass the time. She climbed the wide staircase to deck seven. The promenade deck doors were cordoned off and closed again, and it was easy to see why. Outside the wind groaned and through the window she could see thirty-foot rollers queueing up behind one another, waiting their turn to hammer into the ship's starboard flank, which they did frequently with a loud 'boom'.

As she sat eating her fruit salad and staring out of the window, she noticed snow flurries every now and again. How did those tiny petrels survive in this? How could any mammal survive out here? Other than whales and dolphins of course.

She only had the sweet – she wanted to make sure she had an appetite for the meal with Russell. It was going to be strange, having a date and not being able to indulge in any hanky-panky, certainly not in the ship, and judging by the weather, outside was entirely out unless they wanted to freeze in a romantic embrace. But she was being presumptuous again wasn't she? Russell might have no inclinations in that direction whatsoever. Nothing so far had given her that idea anyway. She thought about the cabin again, maybe she could smuggle him in? But imagined the penalty for being caught with a passenger in their room was probably death. Russell also had a very shy side to him; it would be hard to imagine him lunging at her and tearing off her clothes (more was the pity). No, they'd eat, talk, and say goodbye with maybe a peck on the cheek if she was lucky, either way it would have to look brotherly just in case the 'Cunard Undercover Naughtiness Teams' were around. She laughed when she realised the abbreviation of her imaginary outfit. Either way, sex or no sex she hoped it went well, and one way of assuring that was to keep off the obvious subjects – the environment, and attacking the USA – as he seemed sensitive to that in their previous conversation as well. Maybe he was just a fierce patriot, or even an undercover agent. Seeking out left wing subversives entering the USA. The CIA were capable of anything; she'd watched *Homeland*.

To pass the time in the afternoon Connie went to see the RADA group again, this time performing *The Importance of Being Ernest* in the Royal Court. It was a comedy about name changing. Jack calls himself Ernest, whilst Algernon wishes that was his name, Jack then discovers he's Algernon's brother and his real name is Ernest, or something like that. Connie lost the plot a few times, not because she was stupid or fell asleep but because she was listening to the building storm outside, and wondering whether any of the actors would fall off the stage due to the increasing pitching and rolling of the ship. What she did remember was well acted, and full of typical Oscar Wilde lines: 'I never travel without my diary, one should always have something sensational to read on the train.' Or 'The truth is rarely pure and never simple' and Connie's favourite: 'All women become like their mothers.

That is their tragedy. No man does, and that is his.' Though Jim was like her mother, but she didn't imagine that counted.

She felt tired again after the show and decided to go outside onto her balcony for a blast of Arctic air. She put on her coat and scarf, pulled on her gloves and pushed open the door which as usual required all the strength she could muster. Powdered snow lay on the steel floor and she stepped carefully so as not to slip over.

The waves were now thirty-five to forty feet high and when they collided with the ship's bow wave sent up a huge column of spray, but this time it turned to powdered ice and blasted into Connie's face taking her breath away. Every time a roller exploded, she screamed with delight in anticipation of the numbing facial. However, after a few minutes she was frozen to the bone as before, and quickly re-entered the warmth of the cabin. She looked in the mirror and laughed out loud. She was the image of Jack Frost, her hair and eyebrows white with ice. Her fingers were also freezing, even though she wore gloves. She took them off and rubbed her hands together for warmth. She began to get painful 'hot aches' that she hadn't felt since playing snowballs as a child. It was agony for a short while, but worth it.

She lay on the bed she thought about her childhood, and remembered a quote from L P Hartley's 'Blue Remembered Hills; 'The past is a foreign country, they do thing differently there.' It was, it felt like someone else's life, not her own. Thoughts of death arrived again, so Connie quickly got up, and poured herself a gin and tonic whilst deciding what to wear in the evening. She would only have the one drink, although a second was always tempting.

Feeling just on the right side of merry after two gin and tonics, she walked down the Grand Hallway toward the Chart Room. At various intervals canvas backdrops of the ocean or the ship had been erected on frames, in front of which were chairs or stools, flash umbrellas and a camera. They were doing passenger portraits, no doubt for those disembarking in New York.

Connie wasn't remotely interested, who'd want a picture of her anyway? As she entered the Grand Lobby there were more photo stations, one of which had the arrogant balding man grinning like an idiot posing for his picture. Who'd want a bloody picture of him other than to throw darts at? She avoided catching his eye and walked around the opposite side of the circular upper balcony toward the Champagne bar, and decided to stop off for one.

She'd chosen to wear her black two-piece suit again with a white blouse and black necklace. It was only when she sat down and noticed most of the other women wearing pastel shades, she realised she looked funereal. The odd person in the bar glanced at her, maybe they thought she was the ship's undertaker? If such a thing existed?

She removed her jacket in order to look more casual, sipped her Champagne and heard the jazz band strike up next door. She looked out the window at the black night and saw the odd white plume of a wave. The ship still rocked but not as violently as it had earlier.

She took her Champagne glass and moved into the Chart Room, and as before found seats out of view of the band. She was getting quite excited but told herself to calm down, then asked herself why? If she wasn't allowed some pleasure now, then when? A waiter passed and she ordered another drink, this time a soda, she didn't want to be pissed when he arrived, did she? She also felt it was unfair to drink when he couldn't. Added to that, it was very easy to tell that someone was drunk when you were sober.

Russell was punctual as before, clearly life aboard ship runs like clockwork. He wasn't in the usual dark blazer, white shirt and Cunard tie he wore when performing, but a grey cardigan and white T-shirt that was more appropriate for his casual look. He smiled as he arrived, raised her hand and quickly kissed it, which she guessed was rather un-brother like, so maybe he didn't care. He sat next to her and not opposite like the previous time.

'I booked the table for seven thirty.'

'An hour and a half before we eat? Do you think we can manage that long together? What on earth are we going to talk about?' said Connie smiling.

'Who said anything about talking?'

'That has to be a quote from a film?' said Connie laughing

'If it isn't maybe it should be,' said Russell. The waiter arrived with Connie's soda and Russell ordered a cranberry juice.

'So, how's your day been?' asked Russell.

'I've forgotten. Same as the day before?'

'You getting bored?'

'I wouldn't say bored. More lobotomised. But don't get me wrong, I still love the sea and all who swim in and fly above her. But as for the ship. Well let's just say another week on board I'd be taking Valium. Or to quote an old school joke, shaking at the bottom of the sea.'

'Huh?'

'A nervous wreck.' Russell groaned.

'OK. You got me there,' he said. Connie took a drink of soda and Russell studied her closely. She put her drink back down on the paper mat and turned to him.

'So, how do you survive on here for three months?'

'It's called needs must.'

'Sorry, I didn't mean to sound like a spoilt child. It's just not my thing.'

'So why did you come?'

'Needs must?' Russell smiled. They talked about life on the ship, the dining room where the entertainment staff ate, the shared cabin with four other musicians, and the small cinema with ten seats. Connie still found it strange that many crew members weren't allowed in the passenger recreation areas. Russell pointed out that if they were it wouldn't just be over crowded, but full of gamblers and alcoholics as a fair number of the crew go to sea in order to kick their addictions and save some money. Connie asked if he was one of them, to which he replied 'definitely not.'

They made their way to the stern of the ship and entered the discreet foyer of the Veranda Restaurant. The maître d' stood next to a large elaborate flower display and asked Russell for his name.

'Travis Bickle,' he said confidently, and winked at Connie. They were led to a discreet table near the window that looked out onto the rear deck and covered pool. The restaurant had a lower roof than the others, was a lot smaller and felt more intimate. In fact, it was more like an upmarket high street Chinese. The waiter lit the single candle and asked if they wanted drinks. Connie had another soda, and Russell a fresh orange juice. He reached across the table and briefly touched Connie's hand.

'This is fun,' he said smiling like a naughty schoolboy.

'You enjoy deception?'

'Love it.'

'But Travis Bickle, honestly!'

'Best film ever made.'

'I could argue that but won't.'

'Why?'

'Because I can never remember films in these situations, for some reason my mind goes blank.'

'I have the same problem with phone numbers, so can you write yours down?'

'Ha! Maybe tomorrow, let's see how you behave.'

'I always behave impeccably.'

'Now who said I wanted you to be good?' said Connie alluringly. The drinks arrived and menus were placed in front of them. Connie chose the lobster, having not eaten it for at least twenty years. Russell went for steak, which didn't surprise her with him being American. He obviously hadn't considered the environmental impact of meat, or maybe he was just treating himself?

'We could have some surf and turf action going here?' said Russell.

'Midnight Run,' said Connie quick as a flash.

'Very good,' said Russell impressed. 'So, what's your favourite movie?'

'My favourite movie? Well I love *When Harry Met Sally…*'

'I agree. Best romantic comedy ever made. Anything else?'

'Now I've gone blank again.'

'Don't worry, it happens to everyone.'

'Over sixty,' added Connie.

'You never are?' said Russell with genuine surprise.

'Unfortunately. Sixty-three.'

'I would have never guessed. Fifty maybe? Fifty-five pushing it.'

'Thank you, Russell. I suppose I'm meant to guess your age now? And I have to be very conservative as you've been so kind to me.'

'No, just go for it.'

'Sixty-three?'

'Asshole!'

'Joking. Take off ten.'

'Bingo! So, there's ten years between us? I've always been keen on older women. Mature like a fine wine or a good cheese, and have been around the block.'

'Hey, kid! If you wanna see tomorrow don't push it,' said Connie in a classic femme fatale voice.

'Who said that?'

'I just did, you idiot.' Russell laughed out loud, looked around and cowered slightly not wanting to attract attention. 'You'll get me kicked off the ship.'

'That's a nice idea,' said Connie sincerely. Russell smiled and touched her hand again.

They talked about America, England, films, music and their childhood as they ate their meals. Connie made a point of not bringing up politics or the environment. Russell did talk briefly about his love for wildlife, especially birds, and how a quarter of the world's species had become extinct due to man, nevertheless Connie didn't pursue it.

As they walked quietly back along the narrow corridor Russell manoeuvred Connie into a doorway and kissed her passionately, Connie reciprocated. Russell heard someone approaching and they stopped.

'I might get away with taking my sister to the restaurant, but sticking my tongue down her throat will definitely get my ass kicked off the ship.' Connie giggled. The steward passed, Russell kissed her briefly again, said goodbye, kissed her again and walked away.

He was working all the following day so arranged to meet her after the show at ten p.m. in the Commodore Club. It would be their last night together on the ship.

Connie sat in her cabin going through the evening; she'd never imagined it would be such fun. They were just like teenagers, asking questions and discussing subjects whilst flirting with each other, her heart racing all evening. She would have loved to drag him back to her cell, but there you go, typical. She could tell he was fighting with his conscience, but he was clearly in no position to lose his job. Who was? Especially in the USA where health insurance was so costly.

She imagined he had a reasonable salary, and with no food or accommodation to pay his outgoings would be low. Why on earth was she thinking about this? She'd never see him again after tomorrow, would she? Even if she backed out of her plan and waited for his shore leave in a month then what? She stopped the ridiculous line of thinking; nothing would happen so that was the end of it. Suddenly she remembered Sara and Kurt wanted to call their child Russell if it was a boy. *Was it serendipity? Was it a sign? Was it bollocks,* she thought to herself, and picked up the daily guide. They were now crossing the southern edge of the Grand Banks and the ship would begin to steer south west toward Nova Scotia on the 'Rhumb line'. It also reminded her to put her watch back another hour, as she had done daily since they first set sail. She got undressed and lay still in bed, couldn't stop thinking of Russell, and for the first time in years reached down under the covers.

*

She woke on the seventh day with a searing headache, took two prescription painkillers and went back to sleep. When she finally woke an hour later her head felt as if somebody had hit it with a brick. She lay back and stared at the ceiling and thought of Russell again – a relationship that was going nowhere. Was there any point of seeing him tonight? And of all the places to meet a man She laughed to herself at the ridiculousness of it. Last chance of a shag and she meets a man in a monastery. Maybe he'd risk it tonight? But would you risk your job for a quick fuck? She asked herself. Depends on the job and the man. She sighed as she knew the real answer: of course not.

Slowly getting up to avoid the headache kicking in again she made herself a tea and got back in bed. She picked up the last day's guide and noticed that *Mamma Mia! Here We Go Again* was on TV and starting soon so decided to stay in bed and watch it. After the first fifteen minutes she turned it off, it was stupid, mawkish and pointless – sequels often are. However, she had to admit the first one was great, good to see something about older women enjoying themselves, in and out of bed. It was also rare to see a film about a female putting it about a bit – that was normally the preserve of men – in movies and in life. She thought about the regularity of 'Love' as a theme. It was endless, even on the ship: two films, two plays and a poetry reading. She also thought how strange it was that this love didn't extend beyond other humans toward the planet we lived on. If it did, we wouldn't be in such a catastrophic mess.

She finally raised herself out of bed, got dressed and made her way to the Kings Court. The same people were sitting at the same tables, having unofficially commandeered them, like sunbeds on a beach. Connie looked around, found an empty one and sat down to eat her 'to hell with it' fry-up.' She gazed around and realised many were on board for another three weeks. The thought made her shiver, but she imagined it was better than a care home, and probably cheaper than some if you didn't need constant medical attention. It was then she realised this was a twilight cruise for a lot of passengers, and for the first time felt sorry for them. She was also near her journey's end, and was frightened again. The Atlantic crossing had acted as a buffer, making it seem further away, but reality was now on the horizon.

She went for a walk on deck to forget about it. Outside it was cold but not as bad as it had been, and the sea was steady and grey without any anger. She looked out for dolphins or whales, but there wasn't even a seabird in sight. Maybe they preferred it far out where it was wild and away from mankind. She would that's for sure.

Walking on her third circuit she caught sight of two container ships on the starboard side some ten miles north. She imagined they were heading for the Saint Lawrence River and the port of Quebec or Halifax, Nova Scotia. Either way they were no doubt transporting goods from the other side of the world that could just as easily be produced within a hundred or so miles of their doorstep.

She went back inside and strolled around for an hour looking for something to occupy her. Finally, she gave up and returned to her cabin. She'd now achieved a state of boredom with the ship, and idly checked the guide for the afternoon's entertainment; 3.30 p.m. Insights Lecture – Surviving a Disaster. First terrorism, now disasters. They obviously felt something was on the horizon as well, though being at sea could be one way of avoiding it.

She lay down again on the bed that as usual had been pristinely made up while she was out. Danillo's life would consist of making other people's beds and sleeping in his own for nine months of the year. His quarters would be tiny, much smaller than Russell's, and he no doubt shared with others and had little or no privacy. He was a prisoner for all intents and purposes. For some, life in a dystopian future wouldn't be much worse than it already was.

Connie's thoughts returned to her demise, would she be able to do it? She began to fear the whole idea was madness again – because it was. Whatever made her decide to attempt something so preposterous? But it was easy to answer. Anger. Sheer bloody anger at man's fucking stupidity. She was going to kick all those alpha male leaders and corporate CEOs in the fucking face, wasn't she? She bloody well was. She smiled; her resolve strengthened.

She had her last meal in the Britannia Restaurant. As she gazed around the palatial room, she concluded the ship was the mortality hotel – her halfway house between life and death. It was a fitting end, and of course the last leg would be in the Algonquin, with the spirit of her hero close by.

She believed people gave a spiritual sense of place to a location, which had nothing to do with god, in fact he had hijacked real heroes. What had he done? Nothing, he didn't exist. And people did things, horrible things in his name. Some claim Donald Fucking Duck was sent by God. So, if he allows the planet to burn it's God's will. Which just goes to show how fucked up religion has become. Or maybe it's just an excuse, a firewall behind which to hide and justify your actions. As she mulled over religious clap-trap anger rose within her again, and – not for the first time – she wondered if stress had given her the brain tumour in the first place.

She was getting the headache again and skipping the sweet returned to the cabin for another painkiller. The following day's guide was on the bed along with a copy of 'Britain Today' – a brief summary of news back home. She usually didn't bother reading it, but on this occasion picked it up.

On the cover was a headline: 'CO2 levels reach record high in 2018'. It went on to say 'the window of opportunity for action was almost closed', which was an alarmingly honest admission to make on a cruise ship pumping out huge amounts of CO2, sulphur and nitrous oxide. Maybe Cunard had a 'grand plan' for the future: their fleet becoming floating oases away from the madness and starvation on land? Like the spaceship in *Wall-E*, but on the ocean.

She lay down to ease the headache, fell asleep, and woke just in time for the 'Disasters' lecture in the Royal Court Theatre. Outside it announced this lecture was about the sinking of the Titanic, an extraordinary subject to cover whilst on a ship surely? Clearly the entertainment officer had a well-developed sense of irony. A shambolic looking man in his sixties came on stage and stood with his notes at the podium. A few days earlier he'd done a lecture on the Concorde disaster in Paris, so clearly his message here was don't travel by sea or air. His papers fell on the floor and he nervously picked them up. After gathering them back together he pressed a button on his handset and an image of Concorde came up, nervously he went forward and the images quickly changed until he came to the Titanic caption. He smiled, and reached for a glass of water which he knocked to the floor.

A stagehand quickly appeared, picked up the glass, exited, re-appeared with a cloth and mopped up the water. So far, his lecture was a disaster. Finally, the man wiped his mouth with a hankie and began in faltering tones.

The upshot of the lecture was that the survival rate on the first-class upper decks was three times that of those in second class, and five times that of third class on the lowest decks. This was obviously due in part to being trapped below when the ship quickly began to sink. But more importantly, a large number of first-class passengers ignored the 'women and children first' command, grabbed a lifeboat for themselves, rejected other boarders, and were lowered into the sea only half full. Well what else could you expect from the privileged classes? Connie also couldn't help thinking this was a good sales pitch – to make those in the audience book more expensive cabins on a higher deck next time they cruised on 'Mary,' very clever. Another part of the grand plan?

She walked out of the theatre and along the Grand Hallway toward the lobby. On the upper level of the atrium stalls were set up selling Queen Mary souvenirs, perfumes, handbags, jewellery and watches. She was going to buy a present for her daughter, then suddenly realised she would never see her again. The thought made her almost faint, and she sat down on a nearby chair feeling utterly wretched.

This was the first time she'd seriously contemplated backing out of her plan. But she couldn't, could she? How could she?

She remained seated for a while trying to clear her head. She had to remind herself yet again that she didn't want Sara to know about her illness, or be around when she died. So, she had to find the strength to carry out her plan. And if she didn't then who was she? She was nothing but a weakling who lacked commitment. She thought again of Fawcett, King and Parkes, and above all Jan Palach, a student who took his life in

1969 to draw attention to Russia's invasion of Czechoslovakia. She thought of all those who'd made a sacrifice for the greater good, and there'd been many throughout history. She stamped the ground with her foot in determination, got up and strode down the hallway with purpose. She knew her life was over, she also knew if things continued the way they were that her daughter, husband and unborn grandchild's life could conceivably be in danger in the not so distant future. She'd had her life, but maybe she could help save theirs?

Lying on the bed she read the final chapters of the book to galvanize herself. We now had the highest atmospheric CO_2 concentration for four million years, where the temperature was five degrees warmer and the oceans fifty feet higher – we just hadn't caught up yet.

Even if we stopped emitting CO_2 tomorrow the planet would continue to warm and sea level continue to rise for hundreds of years to come. The final paragraph summed up the book:

"For the past 50 years politicians have ignored climate change, and still they equivocate, or refuse point blank to act. It's the worst crime ever committed against humanity, a disgraceful act of negligence, for which those responsible would be imprisoned in a just society. Politicians are nothing more than servants of capitalism, lacking any moral code. It could already be too late to avoid three or even five degrees of warming – two degrees is catastrophic. We need to act **now**, and governments must bring in severe measures to cut emissions entirely, or else the world as we know it will disappear forever."

Connie put down the book Even though she knew the diabolical situation we were in; it was a final paragraph to end all final paragraphs. It wasn't just sobering; it was bloody terrifying. It was the greatest denial in history and even she couldn't quite believe it. It wasn't the end of the world, there would be survivors, just like in the movies, but there'd be huge suffering. She exhaled deeply, got off the bed, opened the mini bar and poured herself a large vodka and tonic and uttered six words to herself:

'What the fuck have we done?' And decided that nothing now would stop her action.

She stood on the balcony as it got dark, a few pinpoints of light could just be seen in the far distance. They were eleven hours from New York, about 250 miles away, so she imagined the lights from the coast could be Cape Cod. She went back inside and realised that now they were close to the US there might be a signal. She turned on the phone and sure enough there was one. She went onto Google for the first time in seven days, and at the top was the only news she needed to finally find the courage for her commitment.

'US President doesn't believe climate report from his own government' and one of his assistants stated 'It's wrong, not based on fact, not data driven'. Which begs the question: What was it driven by then? Hearsay? The president was still in denial, great news! If only she could assassinate Donald Fucking Duck. But maybe he didn't deserve to die, after all you're meant to be kind to dumb animals, aren't you?

She poured herself a second vodka and sat on the sofa with her feet up and toasted: 'To Connie, the goofy brunette who shot Donald Duck' and laughed to herself in a slightly deranged manner.

She knew she had to eat but couldn't face the Kings Court so got room service. Her salmon fishcakes arrived thirty minutes later and she tipped the steward admirably. She played with the peas by throwing them in the air and catching them in her mouth, until she realised she was slightly drunk and stopped. She finished her food and poured herself a glass of mineral water from the bottle and drank it down in one. She now felt more relaxed, but her anger was still simmering, like the bubbles in a shaken Champagne bottle.

She put on the only decent dress she had with her, a maroon velvet, knee-length, V-necked number she'd bought from 'Next' twenty years ago, and had worn only once at a wedding. Whose, she'd now forgotten. She wore it with a black cardigan and heels. She applied lipstick, and wondered again whether anything could happen with Russell. After a day's rehearsing and a show till ten he would no doubt be tired. Too tired? She put the thoughts of intimacy out of her mind, and applied a small amount of eyeshadow, something she hadn't done for years. She looked at herself in the mirror. Well I'd shag you, Connie, she said giggling to herself.

It was still only nine o'clock and she wasn't sure whether to pour herself another vodka. She couldn't be half cut, but maybe quarter? She poured a small shot, and slowly drank it as the ship ploughed on down the eastern seaboard. She went onto the balcony but no coastal lights could be seen, it was now a mere eight hours to New York. It sent a shiver of anticipation through her. The air was raw so she went back inside, finished her drink, and left for the Commodore Club, even though she was going to be half an hour early. She was sick of looking at the four walls of the cabin.

She entered the low-lit lounge. A man played the grand piano and a few couples were at the bar nursing their cocktails whilst the rest lounged on white sofas and armchairs talking in restrained voices. It felt exactly like its title: exclusive, up-market and reserved, which made Connie wonder whether she should actually be there at all. She glanced around and nobody seemed to blink an eye so she looked for a seat, somewhere discreet, but with a view of the entrance. She walked past the curved bar toward the windows which during the day would overlook the prow of the ship, but now the blinds were pulled down to make the space more intimate.

She found a single sofa and table tucked away in a corner, but could still see the door over the piano. She picked up the drinks menu and checked out the cocktails. 'Take it easy, Connie, cocktails are rocket fuel,' she reminded herself, so she kept it simple, and ordered a glass of Prosecco when the waiter arrived.

Sipping her drink, she became increasingly excited about the imminent arrival of Russell. Why? She'd never see him again after tonight. But it was better than sitting here on her own wasn't it. She'd never expected to meet anyone at all. Her mind drifted again, and she imagined what could/would happen if she wasn't dying. Could she have a relationship with him? Would she wait in New York? Would she go with him back to Houston or wherever? She'd never know, would she? But if she lived for say six months. She could have some time with him. Better than one stinking night anyway. But would she want him to fall for her just before she died? Not really, it would hardly be fair would it? However, she still hypothesised three months with him, then carry out her action. But she would lose her resolve, wouldn't she? The more she fell in love with him? She also knew there was a strict time-frame in which to commit the act. Surely, she wasn't going to jeopardise the whole trip for a stupid man? On the other hand? 'Stop it Connie, you're drunk, and being an idiot!' she mumbled to herself.

She instinctively looked up and saw Russell enter the lounge, she raised her arm and he spotted her and walked across the room. He sat down next to her on the sofa and kissed her on the cheek. 'Hi,' he said, and quickly kissed her again.

'Hi.' Said Connie as she handed him the drinks menu. 'Cocktail? Short? Champagne? Water? And don't worry I'll pay, so it won't come up on your account.'

'OK. Hang it, it's your last night, sister, get me a JD and Coke. Thanks, Connie. I owe you,' he said affectionately.

'Forget it.' Connie signalled a waiter, he approached and she ordered his drink.

'I was thinking of your name.'

'My name? What, Russell?'

'No, Ellis. I thought they said no man was an island.'

'Ha. Ha. Do you think I've not heard that one before?'

'Yes, I do actually.'

'Yes, I do actually. You're so English, aren't you?'

'I guess I am.' Russell put his hand on Connie's knee. Another waiter passed by and he quickly withdrew it. Connie laughed.

'What?'

'It's worse than a bloody monastery. Aren't you even allowed to touch someone?'

'No, well maybe. But you get conditioned on board to become a celibate.'

'Are you allowed masturbate?' Russell looked at her mildly shocked.

'Oh sorry. Was that too forward of me?'

'A bit.' Russell laughed.

'Well?'

'You can try, I guess. But only when your cell mate's out, obviously.'

'Oh, obviously.' Connie laughed. The waiter placed the drink in front of Russell and he took a sip.

'One of these and I'll be drunk,' said Russell. Connie raised her glass.

'Here's hoping.' Russell smiled, put down his drink and leant toward Connie and kissed her on the lips. He moved briefly away.

'Oh, what the hell.' And he kissed her again. 'You're really some gal.'

'What a cliché.'

'But it's true.'

'Thanks.' Connie returned Russell's kiss and they moved closer together on the sofa.

'So, another whole month?' stated Connie with a degree of sadness.

'Unfortunately. Will you wait for me?'

'Where?'

'New York, Southampton, London, wherever.'

'I'm not sure I can, Russell.'

'Well, think about it.'

'I will.' Russell kissed her again. Connie smiled and they both took a drink.

Connie talked animatedly about *When Harry Met Sally…* and told him she was going to visit some of the locations when in New York. Russell said he related to Harry's eternal pessimism, but wouldn't go into detail why. She talked about Nora Ephron and how she thought that *Heartburn* was one of the funniest books she'd read, even though it was a true story about when her husband left her for another woman when she was seven months pregnant.

'Yeah, Carl Bernstein, the journalist who broke Watergate,' said Russell. 'Shows even good guys can be assholes.' The comment seemed loaded in some way, as was his previous one about Harry's pessimism.

Connie ordered another Prosecco and Russell said to hell with it and had another Jack Daniels. She began to feel mellow and leaned against his shoulder.

Two large septuagenarian American men sat on a sofa nearby, they poured themselves a glass of Champagne each from a bottle and toasted.

'To the President.' They clinked glasses and drank. Connie went rigid with anger and turned to Russell.

'Did you hear that?'

'What?'

'Those two bastards, toasting Genghis Khan.'

'Who?'

'Fucking Trump.'

'It's a free world, Connie.'

'Is it?'

'Did you hear what that bastard said today?' Russell shook his head.

'He said he didn't believe a recent climate change report. And his fucking secretary or press officer or whoever said "It wasn't data driven". Not data driven? It's driven by over a hundred and twenty thousand published scientific reports since 1990. Fucking morons!'

'Yeah, OK, Connie.'

'What's wrong?'

'Nothing. Just try and keep your voice down.'

'Oh sorry. But your president and all his cronies are full of shit. They're going to keep burning oil and destroy us all.'

'Yeah, OK. But do we have to talk about this now?'

'No! We have to shout about it because nobody else is!' The two men near Connie turned around and stared at her. One of them spoke. 'Hey, Mr. Keep your big-mouthed lady quiet, can you?' Connie replied.

'Hey Mr. Go and fuck yourself.' Russell took her by the arm.

'Come on, let's go.'

'Sure. Absolutely. Anywhere away from these two fat fucking arseholes.' Connie got up. A few people stared as she was led out. They walked briskly down the corridor.

'I'm sorry, Russell. I didn't mean to draw attention to us.'

'It's fine. It's just…'

'What?'

'Why do you have to keep going on about it? You're obsessed with it.'

'Aren't you? You care about the world, don't you? You care about birds and wildlife?'

'Yes. But that doesn't mean I want to talk about it every fucking minute of the day. To be honest I'm sick of it, sick of having it continuously rammed down my throat.'

'By who? Me? I've hardly mentioned it at all until now.'

'I know. I know!' But I feel guilty.'

'Guilty? Why?'

'I just fucking do, OK!'

Russell stopped at the top of the stairwell.

'I'm sorry Connie. Goodbye,' and he quickly disappeared. Was that it? She'd pissed people off before when having a rant but they'd never stormed off like this. She didn't know what to think, but wanted to apologise. But there again, why should she? All she'd done was speak her mind. Then she realised that making a scene could have put his job in jeopardy, and wanted to say sorry for that, but how? She had no idea where he was, nor could she trace him given their tryst was basically illegal. She sat down on the step at the top of the stairs just in case he came back. She waited five minutes.

Well that was sex out the window, assuming it was on the cards in the first place, stupid fucking ship.

'Fuck it!' she said out loud as an elderly couple came up the stairs, and to partly cover herself 'Fuck these shoes' but that got even colder stares.

She returned to the cabin and poured herself a very large gin and tonic, then lay on the bed still annoyed. 'Typical. The first chance of a shag in what? Fifteen years? And no doubt the last, just vanished, puff, like that, because of my big mouth.' She knew that it wasn't just the sex she wanted, though when your days are numbered there's no point in kidding yourself. But if she'd had a life ahead of her maybe she could have been with him?

He was good fun, bright and loved nature, but she'd have to find out what was bugging him, the stuff about feeling guilty and saying even good men were assholes. But she'd probably never see him again. She'd blown it, so fuck it.

No point in mourning his loss now. She finished her drink and poured herself a water, knocked it back in one slug spilling some over her face in the process. She wiped it with her sleeve and collapsed back onto the bed and suddenly felt sad, then angry.

'Fuck it!' she shouted. 'Can't something go right?'

Finally calming down she stopped thinking about Russell and focused on the following day. She'd planned to be up at five a.m. to see the ship enter New York harbour, and go under the Verrazano-Narrows Bridge which the funnel cleared by a mere twelve feet. Above all she wanted to see the dawn rise up over Manhattan and see the city slowly come to life. Whilst thinking of this exciting foreign land she fell asleep. Thirty minutes later she woke with a start, set the alarm on her phone and crashed out again.

***

Chapter 11

The alarm went off at four rather than five a.m. She opened her eyes slowly, picked up the phone and realised her mistake. 'Shit.' She turned off the alarm, and lay still for while realising she needed painkillers but couldn't be bothered to move. She groaned a few times, then looked down to see she was still fully clothed, she even had her shoes on. It was Sunday morning and felt like it, but she was keen to get up and look at America gliding by, even though it would still be dark. She lifted herself up, grabbed her coat and opened the balcony door. A chain of lights was strung out in front of her along the coastline a mile or so away. 'It was America!' But it looked like anywhere else in the oily darkness.

The ship passed a large buoy that clanked and clunked as it rocked in the bow wave. The air was cold, a real cold that felt clean and made your skin tingle. As she watched the scene unfold, she suddenly remembered the previous night and felt guilty. She went through events; she hadn't been that bad had she? She talked too loud, but that was it surely? No, she swore too, oh dear, she told that man to go fuck himself, oh, and swore on the stairs. Oh well, fuck it, if Russell can't deal with a feisty woman that's his problem. Then she remembered it wasn't that, it was something else, wasn't it? She'd pressed his button again, so perhaps it wasn't all her fault after all? Reassured she'd behaved reasonably well, well for her that is, she carried on watching the scenery glide by.

A car or truck slowly travelled along the string of lights, was it a man driving or a woman? Going to work? To New York? Maybe it was a subway driver, or a nurse, or a doctor, or a truck driver going down to Washington or Florida? Normal people doing normal jobs with one difference – they were American – as different to us as Norwegians, even though they spoke the same language, our language, English, how weird was that? We must have been desperate to get out and clear off, even though it was two thousand miles on an angry sea in a wooden tub. Why didn't we just cross the channel over to Europe? Of course, she knew the answer to that, we were constantly at war with Europe. Emigres had left to have a new life, a chance to become wealthy – away from all those who suppressed or persecuted them. However, whichever way you looked at it they'd stolen someone else's land.

At first there was relative harmony between the settlers and indigenous natives, but it didn't last long, once greed took hold. Greed then became a monster that consumed all in its path, and built cities like New York. But whether you love or hate the western Europeans, you had to admire their industry. Three hundred years and they'd turned a virtually empty country into a monolithic power, and spawned a consumer society that had spread across the entire planet. America wasn't to blame for climate change, but they were a major instigator of the capitalist ethos that created it. Connie deplored yet marvelled at the country. She loved and hated it.

She squinted south and noticed a bright clump of lights that seemed to dominate the night skyline. *That must be it*, she thought, and a shiver of excitement ran through her. There were other large clusters of lights appearing on the horizon too, but that must be it surely? That must be Manhattan.

The coast road seemed to be getting busier now with more vehicles heading south toward the city. A tiny flashing light passed overhead, no doubt heading for JFK airport. Yes, they were definitely getting close. She checked her watch, five a.m., they would be docking in Brooklyn at six thirty, another hour and half, and about twenty miles to go.

As she looked north, she saw the lights of other ships waiting to enter the harbour; ten, possibly twenty tailed back into the distance making her realise what a huge seaport New York and New Jersey must be. One ship's entire cargo would maybe stock the city's supermarkets for just one single day. To the south she noticed the chain of lights rise into the sky, with another high above that and realised it must be the suspension bridge across the narrows. Wanting to be on top of the ship when it passed beneath, she quickly went inside, removed her coat and dress, put on slacks and a blouse followed by a thick jumper, then her coat again. She grabbed gloves and scarf out of the drawer and left her cabin.

As she walked briskly down the corridor, she realised she had no headache or hangover – the excitement must have cleared it. She went up the stairs two at a time to deck seven, and into the Kings Court that was surprisingly full for five am. She grabbed a banana and filled a cup with water which she quickly drank, then strode back to the stairwell and up to the observation area on deck eleven.

Opening the doors, she was surprised to find at least two hundred other people lining the rail three to four deep with their cameras and phones. It was as if the passengers had finally come out of hibernation. She moved around trying to find a space but there wasn't any.

She went up to the next deck where there was a small viewing area over the bridge, but that was full too.

Finally, she went up to deck thirteen and out onto the top of the ship, which by comparison was relatively quiet, no doubt because it was freezing cold with no protection from the wind. The bridge slowly approached, and slow was the operative word. It was a good twenty-five minutes before they finally crept beneath it. She guessed it had reduced speed just in case they got their calculations wrong. As they glided under the funnel seemed no more than a few feet below it. A rough sea and you could easily imagine it colliding with the bridge. Above you could hear the rumbling of tyres on the road. She pictured half asleep passengers pinching themselves as they drove over a ship.

Once under most of the people on the top deck vanished, this was obviously what everyone had come out to see, so she made her way down to the larger more sheltered observation area on deck eleven. This was also quieter and she found a spot near the rail and watched as New York grew closer whilst eating her banana.

Within thirty minutes the sky turned from black to slate grey and the illuminated outline of Lower Manhattan became discernible as millions of tiny lights. These were the glass towers of Wall Street, and rising above them all World Trade One, built after 9/11. But the main interest from those around her seemed to be on the port side, as the Statue of Liberty slowly came into view. She studied it with admiration, it was still the most famous landmark of the city, possibly the whole of the United States, even the world. A mile or so away it seemed insignificant compared to the vast buildings of Manhattan, but they just housed businesses, whereas Liberty actually stood for something – enlightenment, and the mottos of the French revolution: liberty, equality and fraternity – these words welcomed immigrants to the new world. Liberty was the mother of exiles, and millions of people had seen this on their arrival, no doubt with tears in their eyes, as Connie did now.

As the ship crept nearer to the statue more and more people came back on deck, many taking pictures, some just watching, but all in some way entranced by this rather modest monument, that still appeared no bigger than a souvenir.

Early morning light gave the pin lit silhouettes of Manhattan buildings detailed facades as they grew in size. With Liberty now behind them the phones and cameras were snapping the city and the crowd in the observation area grew thicker, Connie decided to go down and watch from the promenade deck.

She made her way to the bow of the ship. To her left New Jersey's skyscrapers competed with Manhattan's, she imagined one day they could even outnumber them, not having the restrictions of being on an island. Ferries were now crossing the Hudson, as early morning commuters arrived from Jersey and Staten Island. She wondered how many on board looked out the steaming windows at 'The Queen Mary,' and imagined what it must be like to cross the Atlantic as their forefathers had. She guessed many of them had never been back to their homeland. She was unlikely to be going back either, and suddenly felt very homesick. Why was she here in this grey metropolis? Where she would probably die?

She began to feel light-headed and her chest went tight; she was having a panic attack and knew it, so tried to breathe deeply. She continued to inhale the cold air and slowly calmed, then in one glorious moment everything changed. The rising sun suddenly hit Manhattan, glass and concrete slabs turned gold. Governors Island was revealed beneath the city, small red brick houses surrounded by trees of Autumnal red and bronze. The light struck the city all the way down the East River to the famous Brooklyn Bridge. Manhattan was suddenly magical, as inviting as a picture postcard. For a brief moment she was euphoric, then felt faint and almost blacked out, but supported herself on the rail just before falling. She stayed still a moment and realised it wasn't a panic attack, but possibly the tumour.

She lay in her cabin for half an hour, then felt desperately hungry and went to the Kings Court and ate a huge breakfast of fruit, cereal and a fry up. Afterwards she felt much better and didn't dwell on the incident earlier. Maybe it had nothing to do with the tumour at all, and was just being up early after a heavy night and then out in the cold for almost two hours.

She had to leave by ten thirty, and now she'd seen the city couldn't wait to get off the ship. She hurried back and began to pack, feeling newly invigorated. A knock on the door and Danillo appeared. She knew tipping was essential so removed her purse from her bag, took out a hundred dollars and handed it to him.

'Thanks, Danillo.' He took the money, and rather than smile as he usually did, was deadpan.

'Sorry is that OK?' said Connie not knowing how much she should give him.

'Give what you are happy with,' he said measuring his words carefully. Connie felt slightly annoyed, surely a hundred dollars was plenty? That was seventy pounds, wasn't it? Ten pounds a day? She opened her purse and took out another fifty dollars. Still he didn't smile, he took the money, said 'Thank you' in a flat tone of voice, turned and vanished out of the cabin. Connie was dumbstruck, she was always a good tipper, wasn't she? Maybe she should have given more? But it was his manner. She'd given him a hundred and fifty dollars and he'd not as much as smiled. Maybe she should have just handed over her purse and asked him to take what he thought he deserved? She was still annoyed and continued packing, but couldn't stop feeling guilty. But why should she? You're too bloody soft Connie that's your trouble, she mumbled to herself. She went for a last look out on the balcony. Her view was toward Liberty; in the full light of day it seemed at lot nearer and glowed an iridescent green in the morning sunlight.

She wheeled her suitcase to the purser's office in the Grand Atrium, where she had to settle her bill. It was a lot more than she expected and noticed a service charge of eleven dollars a day had been added as well. She paid it and at the same time asked how much you should tip the cabin steward. 'Whatever you think they deserved' was the simple answer.

'Do you think a hundred and fifty dollars adequate?'

'Adequate? Very generous I'd say,' said the purser.

'Hmm. So would I,' said Connie firmly, taking her credit card back. 'Thank you. Oh, and if you have any vacancies for cabin stewards, let me know.' The purser smiled. She was surprised Danillo had made her feel guilty about the tip, but could she really blame him? After all, who would want to be locked up for nine months every year?

She walked down the covered ramp and entered a large hangar. She followed the arrows on the floor as fork lift trucks whirred around a number of stevedores loading and unloading suitcases and replenishing supplies for the ship. She was now on American soil. She was in America, she was in America, she repeated to herself a few times, unable to relate to the reality. She entered a hall with people queueing at immigration. She joined the line and it took a good forty minutes before she was finally called forward. She guessed customs was far tighter since 9/11. The officer of Homeland

Security studied her passport carefully and she handed over her ESTA Visa paper. He asked whether she was in the USA for business or pleasure, she said pleasure, though that wouldn't exactly be the word she'd use. He cross-checked her details on the computer as she stood smiling nervously.

In a few days' time she imagined the officer telling his workmates and family that he let her into the country, but how could he have known? He waved her on and she breathed a sigh of relief, even though there was no reason to stop her. But you never could tell, could you? Especially with Donald Fucking Duck in charge. He'd have you detained for smelling of tabbouleh.

She stepped outside the Brooklyn Cruise Terminal, a line of yellow cabs stood in front of her and she joined the short queue. A driver got out, a tall swarthy grey-haired man with a moustache. He grabbed her case, put it in the trunk and slammed the lid down hard. Connie got in the back and the driver slid in the front and turned toward her.

'Where to, lady?' he said in accent that didn't sound American.

'The Algonquin, midtown.'

'I know where the Algonquin is,' he replied and turned back.

She stared out the window at the non-descript warehouses and factories they passed; nothing to tell you this was America apart from the cars and the odd trucks with their aggressive looking bulging bonnets, bull bars and array of spotlights on the cab rooves.

They filtered into a stream of traffic and entered an underpass. The driver looked into his rear-view mirror and cursed.

'Goddam Rookies!' Connie turned to look and saw her first patrol car with its light flashing, give a quick burst of its siren. The cab driver pulled out of the traffic lane, onto the hard shoulder and stopped.

'Goddam Rookies! They've got nothing better to do than send these goons over from Jersey on Sundays for a bit of City action.' A young cop appeared at the window and tapped on it. The driver wound it down – it was an old cab.

'Your rear light's out, sir,' said the cop.

'OK. I'll fix it; now can I go? Got a fare here in the back and a living to make.'

'Can I see your ID and licence?' The taxi driver exhaled deeply and removed his ID from above the visor and his taxi permit off the dash, and handed it to the cop.

'Just be a minute, sir.' The cop walked back to the patrol car. Connie felt she was in a movie and had half expected the cab driver to pull a gun from the glove compartment. He sat impatiently tapping his hands on the steering wheel. 'Goddam Rookies! Got nothing better to do than stop a cab driver for a rear goddam brake light.' Connie felt sorry for him and spoke.

'Where are you from? You don't sound American.'

'Israel, Haifa. I've been here twenty-five years, like an idiot.'

'As a cab driver?' asked Connie.

'As lots of things. Should have stayed at home and looked after goats.' Connie smiled. 'You English?'

'Yes.'

'Yeah, I've been to London, got relations in Hendon, you know it?'

'Sure, it's about four miles from where I live.'

'Where's this goddam cop!' Connie sat in silence as the cab driver banged the wheel a few times again. The cop then arrived handed the licences back to the driver.

'Be sure to get that tail light fixed.' The cab driver grabbed the licenses, wound up the window without a word, checked his mirror and pulled away into the traffic. 'Assholes,' he said quietly to himself.

The cab drove down a long ramp into a tunnel, within a minute it was rising again encountering the daylight, and there was Manhattan towering above them. Connie was awestruck. She remembered what Cathy had said, and imagined at night it would be even more spectacular. It was the sheer scale of things that was mind-boggling, even the small skyscrapers were larger than anything in London, except maybe the Shard and Canary Wharf Tower. Most reached skyward out of view, even if you pressed your face to the window. The only way to really view them was to open it and lean out which she did.

Monumental stone buildings from the thirties were side by side with the modern glass towers, but there was no competition from modernity. The beautiful wedding cake shaped granite towers with their ornate castellation's won hands down and reminded her of the metropolis in *Batman*.

These buildings embodied the aspirations of America when somehow it was wholesome and clean, whereas the modern glass towers seemed aggressively corporate, bereft of any humanity, anaesthetic icons to wealth. Even so, for a first-time visitor they were impressive, as was the sheer scale of the broad avenues that ran between these towers of Babel. However, every now and again shoehorned between the monoliths were the old tenements of New York, with their zig-zag fire escapes that looked like film sets. The city had become so famous in movies, it was hard to imagine any of it was real. For a brief moment she caught sight of the Empire State, and imagined King Kong at the top of it. Even the tiny delicatessens and bars she passed reminded her of countless films and TV series past and present, and of course all the people she saw on the streets were the actors.

They stood at the lights of an intersection into even larger avenue. As the lights changed and they turned she saw the Broadway sign, and if ever there was a road more perfectly named it was this one. As she looked down its length the skyscrapers seemed to vanish into infinity, as if this strip went all the way across America. At the very end she could just make out a few trees, maybe it was Central Park? But it could have been the mid-west.

The cab continued up Broadway with Connie's head hanging out the window like a dog's. Another junction and the cab forked right down the Avenue of the Americas. This was also an infinity strip, with a name that was even more appropriate, and just in case you were unsure huge star-spangled banners flew from a number of buildings along its length. Connie now had no doubt, to come here was the best decision she'd ever made in her life.

Excitement bubbled inside her like a child. Cathy was right, the whole city was like a dream, impossible to come to terms with at first sight. New York was indeed magical, but as Connie was aware, a perfect example of why the world was currently in such a state of flux.

They turned into 44th and drove down the narrow hotel lined street stopping outside the Algonquin, a sixteen-story brick and stone building with an unassuming front. Connie paid the thirty-dollar fare, a generous tip and got out the cab. The driver took her suitcase from the trunk and immediately hailed a porter who was standing outside the entrance. He quickly crossed the street and picked up the case as she bid farewell to the driver.

They entered the hotel through the glass doors. She stood for a few moments to take it in. The dark wood panelled lounge was like a set from a thirties Hollywood Christmas movie, even though it was still November. A large glittering tree stood in the middle of the room, and fairy lights adorned the large pillars and multiple mirrors on the walls. At picture rail height there was a garland of greenery entwined with more white fairy lights. The sofas and armchairs were beige and looked comfortable and deep. The main source of light came from strategically placed table lamps making the room feel cosy and intimate. In fact, Connie couldn't imagine a hotel lounge that looked more inviting and wonderful than this.

She smiled as she turned to the reception desk, where a woman in a dark suit asked for her name and passport. The porter hovered nearby, he wore a long dark coat with a peaked cap and played the part perfectly. A cat jumped up onto the desk purring loudly.

'Is this Hamlet or Matilda?'

'Hamlet,' said the receptionist. Connie knew all about the Algonquin cats, they went back to the 1930s when the actor John Barrymore first christened the hotel cat 'Hamlet.' To date they'd been three Matilda's and this was the eighth Hamlet. She stroked him but he jumped back down behind the desk. Connie asked where The Round Table Restaurant was.

'You're in it,' said the receptionist and she pointed across the room to a dining area at the back with a large painting on the wall. 'Below the picture's the table.' Connie slowly walked across the plush carpet and gazed up. The picture depicted the

'Vicious Circle' of artists, novelists and critics, and it was obvious which one was Dorothy Parker – she was scowling. Connie stared at it for a while, then gently laid her hand on the table. *This has been touched by greatness,* she thought to herself, and wished she could be transported back in time. She looked up at the picture again and tried to imagine the debates, arguments and laughter. She felt envious that she'd never managed to surround herself with people who didn't mind if you launched into a tirade when something or other angered you. She stroked the table lovingly and stood in awe for a while then strolled back to the desk and the receptionist handed her the key card.

'One, one three. Eleventh floor, enjoy your stay.'

'I will,' said Connie determinedly. 'What a wonderful hotel.'

'It is,' said the receptionist smiling at Connie's childlike enthusiasm. She was shown to the lift by the Porter. He led the way to her room. She opened the door with her card and he wheeled the case inside. Connie took out her purse and gave him five dollars. He touched his cap and smiled.

'Thank you, madam.'

The room was small but attractive, done out in nicotine yellow and black, perfectly appropriate for the era. On the wall behind the king-sized bed was a large black and white photo of the South Street Seaport in the thirties, showing the wonderful granite skyscrapers of the period. A black lacquered desk and chair sat in front of the large window, and it was easy to imagine Dorothy sitting here, cigarette in mouth, hammering away on a black Remington whilst cursing her typos. Looking out the window all she would see was the fire escape on the building opposite – the quintessential view for a

New York writer. Connie pressed her face against the glass and followed the ladder down, but they were too high up to see the ground.

On the bedside table was a copy of the *New Yorker* magazine, complimentary because it germinated here, and was contributed to by a number of writers who were members of the 'Vicious Circle', most notably Dorothy.

Connie made herself a tea, and sat back on the bed to enjoy the vibe, though she knew it wasn't all jollity at the 'Gonk' as the members of the circle liked to call it. In 1932 Dorothy attempted suicide in her suite on the second floor, and a few other occasions elsewhere. She was a funny, sad, passionate, brittle person, in some ways a cross between herself and Cathy.

The noises from the streets below were magnified by the building's close proximity to each other, creating a funnel for sound. She listened to the city, the low buzz of traffic, car horns sounding, somebody shouting and the inevitable police siren. She was in a foreign place where everything was alien, but had been made familiar by the silver screen and therefore felt like home. She was desperate to go out and explore, but first needed to contact Sara. Sydney was now sixteen hours ahead, so she tried to work out the best time to call. It was now one in the afternoon, which would be five a.m. the following morning in Sydney, so she texted to arrange to call her at ten in the morning, six this evening New York time. Having double then treble checked she'd got the calculations right she left the room.

She walked out the glass door into the sunny and mild afternoon and followed her nose toward the busy road at the end of the street. She came to the crossing where large crowds were waiting for the walk sign to appear. She crossed the

Avenue of the Americas and continued down 44th as she noticed a lot of activity at the end of the street.

She passed a hotel, a night club, a deli and The Belasco Theatre where Bryan Cranston was appearing in *Network*. She went into a shop and bought a small street map and bottle of water. She guessed the small oriental girl who served her was Korean. She'd heard about the Korean shop keepers in New York, but wasn't sure from where, no doubt a film. When she arrived at the end of the street she walked into a river of pedestrians. Looking to her left then right she quickly realised why, she was in Times Square, the equivalent of London's Piccadilly Circus, somewhere she always avoided like the plague.

The skyscrapers surrounding the area were covered in huge video screens – some a hundred feet high. Adverts continually rolled refreshing themselves every thirty seconds or so, one of them in particular had a large crowd standing beneath it. Connie was curious so crossed Broadway onto a wide paved area and joined the crowd who were all looking up at a huge electronic advert for *Spiderman*. Nothing seemed to be happening until the giant screen suddenly showed the view of the square below, and everyone in it. The crowd jumped up and down now billboard stars in their own right whilst taking selfies of themselves within the advert, which was obviously a very clever way of getting the crowd to look at it in the first place. Within ten seconds the poster reverted back to the advert and the crowd waited eagerly for themselves to return and become stars yet again. She thought selfies were stupid, but a selfie of a selfie?

Connie strolled across the square past a gaudy taco and hot dog shack surrounded by Mickey and Minnie Mouse's distributing leaflets for the Disney Christmas store. Two jugglers juggled, a gang of Japanese tourists were eating big macs, a performing dog was standing on its back legs, whilst above them all Sony, Swarovski, Coke, TDK, American Eagle, Prudential, Adidas, Levi's and Connor Maynard – whoever he was – flashed, blinked and pulsated in attempt to grab attention. She realised these adverts were at the very core of our global problem, they were the poison pen letters.

She quickly moved on from the tackiest part of the city, and continued up Broadway into Seventh Avenue toward Central Park. A psychedelic painted camper van was parked up, written boldly on its side was 'Weed World Candies'. Were they marijuana sweets? She didn't know it was legal in New York? As she got closer the smell of weed was overpowering – a Rastafarian man was at the tiny window hatch inhaling a large joint. He smiled at Connie and exhaled.

'Come and get your candies, man,' he said in a slow, stoned voice. Connie was half tempted but declined with a smile.

'Some other time maybe.'

'No time like now, sister, who knows about tomorrow?' Connie smiled again. He was of course right, even prophetic.

She crossed the busy road into Central Park and a peace suddenly descended. What a wonderful idea it was to leave such a huge space on a small island, keep one part of Manhattan the way it was. She walked under the trees that had now lost their splendid chlorophyll red leaves always associated with New York in the fall. Now they were brown and lifeless and trodden underfoot, and the trees mere skeletons, but the park still looked splendid under the low afternoon sun. She strolled down a wide pedestrian thoroughfare and sat on a bench, took out her map, got her bearings for the boathouse and took a swig of water. She was aware how well she felt now off the ship, and that maybe her headaches had simply been the movement of the ocean or stuffiness in the cabin. Either way she felt great.

A kindly faced man sat on a bench across from her, took a saxophone out of its case and began to play a laid-back jazz piece. She was immediately reminded of Woody Allen's *Manhattan* as she stared over the tree tops to the grand old buildings lining the park on the Upper West Side, however to the south toward mid-town it was a different story. She had no idea what they were but pencil-thin towers were shooting up, some already twice as high as the surrounding skyscrapers; they looked like daggers driven into the heart of the city by an alien force from above. Why did everything have to be bigger, better, updated and inflated? The answer was obvious but it always came at a huge price – destruction of beauty.

Connie watched the dog walkers, joggers, roller bladders, skate boarders and afternoon strollers pass by. They were New Yorkers and she wished she could stay and get to know them better, find out how their lives differed to her own. But guessed they weren't that dissimilar to Londoners; they weren't exactly friends with Donald Fucking Duck either, were they? The city had always been heavily Democrat, like most US cities.

It seemed those who lived shoulder to shoulder with other races were less prejudiced than those in rural areas, why was that? Ignorance? Fear? Who knows? Maybe they were more territorial outside the cities, felt a need to protect their patch from invaders? Or perhaps they were simply less 'open minded.' Either way it created the great divide between left and right-wing politics as it did in the UK.

Here in America she would be labelled a middle class liberal, ridiculed by the right as 'privileged' and 'weak', but she certainly wasn't privileged – having been brought up on a Manchester council estate – and since when were 'decency' and 'justice' signs of weakness? It seemed anything that wasn't dogmatic and dealt with a blunt instrument was lame in today's politics, especially here under Donald Fucking Duck. She could feel herself getting angry and wound up again so told herself off, and concentrated on her surroundings.

She walked further into the park and approached the boating lake. On the Upper West Side one particular building looked like a Bavarian castle, its twin towers reflecting in the water more akin to a fairy tale than a twentieth century city.

Through the trees she caught sight of the famous Loeb Boathouse with its green weatherworn copper roof, large windows and striped awnings. Her heart rate increased; this was her first film location. She knew it was ridiculous, an intelligent woman like her coming to New York and seeking out *Harry Met Sally* locations, but that was the power of the film. One critic called it iridescent, and that was it in a nutshell. Connie had never heard dialogue that sparkled with such emotional accuracy before. That was its core, a great script, so naturally when you added sympathetic direction and wonderful acting you had a genuine classic.

She stood outside the Loeb and looked at the menu: nineteen dollars for eggs Benedict, and twenty-six for fish and chips. Not that she wanted either. She'd have a coffee and find a table near where Sally sat with her friend Maria.

She entered the warm dark interior; which again reminded her of a set from a thirties Christmas movie. There was a polished wooden bar surrounded by high stools, and to one side armchairs and sofas facing a log fire, its mantelpiece decorated with holly and fairy lights. The main part of the restaurant was down steps into a large sunlit room that had a splendid view over the lake through the large picture windows.

Most of the forty odd tables were taken, but Connie could see a vacant one. She went down the steps and approached the elegantly dressed female maître d' and asked if she could have the table near the window. Yes, it was free for an hour. Connie was given a menu and made her way toward it. She tried to image the scene; it was outside but realised in summer all the windows would be open so it would seem like an exterior. She sat and took in the view, yes this was definitely close, but not quite right. She looked around the room, then got up and walked past other tables. Some people stared at her but Connie remained unperturbed. She'd come all this way to find the locations and she wasn't going to give up easily.

She asked a waitress, she'd never heard of the film, but was no older than eighteen and spoke with a Spanish accent, even so everyone knew *When Harry Met Sally...*, surely? She stopped and stared at the lake again, trying to recall the background. In the film it was summer but now the trees were leafless, so it was hard to tell. Then, as if by instinct, she turned to her right. Beyond the windows outside she could just make out a terrace, and a few metal tables and chairs.

That was it! It was outside after all! Connie quickly strode out the restaurant and turned left following the path around through the garden, twenty metres and it came to an abrupt end in front of a large pair of six-foot-high double gates. This was the entrance, but was clearly closed for winter, as a large padlock and chain hung from them.

'Shit,' said Connie out loud. 'Bollocks and shit.' Then she realised how childish her pursuit of the film locations was.

'For god's sake, grow up,' she mumbled to herself. But she had to see it, gate or no gate. She gave a push wondering if the lock and chain were merely cosmetic, and sure enough they began to open, not far, maybe a foot. She tried to peer in but all she could see was a large dumpster brimming with rubbish bags. If she could only move the gates another few inches she could squeeze through. Looking at the chain she realised the end was just looped through itself, so pulled and it gave her a bit more slack, maybe just enough. She pushed the gate and it opened another couple of inches. She looked around, it was unlikely anyone else would come down the path being a dead end, and leading nowhere now the terrace was closed, so she began to squeeze herself through the tiny gap. *Good job there's nothing of me*, she thought as she forced herself sideways. She was almost through when her coat snagged on a small piece of wire. She tried to manoeuvre herself off it, but it wouldn't let her go. 'Oh, shit to it,' Connie just pulled and it tore her coat slightly but she was through.

She stood in the yard, to her left through the window she could see into a large banquet hall with chairs and tables stacked to one side. Nobody was inside so she quickly moved to the end of the building. Peering around the corner made her gasp with excitement, there it was, the patio, metal tables and chairs with the lake beyond. She moved slowly forward in disbelief, this was it, the exact place where Meg Ryan, Carrie Fisher, Director Rob Reiner and even Nora Ephron would have been thirty years ago.

Connie sat reverently in one of the chairs, the one in which Sally sat, camera right as she remembered it. She tried to recall the lines but couldn't. All she remembered was Marie going through a rolodex of available men, and Sally saying she wasn't ready yet. Marie then mentions one of the desirable men in her book has already died, prompting Sally to say, 'So you're saying I should hook up with someone now before they drop dead?' Connie smiled to herself at the recollection.

She remained seated for a short while to absorb the atmosphere. What was it that drew people to film locations? Reinforcement that they were real, and not entirely make-believe? Or, was it just sad? An attempt to feel closer to the stars? Either way it probably meant not much had happened in your own life, which was certainly true for Connie, and for most mere mortals.

She pondered this for a while, then realised visiting these places did give your life excitement in a world where there were precious few heroes anymore. After all, we all needed heroes. Would she go down in history as a hero? Or at least brave? She would never know.

She walked along the wide avenues that intersected the park, horse-drawn carriages frequently passed by, reminding her of *Annie Hall*. Every now and again large rock outcrops appeared. Unlike parks in London these were real and not ornamental, which somehow made it easier to imagine what it would have looked look before mass colonisation; a rocky wilderness covered in trees and scrub, with bears, cougars, wild boar and even moose roaming freely. The Algonquin hotel was named after the tribe of American Indians that once lived here. Would it have been a better place to live then? Who knows? she thought. You'd be lucky to live beyond forty that's for sure.

She passed the Conservatory Pond, manmade yet elegant with its old Upper East Side buildings reflected in the still water. A child's bubbles drifted over its surface and she imagined what it would have been like in the nineteen-thirties; a primly dressed nanny pushes a pram, whilst trying to control a three-year-old who is dangerously close to the water's edge, the oldest is blowing the bubbles. The parent's house is a three-story brownstone a block away, a log fire burning in the living room and a ten-foot tree with presents stacked beneath. A servant called Stokes enters, bringing in a new basket of logs. The children return home, the mother and the father arrive from work and the whole family hug in front of the holly strewn mantelpiece. The scene reminded her of the film *It's a Wonderful Life'*, with the happy Christmas time ending – which would be a far cry from her own, or maybe Clarence the guardian angel will save her?

She saw a statue of Hans Christian Anderson next to the pathway. She read the plaque beneath. It was celebrating his 150th birthday, and was donated by the Danish Women's Association. He was sitting down reading *The Ugly Duckling,* with a sculpted duck at his feet looking up at him. She remembered the 'Ugly Duckling' song by Danny Kaye from when she was a child; the way it was scorned and shooed away made her cry. Even now as she recalled the song, she felt an aching sadness, which then morphed into her own death. It hit her again like a rock to the forehead. So, she sat on a bench and rested for a few minutes.

The thought that everything she was seeing was for the last time shocked her, even though she would never come back to New York if she lived to be a hundred. A hundred years old? Imagine that? From her birth to thirty-seven again, it was another fucking lifetime. She tried to stop thinking about it, what was the point?

She was beginning to feel exhausted, so decided to head back to the hotel for a rest. The pathway became busier as she neared the edge of the park. She spotted a pool of penguins, which took a few moments to sink in, until she realised it was the zoo. Another film location made famous in the animation

Madagascar which had been her daughter's favourite film, because it was about animals escaping captivity. If only the penguins could escape now? On the other hand, those in captivity might be the only ones left in half a century or so.

Crossing busy Central Park South, she noticed a Pret a Manger sandwich bar and realised that hunger could be the cause of her tiredness, as she hadn't eaten since breakfast nine hours ago. She felt a bit parochial going into an English chain in New York, but was too hungry to search for a genuine deli. Inside the sandwiches were exactly the same as in London with one difference: the Christmas special turkey sandwich with stuffing and cranberry sauce, (which she always had because of the charitable donation), cost eighteen dollars, thirteen pounds! It was three pounds fifty in London. She was astonished. How could anyone possibly afford that? She mentioned the hideous price to the guy serving who just shrugged and took her money. *Thirteen quid for a fucking sandwich, and I bet they still pay him a pittance,* she thought to herself as she walked out the shop. He probably sleeps in the park under a copy of the *New York Times.*

She walked down the Avenue of the Americas. On one side were the corporate buildings of Time Life, Exxon (that deserved bombing) and McGraw Hill. On the plazas in front of them were various festive decorations but at present unlit. Further on she passed CBS, the Rockefeller Centre and the beautiful art deco Radio City Music Hall with a fifty-foot Christmas tree above its entrance. She imagined it would look splendid at night, so decided to come back later. She turned into 44th Street and entered the hotel, hiding her sandwich bag as best she could.

Back in the room she ate her food, then set the alarm on her phone for five forty-five to give her time to wake up before calling Sara at six.

This was going to be the last time she ever spoke to her daughter and she couldn't give anything away. If Sara sensed something was amiss, she'd panic. So, she'd act bright, breezy and excited about being in New York, which of course she was, regardless of what she might be doing in two days' time.

The phone rang: the alarm hadn't gone off. Connie gathered her senses, adjusted her hair, rubbed her eyes. She picked up the phone off the bedside table, pressed the button and swiped the screen to see Sara.

'Hi, Mum. You OK?'

'Just woken up, Sara, give me a moment.'

'Where are you? In the hotel?' Connie nodded. 'Is it nice?'

'Fine, yeah. Cost a fortune but that's New York. I paid thirteen pounds for a sandwich earlier on.'

'Good god, really?' Connie nodded. 'But are you enjoying yourself?'

'Immensely.'

'Good. Tell us about life aboard the ship then?' Connie talked about the voyage, then mentioned Russell. Sara was equally as intrigued as to why he went cold whenever she mentioned climate change.

'Maybe he was a closet oil magnate? Or just an avid Trump fan. Oh god did you hear what the idiot said yesterday? He didn't believe it, didn't believe his own government's climate change report?'

'But I bet he believes in Dr Seuss, Disneyland and Mother Goose though,' said Connie.

'Yeah, he believes in make-believe. All the shit that's going on in his head.'

'I'm afraid he does, Sara.'

'Can't you plant a bomb in Trump Tower?'

'I wish,' said Connie realising her daughter's mind worked just like her own.

'So, what's happening tonight in the Big Apple?'

'Well, I'll check out a few bins for my tea, see the lights, go to a bar and get hammered.'

'Sounds good. Wish I was with you, Mum.'

'So do I,' said Connie trying her best to hide the sadness.

'How much longer are you staying?'

'A week.'

'Call me when you back home Mum. I better get to work.'

'Sure, sure, Sara. And love to Kurt.'

'Will do.'

'And, Sara, I love you.'

'Love you too, Mum.'

'And don't worry.'

'About what?'

'Me.'

'I'm not.'

'Good.'

'Why should I?'

'No reason. Bye, darling.'

'Bye,' said Sara and the screen went blank. Connie burst into tears.

An hour later she was strolling back toward Radio City. She crossed the busy Avenue with a hundred or so other people and walked up to the plazas that were now ablaze with colour. On the first all the trees were lit up, and alongside were twenty-foot-high reindeers covered in tiny white lights. In front of the next building was a stack of giant six-foot fairy lights, their leads winding around the red, green, yellow, and white bulbs. At the next plaza was a pond and fountain, in which were stacked ten giant red baubles. But the piece de resistance was still Radio City. Its huge tree now flickering from red to green, and two giant blue and white neon signs a monument to the splendid art deco of the 1930's.

She thought about going up the Rockefeller Building to the Top of the Rock, a viewing area seventy floors up. But it cost forty dollars, and there was a huge queue. She also suffered from mild vertigo, so decided to give it a miss. Instead she walked down West 51st to look at the famous ice rink. Fairy lights covered every square inch of the area; there were trumpeting angels in the garden and the inevitable fifty-foot Christmas tree. She couldn't deny she'd chosen the best time of year to come to the city.

Going back down 51st she re-crossed the Avenue of the Americas and continued until she came to Fifth Avenue, and walked toward Times Square. At night it was all aglow from the mass of illuminated adverts, and reminded her of *Blade Runner*. Steam vapour rose from the heat vents in the road adding to the effect. It then began to rain and the scene was complete. The area was now twice as busy as it had been during the day, the tourists now mixing with commuters who were flocking to Times Square subway. In many ways it was a vision of hell – the future – a world with even more inhabitants and advertising. In the final analysis was it the expanding population that was really jeopardising our future? Another three billion in the last thirty years was certainly stretching the planets resources to the limit. However, Connie knew the First World was really to blame, the wealthy all-consuming one, with China and India close on their heels.

She pushed her way through the crowds and quickly dived into a side street. A hundred metres down she came to O'Brien's Bar. The rain was now falling heavily and the low warm lights from inside were inviting, so she went in. The seats with tables to her left were full, and the long bar to the right seemed the same with men facing numerous TV sets showing sports.

Connie walked down the line of backs and found one vacant position into which she shoehorned herself. The man to her left glanced in her direction as the barman approached. Connie looked at what he was drinking.

'I'll have the same.'

'Which whiskey?' he said in an Irish accent.

'Irish, Glenlivet?'

'That's scotch,' said the barman.

'Oh sorry. Jameson's?'

'Double?'

'Sure, why not?' she said as the man next to her turned and grinned. He was in his forties and wore a baseball cap and a dark blue fleece.

'Wish my wife drank pints and doubles.'

'Why?' asked Connie.

'We could go out and get drunk together.'

'And end up broke and in AA?'

'True that,' said the man laughing. The barman placed the pint of Guinness and Jameson's chaser in front of her and stuck the tab under a shot glass. She looked at the screens, on one was basketball, another baseball, a third was showing American Football and a fourth English soccer. The man next to her was watching American Football. Denver Broncos v Kansas City Chiefs. Connie asked what his team was.

'Neither, Pittsburgh Steelers from the Northern League, this is the AFC West.'

'OK,' said Connie, not really wanting to pursue the line of conversation.

'You English?' said the man.

'Yeah,' said Connie.

'Where from?'

'London.'

'Yeah I been to London.'

'Did you like it?'

'Sure. Got lost though, couldn't find the subway.'

'We call it the underground.'

'Right. That explains it.' The man laughed. 'No, I'm just kidding.'

'Are you from Pittsburgh then?'

'Yeah. Just here for the weekend with my wife and two daughters. They wanted to see *Mean Girls*. Now they're out shopping, costing me a goddam fortune. Flight, hotel and the show – that cost a hundred bucks each. Whole trip be over a thousand bucks.'

'They're worth it though, eh?' said Connie smiling.

'Yeah. Every cent,' said the man. Connie sipped her Guinness and was surprised how sweet and palatable it was, she'd never drank it before. They chatted and Connie told him how she'd come over on the Queen Mary. He said how he'd love to take his family on it someday, especially as there'd be no big shops for them to spend money in and the shows would be free. She asked him how old his girls where and what they wanted to be when they grew up. He said they were twelve and fourteen and both wanted to sing and dance in musical theatre. He said what lovely talented girls they were and got very sentimental, possibly due to the drink.

'Can I ask you a question?' said Connie tentatively.

'Sure.'

'Do you worry about your children's future?'

'Too right I do!'

'So, what do you think about climate change?'

'Climate change? Hmm. Well, I'm not too worried because Donald Trump said he's now gonna fight it.'

'Really?' said Connie in disbelief.

'Yeah. He's sending 20,000 troops to the sun.' Connie laughed and the man finished his pint, then knocked back the remains of his chaser. 'Have a nice time in New York.'

'Thanks. Enjoy the rest of your trip.'

'I will once I'm home.' The man left and Connie took a large gulp of whiskey that made her shudder, but then it slowly warmed her and she began to feel mellow. She thought about the man's joke, it was funny and maybe having a sense of humour was the only way to deal with the things happening in the world. But he still didn't answer her question, did he? Maybe he was scared to death about their future and couldn't discuss it with anyone, even his own family? The more likely scenario was he didn't want to discuss it with her, a relative stranger, which then made her think about Russell and his avoidance of the subject.

As she sat in the crowded bar she was reminded again of '*It's a Wonderful Life,*' and George Bailey, drunk, just before his attempted suicide. Is that why she was drinking so much?

Either way she decided to have another Guinness and double Irish whiskey '*For the pavement*' she thought jokingly to herself, then realised it should be 'sidewalk' which was obviously a better word than ours. She liked 'dumpster' too, very onomatopoeic. But thought that colour spelt without a 'u' was lazy, and the phrase 'To go' lazier still.

She played with words for a while, particularly her favourite 'Navajo' which wasn't exactly a word as such but an American Indian tribe. Connie Navajo, what a great name. In many ways she saw herself as an Indian, the member of an indigenous tribe trying to protect and hold onto an ancient way of life that's in harmony with its surroundings. She thought about the original inhabitants of Manhattan Island and felt their spirits around her, even though she wasn't particularly spiritual. She saw faces, faces of ageing elders with long hair and headdresses. She even began to talk to them, her lips involuntarily moving, then quickly realised the man next to her was staring.

'Are you OK?' he said in an English accent.

'I believe I'm drunk,' said Connie and she laughed. The man smiled awkwardly and quickly turned away. She realised it was time to go and eat something.

She walked down Avenue of the Americas where a group of break dancers performed on the wide sidewalk Connie watched their gyrations a while, but it made her feel dizzy. She threw a five-dollar bill into an upturned baseball cap and crossed into her street.

Thirty metres down was a Chinese restaurant. She entered, and sat down at one of the Formica tables for a few minutes, until she realised she had to order at the till. She picked up the extensive menu, couldn't be bothered to read it and simply ordered a chicken chow mien with sesame toast, and plonked herself back down at the table. It reminded her of going out with Cathy at university. Friday night they'd get drunk, tease boys, then march off on their own to eat at a Chinese or

Indian. If they chose to bring any boys with them, they were definitely at the 'high table' and would maybe get a chance to spend the night with them. The two girls could pick and choose men like sweets in a sweetshop, but never put themselves about too much for fear of a bad reputation. If only Cathy were here now, what fun they'd have.

The food arrived and Connie was so hungry she chose the fork over the chopsticks. Once finished she felt satisfied yet shattered and returned to the hotel.

On entering she felt the warmth and cosiness of the lounge and sunk into one of the armchairs. She glanced at the painting of the round table and thought about Dorothy Parker again. She wasn't just a great writer and wit, but also a passionate civil rights activist, setting up the Los Angeles Anti-Nazi League when she worked in Hollywood. When she died in 1967, she left everything to Martin Luther King Junior to help the civil rights movement. His famous quote 'Our lives begin to end the day we remain quiet about things that matter' had always been a source of inspiration for Connie, as was Rosa Parks 'You must never be fearful about what you're doing when it's "right".' Was it right what she was about to do herself?' Unequivocally yes, and now she was here it made even more sense, now she could hear the voices of those she admired.

She drifted to sleep briefly, then raised herself from the chair, smiled to the receptionist and stroked Hamlet who was sitting on the desk. He rolled over in ecstasy to have his stomach stroked.

'Isn't he lovely?'

'Sure is, when he wants something,' said the receptionist, smiling.

'Typical man eh?' said Connie. The receptionist laughed at her joke.

'I'll say.'

'Goodnight,' said Connie.

'Goodnight, Mrs Noble,' said the receptionist smiling. The familiarity gave her a warm feeling, as if she were home.

Lying in bed a saxophone drifted up from the streets, the traffic and air conditioning vent outside hummed, above it all the proverbial police siren wailed. This was New York, maybe her final resting place, and it felt right.

***

Chapter 12

She woke early, this would be her final full day and she didn't intend to waste it. She wasn't doing the museums or art galleries or taking in a show, she just wanted to walk the streets, soak up more of the atmosphere. She'd never been one for collections of things in vast high vaulted halls, and what's Van Gogh, Cezanne or Matisse got to do with New York? Of course, there were American painters, but you could see those in London. Broadway shows ditto, once they transferred to the West End. It's not that she wasn't cultured, but it was real life that captured her imagination, she didn't need to have it captured for her. She would just get more pleasure people watching in a diner than looking at a Ruben's.

She got dressed and went down to breakfast; to her surprise twenty-odd people were already eating. Then she realised it was Monday, and these probably weren't tourists but here on business. She sat at a vacant table and received a menu from the polite waiter who sounded Eastern European. She hadn't remembered what the Chinese meal had cost the previous night, but was quickly reminded how expensive food was. Tea and toast – seventeen pounds, and if you actually ate a breakfast it would set you back twenty-five for eggs benedict, and thirty for a full one. However, what was the point in worrying about money now? So, she went for the eggs Florentine, a New York favourite.

Whilst waiting she turned on her phone and checked Google News. Top of the stories was an article about the global economy. By 2050 it could easily treble. Three times more production and consumption. And how were you going to stop that, when every company and its share-holders wanted more profit? Did you force them to stop advertising? Force them to produce items that lasted a lifetime? Highly unlikely. Connie looked around at the suits having breakfast. These were no doubt people at the heart of the problem, MBAs and lawyers working in corporations and finance institutions on Wall Street. What did she have to do to stop the rot? Shoot them all? Yes, the world was slowly dying, and the closer you looked the more impossible it was to find a cure.

She went back to her room and lay on the bed, another twenty-four hours and if she succeeded that was it – all over – no more stressing out over everything that was being wrecked and plundered. But she was still terrified of going through with it, who wouldn't be?

A few weeks earlier when she knew the action she wanted to take she'd contacted an activist group in the city. Before she travelled three thousand miles, she had to find out whether her idea was possible. Not wanting to implicate or scare anyone she toned down the details of the protest. After a few days she received an anonymous response – two pages of detailed reconnaissance, a step by step guide outlining exactly what she should do, and what she would need to do it. She'd printed it out, and as per instructions deleted the email and address from her system. She took the sheets of paper out of her suitcase and re-read them for the hundredth time. She needed a pocketable heavy-duty pair of wire cutters, so googled hardware stores downtown. To distract herself she'd planned to visit two more *When Harry Met Sally* locations, Washington Square, and Katz's Deli on Houston in the East Village. There was a store a few blocks away, perfect.

She walked to Times Square station and took the '1' train to Sheridan Square. Sitting in the carriage was no different to the underground in London, people stared down at their papers or books or phones. She'd imagined New Yorkers all chatting with each other, some even singing duets, well that or being held up at gunpoint. New York was unlike the movies in the same way London wasn't filled with cheerful Cockneys and friendly Bobbies. They passed 34th, 28th, 23rd, 18th and 14th until they finally came to Sheridan Square. As Connie stood, she felt momentarily faint, then dizzy. The same had happened in the park the previous day and she wondered again if it was the tumour. Once outside the station she found a bench and sat down. She was now in Greenwich Village and the buildings around her were older and had far fewer floors, this felt like the real New York, where people sat on steps and chatted while kids played under fire hydrants in the summer. But she was probably wrong there too, as she'd heard Greenwich Village was now hugely expensive and full of wealthy bankers and stock brokers.

After a few minutes she felt better, and walked the few blocks to Washington Square past three story brownstones on tree-lined streets. As she entered the large paved and grassed area, she saw the arched monument ahead of her. This was it; this was where Sally dropped off Harry after their eighteen-hour car journey from Chicago together. Harry nonchalantly gets out the car, grabs his stuff, says thanks and walks off. Rather perturbed by his coldness Sally simply says 'Have a nice life' and he's gone. Connie walked over to the arch and stood at the exact spot where the scene took place. She looked up at the monument, as did Harry at the end of the film on

New Year's Eve. Flashbacks of their topsy-turvy relationship over the years makes Harry realise he loves her, and he rushes to the celebration ball she's at to tell her so. The thoughts of the scene brought tears to her eyes, even though it was the classic romantic schmaltzy ending. But she knew it wasn't just the movie, it was her own life. She cried because she'd never experienced that kind of romanticism with anyone. Her boyfriends were largely self-obsessed, and Jim was practical, not a romantic. She'd led a life without sparks, maybe this was why it had to end with purpose, with an explosion of fireworks? Maybe her concern for the world was a substitute for the lack of excitement in her life, so that's where all her energy went. She looked up again and this time felt consoled, she was lucky to have something she felt deeply about, something she could commit her body and soul to.

She walked out of the square, crossed Broadway and down 4th Street toward the Bowery. During those few blocks everything changed. The buildings weren't well maintained, people on the street looked poorer and there was a different vibe to the area. As she walked down toward East Houston Street, she passed a number of people smoking dope, the pungent smell hanging in the cold damp air. One alleyway revealed cardboard box dwellings with blankets and a scuffed-out fire. As she turned down Houston there was a dishevelled-looking group who eyed her up as she passed. She wanted to stop and give them money, but that might seem patronising as they weren't actually begging. She saw more boxes, sleeping bags and blankets scattered around a small fenced-off grassy area, a couple of supermarket trolleys were loaded with clothes, shoes and other various items. This was clearly an enclave for the homeless, no doubt one of many in the city.

Here was the 'other side' of New York and unlike the prosperous quarters these people contributed nothing to the CO_2 emissions. A couple of men stared at her as she walked past. Connie knew she was the enemy, and this didn't sit well with her. But at least she could say it wasn't for much longer.

She crossed Houston and brightened when she saw the large neon sign for Katz's. She entered, it was much bigger than she imagined and packed to the rafters. There were six queues ten deep at the counter, and at least a hundred tables. She joined one of the lines and slowly inched forward. She'd decided to have the turkey sandwich from the extensive menu chalked up on the board. The man produced a tray and slapped two pieces of rye bread on a plate, then proceeded to carve slices of turkey and pile them onto the bread until it was at least six inches high – enough for ten sandwiches, let alone one. He asked her if she wanted a stick, and she nodded. Another plate appeared and a stick of cucumber and gherkin were dropped on. The man added the check and made quick eye contact with his dollar bill stuffed tip jar and Connie obliged. She picked up the tray and glanced down at the till receipt – twenty-seven dollars! Twenty-seven dollars! Being in a pretty run-down area she was shocked. How on earth could the people she'd seen on the streets survive if this was the cost of a sandwich at what was essentially a café? Maybe the prices had skyrocketed after the film was made here, but she doubted it.

She slowly walked down the row of busy tables, trying to approximate which one the scene had been shot at. In the background she remembered there was a kind of grill area, with an extraction hood, and once she'd passed the sandwich queues came to the exact spot. She looked at three tables that were the likely candidates and chose to sit down at the middle one. A young couple sat opposite each other, coincidentally in the same positions Harry and Sally had. She asked if it was alright to join them and the man smiled his approval. So, this was it, this was where one of the most memorable movie scenes ever was filmed:

Harry insists that no woman has ever faked an orgasm with him, Sally asks him how he would possibly know. Harry arrogantly says he knows, so she sets out to prove him wrong with a brilliantly faked demonstration of an orgasm in the middle of the busy diner. Connie smiled as she recollected the scene, the young woman caught her eye and smiled back. Did they both know they were sitting in hallowed seats? Or were they too young to know the film at all? Connie felt she had to mention it.

'Did you know a great movie scene was shot here?' The young man turned and smiled then pointed upwards. Connie looked up at the ceiling where a plastic disc hung, an arrow pointed down to their seats and written above it 'Where Harry Met Sally – I'll have what she's having.' Which referred to the line from a woman at a nearby table after Sally's splendid orgasm. Connie smiled sheepishly at the man and began to tackle the ludicrous sandwich.

Like the boathouse, it was exciting to be in a place where reality met fantasy, and you could escape into another world – which was exactly the reason she was here – it was her Mecca.

She left three quarters of the sandwich, and wanted to give it to somebody on the street, but it was obviously wrong to hand out partially eaten food. She walked to the payment kiosk and noticed the walls were covered with pictures of famous actors and sportsmen, including one of Meg Ryan with Billy Crystal and the director Rob Reiner taken pretty much in the exact spot she stood. She stared at it for a while, and realised this was their reality, off set as normal people. And if Meg Ryan walked into Katz's now, she'd no doubt be as excited as Connie was seeing the location of her iconic movie scene. In the end movie stars are no different to us.

She walked out into the cold air and checked her map for the hardware store. It was a couple of blocks to Schames and Son. She brought her wire cutters and proceeded back toward Houston. It was long walk up to Midtown, but what else was she going to do? She felt like a philistine for not wanting to see any art, but would you if it was possibly your last day on Earth? She'd love to have experienced some live music in the city, but a Monday afternoon in November was hardly going to throw up much was it? She was starting to feel tired but pushed on toward the Bowery. Ordinarily she'd take lots of photographs when she was somewhere new, but what was the point? She'd never be showing them anyone, would she?

She realised that now she'd done her homages she was becoming depressed. She was just a terminally ill person on her own in New York, how sad was that? She needed to shake herself out of it but how? She saw the homeless again, there was a scuffle going on between two men, one of them finally backed off calling the others 'motherfuckingcunts'. Somebody threw a brick and it hit him on the shoulder making him scream more. Who knows what the fight was about? She half expected someone to pull out a gun, but these were homeless, how could they afford guns? She also imagined guns were far less in evidence than you'd expect – movies had grossly distorted the truth.

She proceeded up the traffic-clogged street and cut across to Broadway where she came upon a building that looked totally alien in its surroundings – a gothic spired church. It was something you'd expect to see in an English village or town but not here. However, there was one main difference; attached to the railing outside was a sign that read 'No Soliciting'.

Connie decided to take a look inside; old buildings and castles had always captured her imagination, simply because you had to use it in order to picture the past. She walked up the path and saw the sign. It was called 'Grace Church', what a wonderful name, she thought.

On entering she saw the familiar high vaulted ceiling, intricate stonework and majestic stained-glass window behind the altar. An organist was practising and Connie recognised Bach's Fugue in G minor, which conjured up visions of hell, not heaven. She didn't believe in either, but was thinking which one she might go to if they did exist. Maybe the bad place given what she was about to do. Heaven had never appealed to her anyway, all that harp playing and tranquillity, she'd always imagined somewhere in between might be best, a bit of debauchery followed by some peace and quiet.

Half a dozen people sat at pews in silent prayer, though god knows how with the organist playing at full blast. Connie also sat and stared at the intimidating gargoyles high above her, and it was easy to understand why so many people embraced religion in the past. The building itself was enough to get you on your knees praying for mercy and deliverance from Satan. But she also understood how some people found this imposing building comforting, as it echoed back though history and had a timeless quality.

She guessed the word she was looking for was solid – a rock. Something to cling on to when times were hard, or water levels were rising, which might soon be appropriate. The fugue finally ended, but before she left, she said a quick prayer:

'If there is a God, and you do exist, please save this beautiful world of ours. Amen.' She got up and slowly walked out, putting a five-dollar bill into a collection box. As soon as she got outside it began to pour with rain. *So that's a 'no' then I assume?* she thought, laughing to herself.

She approached Union Square and for the second time saw the Empire State Building rising above the skeletal trees, and again couldn't get *King Kong* out of her mind. It was a film that brought tears to her eyes as a child, and was maybe the seed of her love for animals, and when they gunned the gentle giant down, her frequent contempt for humans.

The clouds turned black and rain came down even heavier, so she quickly ran to 14th Street station and rode the subway uptown to Times Square.

She went into The Times Deli and bought a bottle of water, and a half bottle of vodka that she would need the following day. The rain still fell and she was now soaked, so quickly made her way back to the hotel. As she passed the reception desk she was called back and handed a note. She got into the lift and opened it.

'I'm so sorry about the other night, Connie. Will you forgive me and meet at the Long Room on West 44th this evening around seven? Russell.'

***

Chapter 13

Sitting on the bed drying her hair she read the note again. What was he doing here? He should be on the Queen Mary for another month? Surely, he hadn't jumped ship to meet her again? Connie wasn't even sure she wanted to see him, but was interested to know the cause of his abruptness and obvious discomfort whenever she mentioned 'you know what.' And she had to admit she still liked him, and was beginning to feel excited about the evening ahead, even if there was some doubt. He wouldn't be in Manhattan just to have another altercation with her, would he? After all he knew where she was politically, so he'd have to accept it wouldn't he?

She got ready early, and wore the only decent dress she had with her – the maroon one. She couldn't quite believe it; she was actually seeing Russell. Maybe he wanted to marry her? If he did, he'd drawn the short straw there, hadn't he? She wouldn't tell him anything obviously, she wouldn't tell him unless of course marriage **was** the reason he'd turned up, like the ending of *When Harry Met Sally…* They didn't get on at first either, did they? But they'd had years to get to know each other, not days. Either way Connie felt she deserved some excitement, and an apology, after all these might be last hours of her life. She put on a small amount of make-up and lipstick, grabbed her coat and handbag and took the lift down to the lounge or 'Round Table Room' as she preferred to call it. She sank into a deep sofa and ordered a vodka and cranberry – well when in America.

She sipped at the drink and thought again of Dorothy, who would no doubt sink five of these and proceed to expound on art and argue loudly. She was passionate and lived an exciting life, whereas Connie was passionate and lived a mundane one. Her real fun ended once Cathy went off to marry, then she did the same. How many other women fell into the boring husband trap? Millions probably. She knew that all heterosexual couples weren't unhappy, Sara and Kurt seemed well matched, but for every one that is, there's probably three that aren't.

It was six o'clock and she ordered another drink, sod it. Though she didn't want to repeat the last night on the ship and get too pissed, she must remember to eat, that's all. Surely they would be if meeting as early as seven?

A couple of minutes' walk and she was outside the Long Room with its classy awning covering the sidewalk. She hesitated at the door and peered inside, a few tables were near the window and behind was a long bar. Fairy lights adorned the low arched roof and the atmosphere seemed cosy. She went in scanning the room for Russell, moving through the crowd until she reached another seating area at the end. She searched the groups at the tables, and finally spotted him in a corner reading a paper. She approached, and as she neared, he looked up and smiled, then rose to his feet. He seemed awkward and held out his hand, then quickly lowered it, stepped away from his seat and kissed her on the cheek. Connie smiled.

'Hello, Russell,' she said with just a hint of irony.

'Hi, Connie,' he said lowering his eyes as they both sat. 'Drink?'

'Why not? A vodka and cranberry please.' Russell hailed the waiter and ordered her drink and a JD and Coke for himself. They both glanced at each other a few moments before Connie spoke.

'So, I thought you'd another month to go?'

'I have, well had. I jumped ship, told them a relative had died.'

'Why, have they?'

'No. I had to come to apologise.'

'You didn't, Russell, it doesn't matter.'

'It does. To me.' Russell paused. 'I'm sorry.'

'For what?'

'Being obnoxious and rude the other night.' Connie simply nodded. 'It was wrong of me to take it out on you.' Connie shrugged.

'Take what out on me?'

'My… my shit,'

'That's none of my business, Russell.'

'It is when you're on the sharp end of it, Connie.' she shrugged again. 'I did some bad stuff.'

'You don't have to tell me.'

'I have to, I want to.' The drinks arrived. 'Do you want to order some food?' Connie shook her head. 'Me neither.' They both took sips of their drinks. Russell put his glass down. But remained staring into it as he spoke.

'I worked as a lawyer for a big oil company in Houston. I acquired land for them to drill on. Farmsteads, public parks even a nature reserve that we insisted we'd maintain which was bullshit. If we couldn't get the land we'd bribe and sometimes even threaten. That wasn't my department but I still knew it was going on. I did this for over twenty years and hated every minute of it, but had a wife and two kids to support. I know, I know I'm still pathetic. I should have got out. And I finally did when the disaster happened, the Deepwater Horizon.' He took a drink, then continued.

'The devastation was horrific. Hundreds and hundreds of miles of coastline covered in dead marine life.' Russell paused overcome by the memory. 'Billions of fish and crustaceans, six thousand sea turtles, twenty-five thousand dolphins and whales and six hundred thousand seabirds. And there I was in the middle of it, trying to help the company pay out as little as possible for the clean-up and compensation. I felt sick and quit the job, then started to suffer with depression and began drinking. Within a year we lost the house, and my wife left me, taking the kids with her.'

Connie looked at him sympathetically.

'They should have been proud of you, Russell.'

'Proud? I was an asshole for working there all those years.' Russell looked up from his drink.

'But you got out, you did the right thing.'

'Eventually, but look at all the shit I caused on the way.'

'How could that all be your fault?'

'I'm complicit, Connie.'

'We all are if we consume.'

'I didn't just consume, I destroyed.'

'Yeah, and then you sacrificed your job and family to get out. Not many people would have done that.'

'I guess,' said Russell taking a long drink and weakly smiling.

'So, what happened after they'd left?'

'I sobered up, got a small apartment and decided to pick up the guitar again, started playing the bars and clubs, then got a job on the cruise ships.' Connie lifted her glass.

'Well I think you were very brave; most people don't have your principles Russell. To bravery.' Connie lifted her glass and he followed suit.

'To bravery, though I'm not brave.' They both toasted. Russell put down his glass. 'Listen. Connie, jumping ship and finding you were here was a long shot, and I didn't just come to ask you to forgive me and tell you my life story either. I came to see you again and hopefully spend more time with you, if you want to that is?'

'Sure. That would be nice.' Russell leant across the table, Connie moved forward and they kissed though she couldn't help wondering if it was the right thing to do.

They laughed and chatted for a couple of hours in the Long Room. Russell stroked her leg every now and again under the table and Connie was beginning to melt, especially after another two vodka and cranberries. All she wanted to do was get him in bed, but it was still early, and she had to wait a while before putting the idea to him, unless he suggested it first. The subject eventually turned to sex and Connie had no qualms telling him that her own marriage was never great in that department. Russell wasn't as forthcoming but did suggest that after their second child sex went downhill like a bobsled. Connie smiled then asked where he was staying.

'Well I was at a dive in Brooklyn last night, but tonight I'm at The Muse on 46th.'

'That must be near me,' said Connie.

'I know,' said Russell, almost blushing. 'That was the plan.' Connie felt a tingle run through her entire body. 'Should we eat now?' asked Russell.

'No. To hell with food,' said Connie with bravado. 'Let's paint the town red.'

'OK. I'll pay the check.' Russell signalled the waiter.

Stepping out into the cold night air Connie felt the effects of the alcohol and hooked her arm under Russell's then began to talk in a faux inebriated accent.

'I wish I could drink like a lady. I can take one or two at the most. Three, I'm under the table. Four, I'm under the host.' Russell laughed.

'Good ole Dorothy again?' he said.

'Yup. Good Ole Dorothy,' said Connie followed by a feigned hiccup. They came to the Avenue of the Americas and walked up to toward 46th Street.

'We could do the bar at the Top of the Rock,' said Russell.

'I'd rather be on top of your —' Connie stopped mid-sentence. 'Oh my god! What did I just say? I'm really sorry Russell, that was awful.'

'Nicest thing a woman has ever said to me. Your place or mine?'

'Yours?' Both of them laughed.

They approached the Muse Hotel. In the window was a sculpture of trees and tiny reindeer covered in token fairy lights. They entered the reception area that had a Japanese minimal feel, next to it was a small restaurant and bar with a large illuminated wine cabinet along one wall. It lacked the atmosphere of the Long Room which was probably why it was almost empty. Russell glanced at the bar, then at Connie, who gently shook her head. 'We'll get room service,' said Russell. Connie nodded in agreement. They went to the lift. The doors opened and they stepped inside. Russell pressed the 6th floor button and the doors closed. Connie immediately grabbed Russell and kissed him, he reciprocated with equal enthusiasm.

The room was simple, clean and spacious, done out in creams and browns. Russell faded the lights. Connie kissed him again and they made their way across the floor in a kind of clumsy waltz. Then they both fell on the bed and laughed.

'What would my daughter think if she could see me now?' said Connie.

'Be jealous?' said Russell, tongue in cheek. Connie hit him playfully, got up, removed her coat and threw it onto the floor. She sat back on the bed and they kissed again. Russell moved away briefly.

'Room service? Champagne?'

'Later.' Connie drew Russell back toward her and they continued.

She lay in bed smiling. There was only one word for it – wonderful. The whole evening had been perfect, just how she imagined an evening with your boyfriend/lover/husband should be. Relaxed, warm, fun and maybe a bit dirty. His hand under the table stroking her inner thigh at the Long Room had been enough to arouse her and be a prelude to the best orgasm she'd had in forty years. What a night, and it was still only ten thirty. Russell came out of the bathroom, got back in bed, picked up the phone and ordered the Champagne. He turned back toward Connie and started to kiss her again.

'Wow, cowboy! Give me a breather eh? I need a pee too.' Russell smiled as Connie got up taking the duvet with her.

'Thanks!' said Russell grabbing the pillow and hugging it for cover.

Connie smiled at herself in the bathroom mirror. Fancy having to wait all these years for great sex, she thought. And if

I'd not come to New York it wouldn't have happened at all. Fate or karma or whatever has given me a great shag before I pop my clogs. Thank you. Thank you. She laughed out loud to herself. Russell overheard and called to her.

'You OK in there?'

'Fine. Never felt better,' she replied.

She returned to the bedroom a few minutes later and room service arrived, Russell quickly put on his trousers and went to the door.

Back in bed they drank Champagne and he asked her when she was going back to England. Connie was noncommittal, saying she wasn't sure. He asked her if she'd stay with him in New York for a few days. What was she going to do now? Had this made any difference to her plans? She didn't want to think about it so placated Russell by telling him she'd decide the following day. For now, she just wanted to forget about everything and knew the best way to do that was drink more Champagne and have more sex. She took a sip, put the glass back on the bedside table, turned to Russell and began to kiss him on the neck, and he quickly he did the same.

It was well gone midnight and both of them lay talking about the serious threat of continued CO2 emissions. Connie believed there was still time to avoid global catastrophe, but Russell was far more pessimistic. 'I've seen big business and I know how it works. It's ruthless and answers to nobody but its shareholders. The only way we can survive is not just by halting the use of carbon fuels, but by destroying consumerism and that won't ever happen. It'll be like trying to take an ice cream off a child whose got an AK47. And short-term governments have short-term goals, and are only concerned with being "popular", which is why we need to change the political system. And I can't see that happening either.'

'So, you think there's nothing we can do?' said Connie.

'No there isn't. I think we're fucked.'

'I don't agree. Maybe desperate times call for desperate measures.'

'What do you mean exactly?' asked Russell.

'Revolution?' said Connie.

'In a world controlled by the police and armies? Best of luck with that.'

'But we have to try.'

'I agree, and maybe in the final moment our love for the natural world and wildlife will triumph, but I'm not holding my breath any longer that's all.' Russell kissed her on the cheek and smiled. 'Thanks for a wonderful evening Connie.'

'You too, Russell.'

'I'm shattered. How about you?'

'I'm OK. But you go to sleep, don't worry about me. You can turn off the light if you want.'

'You sure?'

'Yeah, I'm fine.'

See you in the morning?'

'Yes.' They kissed briefly again, Russell turned off the light and rolled over. Connie lay staring at the ceiling. She knew Russell was right, we'd ignored the facts for far too long so now it was simply damage limitation. Some governments were trying to respond but it was probably too little too late. But we still had to try.

*

She'd had doubts about her action, but now it was crystal clear; there was only one choice, and had been all along. Times were desperate as she'd said. There was of course Russell to consider, but it would only be a matter of weeks with him, and what did that count for in the big picture?

*

She listened to the sounds of the night, creaks and groans form the air conditioning, the muffled sound of a TV, a banging somewhere outside, the flutter of a pigeon, a police or ambulance siren, a helicopter, a propeller-driven private plane, a car alarm, all underscored by a low hum of traffic. Her head buzzed from the alcohol. She checked her watch; three a.m.

*

Still dark outside, the hum of traffic, the comfort of dark, the light of the dreaded day yet to arrive. Making out shapes on the curtains. Was it only a few weeks ago she stared at the ones in her bedroom? She checked her watch; four a.m.

*

She felt spaced out, adrenalin pumping through her veins, she couldn't do it surely? Stay in bed stay with Russell a week? Two weeks? Longer? No, that's a coward's way out. What was a few more weeks anyway? If she actually felt ill it would make everything a lot easier. Four forty-five a.m.

*

Russell snored, stirred and went back to sleep. What will happen to Sara? Kurt? And their child? It will have no future, unless, unless you at least try. Unless you have the strength to overcome the fear. She ran the quotes again:

'You must never be fearful about what you are doing when it's right.' 'Our lives begin to end the day we become silent about things that matter.' This is bigger than you, Connie. Five fifteen a.m.

*

She told herself she had power, and could pass this on to people for the real uprising that had yet to happen. And it could start today. It could begin in a few hours. It was six a.m, she slowly moved the duvet, slipped out of bed and put on her clothes, kissed Russell on the cheek and silently left the room.

*

She walked toward the Avenue, and was still torn. She didn't have to carry out the action today, did she? But she also knew the longer she stayed with Russell the more her resolve could weaken. No, this had to be it. She'd had a great night – the perfect ending – and that could never be repeated. It was today or never, and in the email, it had clearly stated that security could change the longer she left it.

*

She stood waiting to cross the already busy road, experienced a dizzy spell, almost blacked out, and had to lean on a fire hydrant for support. Her vision briefly went, then returned a few moments later. This was definitely the tumour. If she collapsed now that would put an end to it. Her mind was now finally made up. She took deep breaths, quickly recovered, and with renewed determination walked the short distance to the hotel.

She greeted Hamlet the cat and the receptionist as she approached the lift and punched the button to floor eleven. She entered her room, had a quick shower, packed her suitcase then made tea. She sat the desk, removed her phone from her coat pocket and proceeded to record a video message.

She went into the bathroom, poured the water from the small plastic bottle and filled it up with vodka and put it back inside the plastic bag. She slipped the wire cutters into the inside pocket of her coat, sat on the bed and double-checked she had the entry ticket. She drank another cup of tea and checked her watch. Seven thirty. She needed to be there in an hour. She left the suitcase on the bed, closed the door and handed the key into reception. She was booked in for another day and had pre-paid so didn't need to worry about settling up.

Adrenalin was now coursing through her system; she was ready and charged up like a soldier waiting to go into battle. She walked out into the street and travelled with the crowds to Times Square subway. She bought a ticket from the kiosk and got on the '1' train to South Ferry. Most of the morning passengers were coming up town so there was plenty of room in her carriage.

She sat and looked at the other passengers all with their heads down avoiding eye contact, some with papers but mostly looking at their phones. Would they be reading about her on their journey home tonight? That was the plan. That everybody throughout the world would know her in eight hours' time, maybe sooner. She didn't have faith it would change anything, but she had to try.

She stepped off the train now on autopilot, she had to remain calm and composed and pray security was still as lax as it had been three weeks ago. If it wasn't the whole exercise would be over before it had begun. As she walked through Battery Park it began to drizzle with rain and she momentarily panicked, would the rain cause a problem? No, probably not unless it was very heavy. She saw Fort Clinton ahead of her, an old coastal fortification, now the ticket office. She'd been instructed to take the first ferry of the day so it would be quietest

She walked through the arched entrance to an open courtyard and stood in a short queue at the kiosk. Once at the window she handed in the ticket she'd printed out at home and was given a yellow paper wristband that she attached. She was then told to join another queue outside the fort. She followed the signs and stood in line with about twenty other people ahead of her. The line stopped short of a large marquee-like structure beyond which was the quayside, no doubt where the boat moored up.

She went over again what she must do as she stood in the drizzle. Behind her now were at least another hundred people and she was beginning to realise the importance of being first off the boat once it docked at its destination.

She shuffled forward inch by inch, the security inside was taking a while, as the line turned a corner, she had a glimpse of the guards alongside the X-ray machine and body scanner. Nearby were two police wearing flak jackets and holding machine guns. What were they doing there? It's not Fort Knox for god's sake. Maybe somebody had tipped them off? Then she remembered the twin tower attack again, and that New York had probably been on a high security alert ever since.

The queue moved forward and she was approaching the entrance. She had to remain calm at all costs, if they found the cutters, then they found them. She was a sixty-three-year-old woman, what did they think she was going to do with them anyway? She could say she forget they were in there, that they were her husband's, or she'd been out fixing a fence. And if they did find them, she'd simply apologise and let them keep them until she returned. But it would certainly scupper the plan.

Finally, she was inside and beginning to sweat. The couple in front put their metal objects and small rucksack into a tray and onto the conveyor. Connie stepped forward and did likewise with her phone, coins and the plastic bag with the allowed bottle of water. She then stood behind the woman who was waiting to enter the scanner. She'd never been so nervous in her life, and couldn't imagine how she was going to get away with it, but unless the machine had been changed or repaired, she would.

A security guard beckoned her forward and she moved slowly trying not to screw up her face in anticipation. She passed under the arch numb with fear, but sure enough nothing happened, nothing at all. How could they be so incompetent? Connie smiled at the guard. Maybe the scanners were dummies? Security certainly were, a good job too!

She took her belongings out of the tray and joined the queue that led outside. She could see the water was lapping the quay and when the ferry docked it came over the top. A boarding ramp was positioned and passengers were helped onto the ferry between the wash. Connie did a quick hop up the gangway and went inside. A small snack bar was at one end, but she didn't want anything so sat on a bench near the door. As the passengers slowly came aboard most went upstairs onto the viewing deck outside.

Fifteen minutes later the ferry cast off. Connie got up and went out onto a sheltered lower deck as Manhattan receded. An orange coastguard power boat pulled up alongside, a man stood on the front deck next to a large machine gun. Were they looking for her? The boat then shot off, turned and did another slow pass.

She was now in panic mode. But the man simply waved at those on the top deck, and the boat finally powered away up the Hudson toward New Jersey. Connie sighed with relief.

The ferry stopped at Ellis Island where immigrants were held in their thousands before being allowed to enter the USA. She thought of Russell briefly but realised she had to blank him out, she had to blank everyone out.

 A few people got off to visit the museum but most stayed on board. Within a few minutes they neared their destination – Liberty Island – and Connie stared up the majestic three-hundred-foot monument.

She was here at last and her heart beat rapidly with anticipation. She went back inside as the ferry approached the landing pier, and as instructed kept near the exit door, so she could be first off. She noticed that water was lapping up through the slats. *It must be high tide,* she thought. The ferry docked and the passengers from the upper deck crowded into the saloon. Ropes were thrown and the boat came alongside and was secured.

The doors opened and Connie went down the gangway. She walked the fifty metres to shore avoiding the water that bubbled up through the wooden slats.

A park ranger greeted her and said there wouldn't be another ferry for two hours due to the exceptional high tide. For some reason this made her feel safer, as there'd be even fewer people around.

Walking down the esplanade she passed the restaurant/gift shop and approached another ticket kiosk; she showed the wristband and the woman waved her on. She could see another white marquee style building ahead and assumed this was the main entrance. She moved quickly knowing full well she had to be first inside. Her phone rang. Who the hell could it be? She removed it from her pocket and looked at the caller. It was Cathy. Oh god, what should she do? Now of all times?

She stared at the phone as it rang. She was desperate to talk to her, but how could she possibly have a normal conversation at a moment like this? She wanted to say she loved her and was sorry. But if she answered how would Cathy react later when she discovered what she was about to do? She'd think she could have stopped her, wouldn't she? She'd be wracked with guilt and probably kill herself. No, she couldn't answer.

Finally, the ringing stopped. Connie continued toward the entrance feeling wretched, Cathy may still kill herself when she finds out? God, what the hell was she doing?

Sara, Kurt, Cathy, Russell, they would all be devastated, how could she do this to them? But she had to blank them, she had to blank them. It was now too late, far too late to turn back. Gritting her teeth, she opened the door and entered the building trying to keep her mind focused.

Ahead of her were rows of tacky souvenirs, and at the end she could see another a door marked 'Entrance'. She walked through the shop area, two young women stood chatting behind the check-out tills, one of them looked up and glanced at her briefly. What a story she may have to tell?

She passed through the zig-zag queueing cordon leading toward the door, paused, and slowly opened it. Immediately she was chastised by a loud voice.

'Go out and shut the door until we tell you!' Connie saw the man was wearing a flak jacket and casually holding a machine gun, he was surrounded by three others, one dressed like himself, the other two wearing tawny park ranger uniforms. They gave her a cold stare as she edged backwards and out of the door. She panicked again, they might have been tipped off, and surely they'd fixed this scanning machine? How could it be possible both failed to pick up a pocket full of coins as they did during the reconnaissance?

She waited to be called through trying her best to remain calm, nobody else had arrived in the entrance hall yet so she was still had a good lead on the rest. However, the longer she was kept the quicker she would have to ascend the statue, and she was wasn't exactly in her prime.

It was imperative she was at least five minutes ahead of the person behind her. As every second passed, she became more frantic. What were they doing in there? It was now ten forty and she was due to go up the statue at nine thirty. She heard people enter from behind her and turned to see a group of ten or so ambling in, but fortunately they were browsing in the shop and in no hurry to join the queue.

Ten forty-five, and the waiting was becoming excruciating. Just as Connie thought her heart was about to explode the door opened. A ranger beckoned her in, and casually she followed. She put the plastic bag in the tray along with her phone and coins then waited to be called through the scanner. This was it; she was certain it would go off, how couldn't it? Its only job was to detect metal? How simple a piece of technology was that? And what would be the point in having machines that don't work? But then it became clear to her. Dummy speeding cameras, the concept of the deterrent? Either way when she was finally called through, she was terrified. She stepped into the arch, and off it went. Shit! It did work! Connie all but fainted as the ranger pulled her to one side. He was just about to begin a body search when Connie felt in her pocket, she'd missed a few coins! She removed them, and the ranger smiled and simply nodded her on. She couldn't believe it was that easy to avoid being searched, even though it had been a genuine accident to leave the coins in her pocket.

Feeling relieved she continued out of the white marquee and into the base of the statue. She entered a large stone hall, another ranger stood behind a counter to one side.

'Pedestal or crown?' Connie hesitated.

'Err, crown.'

'Take the lift, or stairs to the left, madam,' Connie walked across the hall and pressed the call button, immediately the doors opened and she stepped in. She stabbed the 'up' button and quickly arrived at the top of the pedestal – the base of the statue. The doors opened and she saw the stairway signposted to the crown. She climbed a short flight and entered a small room with another ranger in attendance. He smiled, removed the wristband from her and pointed toward another narrower stairway ahead. After climbing the small flight, she arrived at a gantry inside the statue itself. Ten feet below her floodlights shone upward, and glass observation windows in the roof of the pedestal allowed people to see up inside. Connie gazed at the mass of criss-cross girders that supported the interior of Liberty's body and skirt. *Like the inside of a jelly mould*, she thought to herself. It was a magnificent piece of sculpture, and Connie was awestruck by its sheer scale, but she didn't have time to ponder.

In the centre a steel spiral staircase led up to the crown and she quickly began to climb whilst avoiding looking down. The last thing she needed now was an attack of vertigo.

The spiral was tight and only a mere eighteen inches wide. Connie knew it was three hundred and fifty-four steps to the top; she became breathless after the first hundred and had to stop at the resting platform. She paused briefly resisting the urge to look down, then climbed the next hundred or so and stopped at the second platform taking deep breaths. The exertion and rising heat from the powerful spotlights below made her brow begin to sweat.

She continued to climb; no voices could be heard below so she had a good head start. She ascended rapidly to the final platform and bent double gasping for breath. She wiped her brow with a handkerchief and made the mistake of quickly glancing down. Suddenly she felt light-headed, and feared she'd pass out. She rested briefly taking deep breaths, refusing to be daunted, straightened and re-galvanised. She was now being driven by a force – the force of nature. She took more deep breaths to calm herself so as not to appear suspicious – she knew two rangers would be in the crown.

She climbed the last few steps and entered the small room with its viewing windows. A male and female ranger smiled weakly at her as she entered. She wasn't interested in the view but needed to show that she was, not that the rangers would have any idea regrading her true purpose. How long could she wait before descending? A minute? Two?

She looked out of the small slits in the crown across to Manhattan, then removed her phone and fired off some pictures, but didn't register anything, her mind now solely concentrated on her next move. She thought she heard voices from far below and this gave her the cue to move on. She smiled at the rangers and walked out of the opposite door. The spiral staircase was a double helix, one up and one down so nobody would descend for some time, and once they arrived in the crown, they'd be there for at least five minutes. However, she still needed to work quickly.

She descended the sixteen steps down to the top platform. In front of her was the metal grill with a padlocked gate, behind which she could see the ladder. She was so near to her goal now she felt a mixture of euphoria and blind panic. She'd been through this a thousand times in her head and now here she was for real. Her heart raced like a pneumatic drill.

She removed the wire cutters from her inside coat pocket and proceeded to cut out a two-foot square hole at knee height whilst leaving the bottom edge intact so she could fold it back into position. It was tough to cut and required all her strength; she had forty odd cuts to do to produce a hole big enough to climb through so had to work quickly. Within a minute she'd done one side and continued across the top, which was when she heard voices and footsteps coming up the ascending spiral, but fortunately she was hidden from view.

She quickly cut across the top hoping and praying a ranger wouldn't decide to descend, but why would they? They'd just arrived and would stay up there for two hours until they changed shifts, as it had stated in the email, but she was fearful nevertheless. She began to cut along the final side and heard the visitors now above her in the crown talking animatedly to the rangers. This gave her real reason to panic as they could descend at any moment. She cut fast as she could and finally finished.

She pushed in the mesh bent it down and stepped inside, then quickly bent it back again into position, attempting to line up the cuts best she could. It wasn't perfect but convincing enough unless you had a close look. She took the phone from her pocket with the pre-recorded message and placed it at the foot of the ladder.

She slowly began to climb the forty rungs up the inside of the arm, holding the carrier bag with her teeth as she needed both hands. As she ascended, she knew the danger of being stopped was now almost over which gave her a thrill. She felt more relaxed and focused as she approached halfway.

She knew what to expect when she got to the top, as the reconnaissance had spoken to a park ranger who replaced the bulbs around the torch, and he'd told them exactly how to get out onto the narrow gantry.

Climbing the last few feet she imagined the outstretched arm, the thought of being this high up made her feel momentarily strange, but she blocked it.

She stepped on the final rung and arrived at the top. To her left was a small door with a bolt. She slid it to one side and gently pushed the creaking flap open. Cool air blew in and the daylight made her squint. She took the bag out of her mouth and placed it outside, then carefully manoeuvred herself through the door onto the narrow parapet. Once she'd crawled out she gingerly moved to one side, closed the door behind her, and leant against it to prevent anyone from entering.

The parapet height was a couple of feet so she couldn't quite see over the edge, which was just as well considering she was now almost three hundred feet up. She looked around at the rows of lights that shone up to the torch, initially the light was within the flame, being translucent, now it was reflected off the new copper one. Would anyone look at it in the same way again? Wasn't it about time it actually gave out what it symbolised: enlightenment to the world in a period of darkness?

She sat back and closed her eyes and said a silent prayer to her loved ones, not a prayer as such but a wish that their futures would be safe, especially her unborn grandchild's.

She opened her eyes, removed the water bottle from the bag, undid the top and sniffed, she couldn't smell a thing! For one awful moment she panicked, thinking it was actually water, so she took a quick swig to check, yes it was vodka, thank god.

She removed the matches from her pocket then slowly emptied the entire bottle over her coat starting with the shoulders and working down until she reached her lap where it emptied. She removed a match from the box, held it a moment, then struck it, but the wind immediately blew it out.

'Shit!'

She removed another and struck, again it blew out.

'Shit! Shit!'

She took out third, struck it, and quickly shielded it.

'Eureka.'

She lowered the match to her waist, touched the flame to the edge of her coat, and held it until the flame died, nothing happened. She lit another and touched it to her sleeve, a blue flame licked up the arm, then slowly died again. She tried again and the same happened, the flame licking the coat and burning off the vodka, but not catching the fabric.

'Shit!' She'd tried the vodka at home and it burnt a coat with ease, but this was a different one, and no doubt made from different materials.

'Shit! Shit! Shit!' she uttered to herself, surely she wasn't going to get this far and fail? How stupid of her! She lit another match and tried again, holding it under the cuff, again the blue tongue of flame licked up the coat, then disappeared. Maybe she should have bought white spirit? Or at least a lighter? Why didn't she bring a fucking lighter? Why didn't she bring a fucking lighter! Idiot! Fucking idiot!

It was then she smelt something acrid, a small wisp of smoke issued from inside her cuff, followed by a tiny yellow flame. She felt the burning, it was the coats polyester lining. A sharp sting ran up her arm like a knife cut, and quickly spread to her chest. Smoke suddenly poured out from under the lapels, and within seconds she was engulfed in flames.

The pain was unbearable, yet she felt ecstatic, like giving birth. Was this really happening to her? How had she arrived here? What on earth was she thinking? When planning it had all seemed so natural, almost routine, until now. Now it was beyond words, beyond anything she could have ever conceived, to end like this, in this way, with this pain. This terrifyingly glorious pain.

Not much longer now before the lights finally go out and she becomes just another fading memory amongst the few, or the many? Who could know? The pain vanished as her body's adrenalin rushed to the rescue.

A plane passed overhead, she thought of Jim, and the sky darkened as if controlled by a dimmer switch. She closed her eyes and said goodbye to her life. Her world faded to black.

***

Russell woke around eight thirty a.m. and was surprised to see Connie gone. He got up, showered, dressed, had breakfast in the hotel and strolled to the Algonquin to check out where she was. He entered the glass swing doors and was confronted by the two doormen, a cleaner and the receptionist all slack-jawed and staring in front of them. He followed their gaze to the television on the wall. A CNN news report showed flames pouring from Liberty's torch. He turned to look at the staff who were still blank-faced, then as he turned back there was the picture of Connie sitting on the bed in the hotel room. The receptionist spoke tearfully.

'She was in one one-five

'Oh my god, it's her,' replied one doorman. Russell put his hand to his mouth in disbelief as she began to speak passionately.

'What I'm about to do is for every animal on Earth, every creature that can't protect itself and relies on us, the so-called "superior race" for its survival. We're a disgrace, a destructive blight to everything in the natural world, and we're ignoring all the warnings we've been given, just so we can carry on with our consumer-obsessed lifestyles.'

She hadn't written down or rehearsed the speech as she wanted it to be authentic and from the heart. She didn't even care if she repeated herself, as this would help her to clarify the message.

'The natural world is beautiful and it's free. But we're destroying it. The forests, the plains, the ice caps and habitable oceans are vanishing, along with all the wildlife. So, in the future where will we go if there's no countryside left, all the beaches are flooded, and there's nothing left in the dead ocean?' She paused.

'Where will we go then? The shopping mall? To buy more of the stuff that wrecked, polluted and drained the planet of all its natural resources in the first place?' She paused to stress her point.

'We can't have our cake and eat it. We can't keep driving, flying and buying, and still have forests with birdsong and butterflies. So, which is it? It's your choice? We carry on the way we are and destroy everything? Or, have a simpler, less consuming lifestyle?' She leaned closer to the camera.

'It's a no-brainer really isn't it? Because if we don't respect nature, it could all disappear, every parrot, every tiger, every turtle, every bat, and a lot sooner than we think. Then there are the people, the millions of blameless poor around the world who've never even owned a fridge or driven a car, they will also die of starvation and disease, as thousands are already because of our increasing greed.' Connie was sombre, then tried to be positive and smiled.

'But just think, life might be even better without all the so-called luxuries and pointless junk we surround ourselves with. Discarding what we don't really need may help us to value the more important things – our family, our friends, and above all the world we live in.'

'So, what are we going to do? Sit back and do nothing? Or change and survive? Are we going to keep on consuming if it means we could be surrounded by dead and barren wasteland? I don't think so. Because we love nature, we love the natural world, and know without it we would perish, and even if we survived our lives would become dark and meaningless. Do we want our children and subsequent generations to inherit that?' Connie became more intense.

'We must stop this happening whatever the cost, and governments have to act immediately to avoid an irreversible catastrophe. We can't let big business tear the world apart any longer, and we can't let those in power turn their backs, like they have done for the past fifty years.' She paused to focus her thoughts.

'We've ignored the scientific evidence for too long, and now there's only one solution; We must cut CO_2 emissions to zero within the next fifteen years, and stop destroying the planet and using it as a garbage tip. We know politicians can be self-serving and corrupt, but they also like to believe they're passionate, caring and humane, so this is their chance to prove it. To prove to us they really do care, and above all, prove to our children they care about their future. So, please, please, don't let them down. Whatever you do, don't let our children down.'

Connie became briefly emotional, but then found all the passion and anger she could muster.

'And if governments don't act, then **we** will have to. **We** will have to go it alone. **We** will have to force change.'

'And if we're ignored. **We** will have to fight like the suffragettes.' Connie stared hard. '**We** will have to start a fucking revolution.' She took a few deep breaths.

'**We** have to be brave and make sacrifices.'

'**We** have to light the way like Lady Liberty.'

'Because if we don't, the light could go out.'

The picture vanished, and the news channel showed the flaming torch again whilst the reporter recapped the incident for those just tuning in. Russell and the hotel staff were stunned and tearful – as were millions around the world who were watching.

***

Epilogue

During the period this novel is set the US administration had no CO_2 emission targets. The UK pledged to become carbon neutral by 2050. However, if you look into the details this translates as an 80% emissions reduction based on 1990s output, which was almost twice that of 2018. So, in reality this is a 40% reduction of current output by 2050. Under the Paris Agreement, countries don't have to take into account international aviation and shipping, or CO_2 emitted from the production of imported goods, which would account for approximately 10% of UK emissions. Therefore, the final UK reduction pledge is a mere 30%. If every country in the world reduced their emissions by 50%, we will still have a two-degree temperature increase – which scientists admit would be catastrophic.

In 2018 world emissions increased by 3%. None of this takes into account the vast amounts of methane now being released from melting permafrost. Methane is ninety times more potent than CO_2 in the first 20 years.

In the 2019 general election UK political parties saw 'tree planting' as the easy fix to climate change – as it avoids bringing in unpopular vote losing measures. The most ambitious target was two billion over the next twenty years. These will take twenty years to grow and remove less than one per cent of carbon from the atmosphere. Perhaps it would make more sense to try and stop the 15 billion mature trees that are cut down around the world each year.

Boris Johnson became Prime Minister, he called those who demonstrated to draw attention to the dire consequences that faced us a bunch of 'ring-nosed uncooperative crusties.' Maybe if the government was doing its best to protect us, and listened to scientists, they wouldn't need to demonstrate in the first place.

In December 2019 Sara, Kurt and their baby daughter Connie fled Australia as thirty percent of the bush burnt. The prime minister denied it was caused by climate change.

In the March 2020 budget, the Tory party pledged £2billion for oil well subsidy in Brazil, Kuwait and Oman.

If the planet warms by 2 degrees the effects on humanity will be a thousand times worse than Covid-19 – and without a cure – as once the 'tipping point' is reached, it's hard to reverse. And if all the CO_2 is removed from the atmosphere to pre-industrial levels, the effects of warming will still continue for many decades.

In June 2020 even after a three-month world lockdown, atmospheric CO_2 was at a record high.

*

This book is dedicated to David Buckel – a lawyer and environmentalist who self-immolated in Prospect Park, Brooklyn on the 14th April 2018, as a protest against climate change and the human destruction of the natural world.

***

Lightning Source UK Ltd.
Milton Keynes UK
UKHW011209051020
371043UK00001B/4

9 781800 317727